What readers are saying about
Sometimes I Wake Up and Think I'm Still in Nebraska

The novel called *Sometimes I Wake Up and Think I'm Still in Nebraska*, authored by Dusty Dowse, is a fine read: It really moves the reader along, via a combination of imagination, intelligence, and humor. One is tempted to describe that work as picaresque (a good thing!); shades of *The Sotweed Factor*. And even though I never met Mr. Barth, the author of that work, I should mention that I have long known Dusty D. Accordingly, I could not help discerning certain autobiographical elements distributed through his book: an extra good thing, owing to the author's rich, full, and interesting life. And even though most readers would not know, or care about that feature of the novel, the key factor is that they are in for a fine reading experience if they opt to acquire, then delve into it, which they should do.

Jeffrey Hall, Ph.D.
Nobel Laureate and author of *The Stand of the U.S. Army at Gettysburg*

Dusty Dowse is a Renaissance-type of man who has a vast range of interests and knowledge. He is not only an author, but also a professor emeritus in biology, a researcher in fields that would be considered esoteric, a Zen baker, and a mountain man. His recently published book, *Sometimes I Wake Up and Think I'm Still in Nebraska*, is fiction, but so compelling in the vivid and detailed descriptions of the protagonist, a leading scientist named Larry Vintner, and one other main character, I can't help but wonder if each of those characters represents an aspect of the author. You will be drawn in by the stories which make the book hard to put down.

Erica M. Elliott, MD
Author, speaker, mountaineer, and Medical Doctor.
Her current work is *From Mountains to Medicine-Scaling the Heights in Search of my Calling.*

The best compliment for any writer is that he told a good story, and it was based on his own life. Dusty Dowse is twice blessed; he lived an original life and came up with an even more original story. His résumé is rich and long and makes a worthy template for Larry, the protagonist of his novel,

Sometimes I Wake Up And Think I'm Still In Nebraska. Larry is a professor of some arcane branch of computer science at an unnamed university in Cambridge, Mass., an unlikely destination for a man who started out oiling in the logging industry of the northern Catskills in Upper New York State. The title has nothing to do with either location but plenty to do with the author and his protagonist and their shared appetite for a pithy line and vivid cultural references cached throughout the narrative like Easter eggs. The presence that looms over everything is the mystique of the old growth forest and its eerie natural phenomena, some explicable, some inexplicable. One of these is a magnificent ash tree that casts its own spell over all who see it and becomes the locus for a violent clash between a youthful Larry, who wants to save it and his employer, Jimmy, who wants to cut it down. Jimmy is a crude, hard drinking backwoods brawler and the fight between them ends with him fleeing into the deep woods believing he has killed Larry. But Larry survives and both men are thrust into their own personal quest for the meaning of what brought them to such a terrible moment. As he pursues a successful career in academia Larry is constantly drawn back to the mountains by his love of climbing, the solace of the forest and the lifelong bonds he forged with those who worked in the woods. When Larry calls on an old friend, Eban, who is splitting wood in the barn the two fit wordlessly into a familiar routine, Larry feeding Eban the rough chunks of wood while Eban works the splitter, a homebuilt tractor driven contraption impressive in its efficiency and durability. The authenticity of the moment is so persuasive you can almost smell the fresh split wood. There are many such moments because Dusty lived them, and the book is richer for them. Every good story needs a compelling denouement and Dusty has come up with a beauty. I won't spoil it here but when the two old combatants meet again, as we know they must, the resolution is as ingenious.as it is astounding. I will say only that Dusty's record as a professor of Biology and Mathematics at UMaine-Orono imbues the metaphysical with the practical in a way that satisfies intellectually and emotionally. I was left wanting more.

Paul Mann

Author of *Season of the Monsoon*, winner of the *New York Times* Notable Book of the Year award.

Sometimes I Wake Up and Think I'm Still in Nebraska is a classic—a hardcore underground working-class novel somewhat reminiscent of nineteenth-century novelist Thomas Hardy with a touch of Nathaniel Hawthorne, Edgar Allen Poe, and Annie Proulx, but more blue-collar and engine-and-motor-savvy. It's a rare novel that can teach you about Johann Sebastian Bach's music and how machines work at the same time.

Richard Grossinger, Ph.D.

Curator of Sacred Planet Books at Inner Traditions, and author of *Bottoming Out the Universe: Why There Is Something Rather Than Nothing.*

Okay, boomers. This is a story for you.

It's about two men, casual friends who are also loggers: one the boss, the other his employee. They've followed different paths to this place in their lives. One day on the job they find themselves faced with events they can't explain. A moment of sudden, jarring violence scatters them into the wide world again, with more questions than ever.

Dusty takes us along their journey through insights and experiences of a life overlapping two centuries. The dialogue is real; the experiences, locations and events of recent decades are familiar to any of us that have lived through them. The story doesn't answer every question raised or tie up every loose end – just like life. It does give the reader much to think about. And that is, in itself, a rare and wonderful thing.

Diane Genthner

Diane Genthner has 20+ years' experience as a trade book buyer at B Dalton and the UMaine Bookstore, and also holds a MA in English. She writes fiction privately as well.

Not often does a longtime friend and colleague from an academic science department ask you to read his novel. Dipping in, I quickly had a pretty good idea that it would be a memoir or at least draw heavily on the author's experiences in New York and New England, and for myself and longtime friends of his, put together some pieces of the puzzle that is Dusty Dowse. Reminiscence or novel, it would be a good story for other readers as well, with its blend of historical facts and quirks of human nature.

The book follows the employments and career of its central character, Larry Vintner. He is presented as a top-notch international climate scientist but who in some respects is a throwback to a time when science was emerging from natural philosophy as a complement to art in understanding the natural world. Larry's "sense of trees" and sensibility to flow allowed him to "hear them talking in the forest floor." But this sense of mysticism and enchantment is blended with scientific discussions of non-equilibrium thermodynamics and heat transfer in self-organizing systems involved in the formation of hurricanes.

Artifactual objects figure throughout the book and give context to the vignettes and the author's life and likes, beginning with an heirloom mantel clock—"a work of art, composed of exotic woods mixed with honest oak"—and a touchstone for a chronobiologist specializing in the mathematical analysis of biological rhythms and the underpinnings of cardiology. Heavy machinery figures prominently. The hardscrabble reality of rural New York is pervasive. Personal dislikes and annoyances feature in the author's academic scientists and curmudgeons rural and urban alike. All these factors give the book its personality.

Professor Dowse is versed in crafting scientific publications, with to-the-point descriptions evincing a careful choice of words and a polished style that avoids complicated sentences. Thus, his novel flows well and is eminently readable.

This marvelous book will be of particular interest to those readers of a certain age who recall how the physical and cultural worlds have changed in the past four-plus decades, for better *or* worse. Academics of various stripes, especially scientists, will enjoy his wry treatment of the familiar politics, culture, and personalities of their domain, but the relevance goes beyond these things. Thoughtful readers will be drawn to reflect on why we are here, where we are headed, and the importance of the relationships that make us human, including our connections with non-humans. Books such as this are good arguments against a voluntary posthuman future, where literature cannot flourish.

Malcolm Shick, Ph.D.
Emeritus Professor of Zoology and Oceanography,
University of Maine; a Fellow of the American Association for the Advancement of Science; and author of *Where Corals Lie.*

SOMETIMES I WAKE UP AND THINK I'M STILL IN NEBRASKA

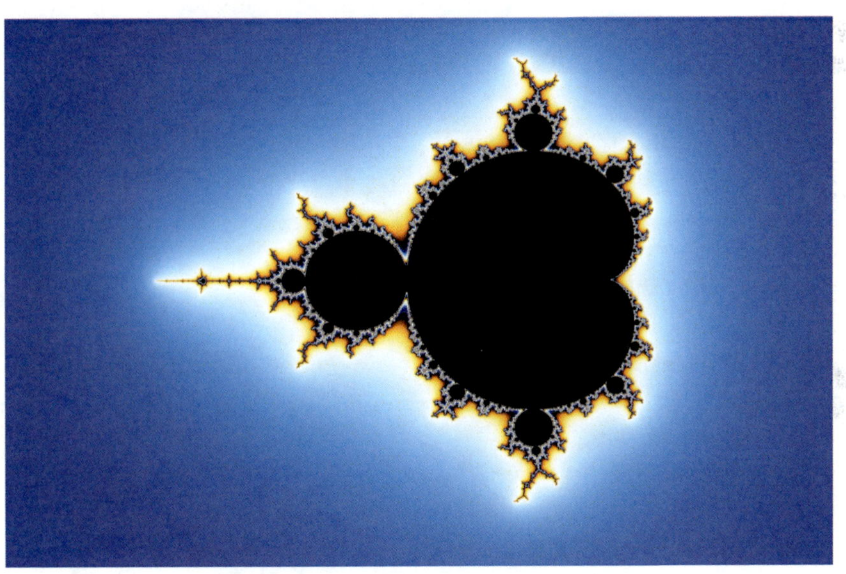

DUSTY DOWSE

Sometimes I Wake up and Think I'm Still in Nebraska
Author: Dusty Dowse
The characters and events in this book are fictitious. Any similarity to real persons other than the author himself, living or dead, is coincidental or inspirational.

Published by Lammastide
946 Dexter Road
Cambridge, Maine 04923
www.lammastide.com

Lammastide is a division of Demeter, LLC

ISBN: 979-8-9876200-2-1

Book and cover design by Barbara Aronica
Cover photo Shutterstock / Design Pics
Mandlebrot set Shutterstock / wirow

I dedicate this work to my Family,

both close and extended.

Thanks for your patience.

“All along the watchtower
Princes kept the view”

Bob Dylan

Prelude (And Fugue)

Over three hundred million years ago, an ancient mountain range, located where the Taconic Hills now stand, gradually eroded away. These remains washed down to the west and south, forming a large delta in an ancient sea. With time, this region rose several thousand feet. Water flow began to erode deep valleys. Glaciers took their toll, further sculpting the landscape. The mountainous terrain you see we now call the Catskills. The northernmost traces reach near Albany and are called the Helderbergs. Owing to their origin, some geologists do not consider the Catskills "real" mountains, but they certainly fill the niche perfectly. And like most mountains, they have a wondrous history and power. Some have called the Catskills one of the pillars holding up the universe.

The humans who arrived in the area many thousands of years ago, after a long trek from Asia, became the tribe known as the Esopus. They were hunter-gatherers with some agriculture. Sadly, they were driven from their homeland and ended up in the Mid-west, where remnants of the tribe remain. There is no reliable record of what they called these mountains. The current name we owe to the Dutch, who explored and settled the region. Kaaterskill, translated, is simply Cat Creek.

The Catskills have a rich lore that includes very spiritual elements. As with most mountains, legends have sprung up. The river passing the range that runs from northern New York down to the sea is called the

Hudson, after the explorer Henry Hudson, who first sailed up it on September 3, 1609, and it has its own stories. When thunder rolls down from the hills, children used to be told that it was Henry Hudson and his crew bowling. And think of one of the greatest sleepers of all time, Rip Van Winkle, who awoke to his long beard, tattered clothing, and hunting musket rusted to ruin. One thoughtful cartographer has even created a new map symbol in a very detailed New York State atlas. This addition is to be found just a bit west of Palenville. It is a tiny reclining figure, with three *z*'s above its head. The intriguing ravines, gorges, streams, and crags were the inspiration for an entire art movement, the Hudson River School, with many truly great works to its credit.

In our own time, a ragtag crew, a half a million strong, on a search for the path back to the Garden, made its way to a hillside on an obscure farm in the foothills, owned by Max Yasgur, in the town of Bethel. Bethel is about sixty miles from the town of Woodstock, for which the gathering was named.

A vast reservoir system was created in this range. When you make your coffee in the morning in your condo on West Eighty-fifth Street in Manhattan, the water from the tap may have fallen as rain on Denman Mountain.

But the eternal question arises: is this power at the heart of the range itself, or is it something the human race has given to it? This is a part of a much larger mystery. In fact, there may be just one mystery. This would be like Escher's paintings, which, as one astute critic once opined, are all connected behind the frames. Or, perhaps better, like the Mandelbrot set. Wherever you are in this most complex of all objects, you can always get to any other part. And as with all true mysteries, there is no way of knowing what's on the other side. But there are windows into these unknown realms that open just a bit from time to time. With "luck," you might be privileged to be there when one of these opens. Real answers never become visible, though, just insights. And there is a price . . .

1

The ancient chime clock groaned, locked into its duty cycle, and tolled out the hour. It was 4:00 P.M., or thereabouts. Afternoon shadows filled the back of the office where late September sunshine had been. It was unlike any other office in the building, looking every bit like it would be more comfortable in the 1870s. It would have liked, presuming a place can be thought to like anything at all, to be listening to horse carriages rather than trucks and buses in the old street below, presuming further that it also possessed the sense of hearing. In the scheme of things, Cambridge, Massachusetts, had seen and heard horses far longer than the grim grinding of the internal combustion engine. But this building had been built with federal matching funds only a few years before and was almost new, so the explanation lay not with the ghosts that haunt ancient places but with the persona of the individual who now dominated this space, Professor Larry Vintner.

The chair in which he sat dated from that ancient equestrian era. It was walnut and upholstered in leather so old that it was cracked in several places, despite the liberal and obvious application of neatsfoot oil. The accompanying desk matched the chair neither in era nor composition, being a mission oak parsonage desk of uncertain vintage but substantial construction. Fairly good quality prints of a number of artists of the Hudson River School hung about with their atmospheric mountainscapes. An antique wooden file cabinet of the type that Bartleby the

Scrivener might have preferred not to use sat with a drawer extended, filled with papers in exquisite disarray. The principal light came from an incandescent bulb housed in a brass laboratory lamp salvaged when the old Biology Building was renovated a few years back. The fluorescent overhead office lights, which would normally come on when the rest of the lights in the lab suite were lit, did not add their bluish offering, having had their bulbs removed. The custodians had given up trying to replace them some time back.

The clock was the heart of the space, and visitors were drawn to it immediately. It was a work of art, composed of exotic woods mixed with honest oak. It did not match the oak of the desk, even to a first approximation, but the mismatch was unimportant. It was much smaller than a grandfather clock, being of the type commonly called a mantel clock, but its presence was nonetheless imposing. The exotic woods that ornamented it were not veneer but solid inlay. They included rosewood, zebrawood, bubinga, and several others that defied identification. It had a great brass pendulum hidden within, as was the custom with this type of timepiece, and it gave off a stately ticking that rumbled up from deep within the case and imposed a serenity that even a modern phone, with its evil warbling, could not dispel.

The phone itself seldom rang in these environs. Few people wanted to disturb the denizen. Even when officers of granting agencies or officials from NOAA called, normally people with strongly developed senses of self, they did so with a certain degree of uneasiness. The man was never unpleasant or rude to them, but one always got the impression that he must have dragged himself back in from a great distance, followed by a gut-wrenching change of gears to figure out how to deal with the caller.

That impression was largely true, and the distance he had covered was not measurable in meters. But he would answer it if he actually heard it ring.

Some time ago, the university, in its wisdom, had equipped all the phones with answering machine service. In this configuration, one could leave a long message, up to ten minutes in length. The dean had been known to fill nearly two ten-minute periods with long, rambling, unfocused messages on some faculty members' phones. But not Larry's, at least as far as anyone knew. Larry had never used the system. It had been in place for a very long time now, and presumably there was an age limit on messages so the earliest must have been purged, but Larry never bothered to learn how to access the calls. The little red message-waiting light burned balefully and eternally, always in vain. If they could not get him fair and square, they would not get him at all.

The phone did not disturb him this afternoon. He was working on a computer set up on another old wooden desk, this one not so imposing as the first. He probably would not have even noticed the phone had it rung. The computer was not physically large but was impressive in power. As he clattered away rapidly on the keyboard, a fraction of his brain pondered its configuration. He had cobbled it together himself using parallel processing among many CPUs. The operating system was of his own devising and the unit could achieve a very respectable speed. Not what the giant supercomputers were capable of, but still enormous. It was more than up to the tasks he assigned it. The teams working on global climate models needed a lot more than he did, and having the whole thing sitting in his lab meant a lot in terms of convenience. What amused him most was that this unit was a linear descendant of the tiny microcomputers of the early eighties. It was related, if not at the level of genus, then at least at the family level, to legendary machines like the old Commodore 64. That had been Larry's first computer, and he had worked on it until the original matte finish had a mirror sheen from his palms.

But it was the mathematical model he was tweaking that was holding the lion's share of his brain on task. He tweaked a few more coefficients and recompiled the FORTRAN code. Like his office, this language was a throwback to a bygone era, akin to Latin. He was equally adept at machine language when he needed to talk directly to his instrumentation. He liked it that way, was comfortable with it, and figured that after the first pass of the compiler they all looked alike anyway. It was image flack. No one in the building was doing anything remotely as close to the edge as he was, and his retention of FORTRAN was one more little fun thing to keep his colleagues guessing and annoyed.

After compiling the source code, he set the model in motion. The screen darkened to reveal a graph of the output of his system of nonlinear differential equations in the "phase plane," a space that did not exist in a real-world sense but displayed the state variables of the model as it evolved. Having satisfied himself that things were in order, he modified the input parameters of the model until the trajectory of the moving spot became erratic. Not just any old erratic, but erratic in a way that "felt right" to him. He switched over to a view of the system in what would pass for real space and time and saw a vortex begin to form in the gray monochrome of the screen. As it did so, colors began to emerge, indicating velocity, with red the fastest and blue grey the slowest. As the system evolved in time, it took on an angry look, organizing itself from the void in what appeared to be a self-aware, methodical manner. Such dynamic structures were common in systems that were far from equilibrium, like a whirlpool in a bathtub. Life itself is such a dynamic, dissipative structure, forming itself in the void where there was the potential for energy flow, maintaining order at the expense of the surrounding universe.

This particular system was behaving precisely as its creator had envisioned. And that creator was vaguely frightened by what he had wrought. He could feel the hair on the back of his neck prickling as the colors moved through greens to yellow and finally to red in the center. A small part of his mind was grateful there was a little hair left back there to rise up. That prickling had served him well over the years, and what little gray hair the barber had left remaining was strategically located. He well knew that the feeling went deeper than the hair, which, in truth, really did not move much at all. What set him on edge was the view this maelstrom gave him of the future; it was, after all, a model of a real system. And now, in the real world the computer modeled, the vaguest hints of the vortex that was coming could be seen in the data that were fed to him by his colleagues from all over the globe. He hit the alt key and the letter S on the keyboard, and thousands of smiley faces were swept up into the most troubled part of the screen. They moved about according to their background color, with the ones in the red zone ripping about with the greatest velocity. It had taken several hours to add them to the code, FORTRAN being fairly stodgy about such things, but it was worth it. He felt like Saint Dunstan, grabbing Satan by the nose with his pliers. If you can't have a little fun with the Devil, what's the point of messing with him?

He was not yet satisfied with the performance, as good as it seemed. There was one parameter in one of the (highly, nastily) nonlinear differential equations defining the system that needed refinement, and he set up an iterative procedure to get a better estimate. Even with the blinding speed of this machine, with its multiple CPU's, it would take about two days to get output data from the huge array of possible starting parameters. He had justified the expense of the computer guts on his last National Science Foundation grant proposal on the strength of computations like this. NSF was inclined to give him what he asked for as long as it was halfway reasonable. His proposals were way more than halfway reasonable. He cast off the program for its long journey, locked the system with his explicitly obscene password, and turned off the monitor.

Larry stretched out to his considerable height: six feet, three inches above the earth. He was a lean man passing through late middle age with a certain style. He was clean-shaven with very short gray hair. It was not a military haircut, which might have labeled him as a veteran who missed the old days, but really had no discernable style at all. It looked as if the barber had been told to remove as much hair as possible, leaving only a uniform short fuzz. In reality, that was not far from what went on every three weeks like clockwork at Tony's barber shop. Tony's Tonsorial Parlor was a relic of an earlier age itself, defying the posh new salons in Cambridge.

But the striking thing about Larry was not his great height, his lean strength, or his unusual hairstyle preference. Rather, one's attention was drawn to two things, in this order. First, he was badly scarred. One noticed his face first. There was an angry white slash that started on his left cheekbone, passed through his lips, went across his chin, and terminated on its point. A second scar was on the back of his head, and it was considerably worse. It was long and deep and occupied the bottom of an alarmingly cavernous depression in his skull. In the proper light, it appeared to be a creek running through a steep mountain ravine. After introductions were over and pleasantries exchanged, the other thing the new acquaintance would see was a strangeness about his eyes. There were few who were curious enough to want to know where that haunted look came from, and none who ever made an effort to find out. One might note a picture of him on his desk from his college graduation. It only added to the oddness one was beginning to perceive about the man. This was a Larry unscarred and young. He had long hair and the beginnings of a full beard. He did not seem to be surrounded by his ghosts. But the picture was still unsettling. He was not looking exactly at the camera but seemed to be glancing over the shoulder of the cameraman at someone or something that perhaps the person taking the picture could not see or even understand.

Larry had a small group of friends, some close. He did not socialize much since his move into Cambridge but did not avoid those who found his company worthwhile. One thing did bemuse him. At work, which was scarcely a social club, he found folks in the unit would drop in from time to time, unannounced, just wanting to spend a few minutes chatting about nothing in particular. He was fine with this and did enjoy the visits. Oddly, the visitors were not always other faculty but included office staff, administrators, technicians, custodians, graduate students of other faculty. Curious, he thought. He had no matching desire to wander the halls of his building or the campus in general to pursue such interactions, he but took it as a given that a number of folks did, and he obliged them with equanimity. It had always been thus.

Larry watered his plants, wound the ancient clock with its heavy brass key, and walked back out through his lab without bothering to lock the inner office. The lab, unlike the office, was very much of this century, decade, and day at the very beginning of a new millennium. One of his grad students was still out there laboring on a large chamber in which the process of cloud formation could be simulated, monitored, and manipulated. The change in phase from liquid to vapor and back transferred the latent heat that powered hurricanes, and he needed to gather much more detailed information about how this heat was used. He wandered over to see what was going on.

The student, Sharon Flagler, was a doctoral candidate with real promise. She was interested in the spatial patterns of heat transfer that occur when hurricanes just begin to form. Right at the moment, she was working on Bénard Cells. These were curious dynamic self-organizing nonlinear systems that form when a sheet of water is heated from below. They reminded her of the multiple thunderstorms that form when hurricanes develop. But those are in air, and Bénard Cells are in liquid. Whether or not this work would shed any serious light on matters at hand was as yet problematic, but he was inclined to let his students wander out East of Eden if they wished, as long as they knew the dangers. He had hauled a few students back in from the howling darkness in time to get a thesis done and go on to a postdoc before they were ready for the old age home. By and large the philosophy worked, and his students were seldom without work for long after leaving his lab. More importantly, he was sure there would be insight, and that was as important as data. A few thousand years ago, a gentleman was settling into a bathtub with a problematic gold crown at the back of his mind. In a flash, he discovered a fundamental law of Physics and went running down the street shouting "Eureka"!

After a few minutes of specific and precise questioning, he headed out of the lab, ventured hesitantly into the hall, and was relieved to see the coast was clear. Suddenly he heard the dread sound of Fred Larch's voice, and all thought of a timely departure was gone.

"Hey! Larry!"

"Aaaay, how's Fred today?" He managed to disguise his dismay with an ultimate act of will.

"Did you hear what the board of trustees wants to do now? They met this morning, and they want to mandate minimum teaching loads for all faculty. Two goddamn courses a semester. Jesus, this place is going to hell. You'd think the president would stand up to these idiots and tell them he knows how to run a research university. That's what they hired him to do for Christ's sake! Look at his fucking salary, three times what I make! They think they have some idea what they're doing, and every time they turn around, they make things tougher for us. If he had any balls, he'd tell them to eat shit and die. "

"Did you go to the BOT meeting?"

"Nah, it was in some fancy-schmancy hotel in downtown Boston. Catered, probably, with fancy pâté and French white wine. Supposed to be an open meeting for anyone, but just try to get in sometime. You know—"

Larry interrupted, seeing a solid fifteen-minute rant, which he hoped he could diffuse. "How did you hear so fast about what went on?"

"You know me, I have fire hydrants I visit. Man, I am so glad I'm getting out of here next year. I hear they are going to give us a golden parachute. They want to dump older faculty and hire youngsters so they can cut faculty salaries. Then they keep raising the bar for tenure and promotion. Work the poor kids to death. Next thing, they'll be trying to get rid of tenure so they can doom all of us to early graves. I don't care, I'm on my way out anyway. Place is a zoo. When I was first hired, I remember they used to give faculty a nice captain's chair for twenty-five years of service. The year before I hit my twenty-five, they stopped, and I got a stinking key ring. Can you imagine that? I took it out to the rifle range I go to out in Wayland and shot the shit out of it."

Larry had his own plastic key ring with its tasteful University logo. He had not shot anything out of it. He kept it as a kind of modern *memento mori*. If he were a biologist, he would probably try to get a genuine human skull to serve that function, being more of a traditionalist, but felt that might be a bit over the top, even in his unusual office.

"You know I was just talking to the chairman . . ."

It was at that point that salvation arrived in the form of the department's administrative assistant. Alice Tétrault was a small dynamo of a woman and a Person to Be Reckoned With. Even the good professor Vintner, a mighty curmudgeon of a man, physically imposing, gruff, brusque, even frightening when he wanted to be, did not say "boo" to Alice. In fact, as he read the look on her face, he began desperately searching for a place to run and hide. She was after Fred, though, and Larry succumbed to the sick guilt-mixed-with-relief of the survivor who has just seen a bad accident that might have involved him but, through chance alone, did not. *The Bridge of San Louis Rey* often figured in his musings.

"Professor Larch, when you gave me your hazmat report last April, you specifically noted that you had no mercury thermometers in your lab. Now the OSHA people are talking about an inspection of your floor, and your grad student says she found four in an old drawer! Do you know we'll get fined over a thousand bucks for each infraction? EACH thermometer is a single infraction, Doctor!" She said this in a tone of voice that was steady, measured, and made of high-carbon tool steel.

"Yeah, I know, but the hazmat team wants almost three hundred dollars apiece just to take them away." By now, Fred was almost whining. Larry sympathized with him, and had wasted a good many hours trying to get up to code himself, with no real success. He survived on the blissful assumption that they would simply leave him alone, deflected by guardian angels, in whom he maintained a staunch disbelief in all cases but this. He saw no inconsistency in that position. Perhaps lamb's blood painted over his lab door would help. Meantime, since Fred seldom ventured into his own lab, there could be a hundred kilos of weapons-grade plutonium dipped in anthrax sitting around and he would not have a glimmering of a notion. Gail was his only graduate student and was really being advised by someone else. She was simply using Fred's space and equipment for a project she largely designed and financed on her own. She would certainly be his last. Fred would likely read her thesis, semi-understand it, ask questions, and demand to be on any resulting publications, reserving the most honorable last spot on the authorship list for himself. But as far as contributing in any meaningful way, forget it.

Larry guessed that four mercury thermometers would be on the bottom of the Charles River in about the time it would take to get to the nearest bridge with a pedestrian walkway at Fred's top speed. Computing this time interval would make a nice, simple word problem for a middle school math/physics text, he mused. Fred was not all that in touch with environmental concerns.

The matter was out of Larry's hands, but he was upset by the interchange. He was ready to do his part for workplace safety, but if that meant not doing his work, he would be taking a walk like Fred's with his own stash of mercury-filled thermometers. He rather liked them better for some applications. And he already had them. But he knew his own territory better than anyone, and even OSHA would be very unlikely to unearth them unless they happened by when the instruments were actually in use. He could just store them at home in his bathroom and bring one or two in when he needed them.

The (largely one way) "discussion" crackled on, and he slipped out through the fire door and into the stairwell. He went down three flights to the parking lot reserved for faculty. In typical bureaucratic fashion, it was grossly oversold. The university's department of public safety was ever vigilant about violations and would happily tow your car if it failed to meet any of their regulations, while getting the princely sum of two hundred dollars per year for a sticker. Larry was one of the first people in the lot in the morning, but that meant that he was trapped for the day. If he needed to leave and return, he might as well park in Springfield and hitchhike in from there. Parking spaces in that lot had a phenomenal vapor pressure. Normally, he walked from his apartment, which was only about ten blocks away, but today he had some gear he needed to pick up for his trip, and he did not feel he could afford the time.

He was headed out of town on a journey that had him deeply occupied. He knew exactly where he was going, but not why. The trip's origins lay deep in an unsettled part of his past that he had never dealt with at any level in all the passing years. It was clear the time for this reckoning was at hand, but the way this would play out lay in darkness. The letter had come from the obscure town of Phoenicia, New York, but a letter from the main offices of the National Science Foundation in Alexandria, Virginia, could not have come close to the reaction it produced.

There was a spot deep down in him that was a haunted room. It came into existence suddenly one day, years ago, and that incident had just come back into the present with a vengeance. It had changed the course of his life profoundly and irrevocably. Who he was now, a leading scientist with a worldwide reputation, was a direct and positive outcome. His marriage and the fact that he had a son were down the road he took that day. But so were the scars, the ones one could see and the ones one could only guess at. Larry was no coward. He would make this trip. But that dark room was filled with howling ghosts, and it was so cold it made a Dewar flask filled with liquid helium look like a hot, freshly brewed cup of oolong tea.

He fired up his old VW Rabbit and headed out for the outfitters. He could not justify the expense of a new car in Boston. A new car had a target painted on it that drew the worst of an already bloodthirsty lot of thieves, vandals, reckless drivers, sociopaths, and otherwise troubled souls. The Rabbit was mechanically sound but looked like it was on its last legs. The license plate was wired on, there was a barely legal crack in the windshield, the radio antenna was a coat hanger, it had no hubcaps, both front fenders were largely unpainted Bondo, and the passenger-side door was from another Rabbit that had tinted glass instead of clear and was of another, clashing color. Camouflage! People left him alone, since it looked as if no matter what they were driving, they had more to lose in any interaction than he. Inside, where it counted, the car was better than new. He changed the oil and filter every three thousand miles, the brakes and shocks were always replaced on schedule, and there were a few parts in there, courtesy of Bernie, the university machinist in the basement of the physics building, that were lots better than Volkswagen new original stock. The Germans were good engineers and manufacturers but seldom used titanium, zirconium, or magnesium/aluminum alloys to build their vehicles. The space shuttle would come off second best going head-to-head for exotic metallurgy. A surprising amount of the car was stainless steel, including something old-time mechanics might recognize as an "X" frame typical of the Buicks of the early fifties. Not a stock configuration, it may be assumed.

Traffic was surprisingly light for this time in the afternoon, even given that it was a Thursday. He was glad he had planned to leave a day early. First of all, it would give him a chance to spend Friday afternoon and evening with his old friend Eban, and second, he would avoid the Friday afternoon crunch. He pointed his miraculous vehicle toward Boston proper and negotiated the back streets that he knew better than most of the natives of this part of town. He figured it paid off to explore any new area, and when he had hit town many years earlier, he'd begun to poke around with a messianic fervor that would have done credit to Lewis and Clark.

His destination today was an outdoor sporting goods store that he frequented regularly. A phone call had confirmed that the parts for his Svea 123 camp stove had arrived. He wondered where they had found them, since the chief curator of antiquities at the Smithsonian was not known for parting with relics of this rarity. The parking lot was almost full, but after a short face-off with a young woman in a brand-new Saab, who caved in rapidly after taking a nanosecond to assess the condition of the Rabbit, he got a choice spot. It was a common occurrence for him, but he savored the tiny victory briefly.

He wandered into the showroom, and old feelings wrapped him up in a familiar embrace. The walls were covered with pitons, crampons, mountain climbing line, all the keen stuff. Rows of hardcore high-angle ice climbing boots greeted him. There were tents that began to show their mettle when you were looking down on fifteen thousand feet of exposure. The effect was always physical for him, almost like having your breath sucked out of your chest. He looked at the youngsters walking about, fondling the gear with knowing looks. They were tanned, with premature age lines from being outdoors so much. Men and women both, they looked like they were made solely of muscle and sinew and bone. Creatures of the high realms. Mixed in were the far more numerous phonies who put carabiners on their bookbags to look cool but lacked the hard-earned look of the real thing.

He envied the youngsters who were genuine mountaineers, but with envy liberally slaked with equanimity. When he was young he had been up there too, as much as he could fit into his life, and his sins were not sins of omission in those halcyon days. What crept in around the edges now was more a melancholy autumnal chill. Any of these kids, with preparation and some good fortune, could climb the highest peaks on earth. Now he was too old. They had no ceiling yet on earth below thirty thousand feet, while his had formed already and had started to drop. He knew that in the high country, the really high country, where our world meets outer space, where even in the brilliance of high noon the stars are almost visible, he could no longer survive. The altitude would kill him—if he even got that far. Each year, the highest point he might achieve came a down bit lower.

He had never traversed the highest country of the Himalayas. There were a lot of formidable peaks that had seen his boots, but never the greatest of them. He had never been able to pull that off. Partly, it was for financial reasons. You can't go traipsing off to Nepal when you are subsisting on poached deer and roadkill rabbit. And when he did have the money, there was no more time. He had done his best climbing when he was broke and getting gas for his old F-100 pickup had been a major problem. Tibet and Nepal were musings of old age now, not dreams of fiery youth.

When the great heights passed through his mind now, he almost always replayed a tale he'd once heard. One of the great climbers of the mid twentieth century, a man who had conquered the west ridge of Everest and a number of other eight-thousand-plus-meter giants had a child, a daughter, whom he named after one of the greatest peaks of them all. Not the tallest, but one that was great in spiritual stature. She grew up in a world that was rich with tales of high ice, talus slopes, vertical rock, cols, long treks in lonely country, and monasteries populated by robed monks turning their prayer wheels endlessly on the roof of the world. She had grown to a woman, and a day came, probably inevitably, when she challenged with her father the peak whose name she shared. It killed her. She became sick with the altitude, and before she could be brought down, it killed her. Larry had never fully found a way to be at peace with this event. There was no way he could find a place for it to rest. It wormed its way through him eternally, like an asbestos fiber, leaving a trail of scar tissue behind.

The story populated a space beyond the bounds of common irony. It was a tale that those monks could likely assimilate and learn from, and then go on about their lives. But not Larry. It was a darkly beautiful parable, and he was ashamed at how much he loved the beauty that such tragedy had hatched. But it was an inhuman beauty, something in the aching, airless darkness between the stars rather than in the hearts of mortals. If she had been his child, he knew he would never have recovered from the agony. He knew that fully, as any parent contemplating that greatest of all fears must. As a parent, Larry knew he never would have had the faith of Abraham as he led Isaac away. But there was something there as well that transcended the sense of loss.

He thought of the name, the mountain's and the woman's, and wondered if there was some supernatural power in this name that mocked his rational mind. Mountains are rock thrust up by unknowing nature, the titanic action of tectonic plates wandering the earth. Just really big bumper cars. The earth itself is, in its turn, dwarfed to the point of meaninglessness by what lies beyond. Humans are animated clay: dissipative, dynamic structures, organized by nonlinear thermodynamics into beings that can think, and be aware, and fear the time when they must return to clay. So why are names so important? Names for people and names for mountains. There are cultures whose people do not like to divulge their "true" names, fearing the power that a name in the wrong hands might convey.

As a person to whom rational inquiry was the only sensible way to understand the universe, he believed in statistics and probability. Two events could occur simultaneously and be unconnected causally. He knew this on a fundamental level and accepted it unequivocally. In any event, the death of the mountaineer's daughter had not been purely a chance occurrence. If you grow up in a mountaineering family, and if you are named after a high peak, presumably, you might want to climb that peak. Mountains are deadly, even little mountains. Her death in the thin air of some peak might have been physiologically inevitable, a cardiovascular/respiratory time bomb. One did not need to consult a cosmology to explain the event. But the success of rational thought in this regard did nothing to diminish the value to Larry of thinking about her death in spiritual terms. Names of mountains and gods are words of great power. Names like Annapurna, Kanchenjunga or, or . . . Nanda Devi.

He walked over to the counter that had the stove display and listened to the kid who lectured him on the features of the new stoves, castigated him (in a nice way, if a bit patronizingly) on his intransigence in maintaining an antique, made the requisite jokes about terrorist weapons, and ultimately sold him the repair parts, some Coleman fuel, a few tent pegs, a new stainless steel vacuum water bottle with a protective cover, a package of moleskin, and a filter element for getting the giardia out of the water. As a kid wandering the high country of New Hampshire, Larry drank the water with complete confidence, and there had been beavers then too. What was happening to the world?

His mind wandered briefly back to a long-dead summer day of furnace heat. He had climbed Mount Moosilauke and was on the way down. The water in his canteen was getting warm, and he came to one of those streams that you see only in mountain country. The bed was rock, both ledge and boulders, and the water was rushing by at a great rate. He drank his fill and topped off his canteen against harder times. In his whole life, he had never drunk anything that tasted any better. There was something else going on. There had been beavers here since before the first migrations out of Asia. He had never even heard of *Giardia lamblia* until ten years ago. Maybe he had just been lucky. Thinking about the Good Old Days was a sign of encroaching dotage.

He paid with his credit card, grabbed the bag, and strode purposefully out of the store.

One of the young gearheads who made this place a second home strolled over to the counter and made a few pleasantries. He queried the clerk who had sold the goods to Larry, asking about who that old guy was. He was told it was just some old professor named Vintner, and that he was in a few times every year.

The young man went back to his group to report.

"Aaaaah, I told you it wasn't anybody major league."

"Yeah, but whoever that guy is, he's the real thing," said a tall, blond, lean man, looking to be in his late twenties. He was the one who had started the speculation on Larry's identity.

"OK, but even if he was, like, some hotshot back when, so what? Dude's way over the hill. Ready for the nursing home," chimed in a third, the youngest of the lot.

The tall, fair man said nothing in reply. He had been climbing in Colorado a couple of years back, trying to make his list of twelve-thousand footers, and sought out a guide. It was late in the year, and snow was in the forecast. An uncertain forecast. He did not mess around with mountains, even little ones, and this was a nasty one even when you hit it in July. The man he finally hired was older than the individual who had just aroused his curiosity. He had inwardly resigned himself to leaving him in the Blazer with his nitro pills and the ball game on the radio when they reached the end of the passable part of the approach road.

But that was not how it worked out when they got to the trail. The old fart was part mountain goat. He just loped along in low gear, low range. The younger man started out almost running on ahead, impatient as hell, bounding up the broken boulders of the lower slopes. This turned out to be a bad move. The old mountain man just kept up that lope, not slowing down, not speeding up. He never broke stride, even though they ended up going almost vertically up the summit cone, close to a rope-up situation.

By unwritten rule, either could have called for ropes or even a belay. Neither did. The guide never seemed tired, while the younger man came close to quitting twice. That he did not do so was a tribute to his youth and a stubborn streak as wide as an interstate. The man with the almost nonexistent gray hair whom he had just seen leaving the store reminded him of that Colorado guide. He thought he might be a bad guy to mess around with on almost any front.

The group broke up and went on about their collective business of spending money on ripstop nylon, exotic alloy, and other wonders. Upon reaching home, the tall blond man, the only serious climber in his small group at the store, idly thumbed through his brittle, worn copy of *Everest: The West Ridge* and other expedition books of that era, expecting to find a familiar face in the old photographs, or the name Vintner in the index.

2

Larry pulled into his parking garage, landed in his spot, and removed the things he was going to leave home. The new gear stayed in the car, as there was no reason to bring it in just to haul it back out. He walked around to the apartment building and headed up to the top floor. He was greeted by T. Hewitt Edward, his ancient male cat. He no longer really had claim to the first name Tom, of course. Larry had resisted the pressure to have him neutered for some time. The unfortunate side effects of this became intolerable fairly quickly. The poor animal, driven by the normal physiology and neurobiology of his species, spent days out in the 'hood, fighting for females. Sometimes he won, sometimes he lost. He always ended up a pus-covered mess. Thinking of his own testicles and identifying with his pet a bit too much, Larry kept the scalpel at bay until one day when T.H.E. had limped in with one game leg. He rested for an hour or so, grabbed some dry cat food, and demanded to be let out again. Not a demand you could resist. He was gone for two days and returned limping on two legs. Same routine, out again. Next time, he dragged himself in limping on three legs. He immediately went to the vet for surgery, antibiotics, and a trip under the knife. This was the end of the problem for them both. His wife was pleased.

The name was a reminder of a long-forgotten TV show—older than the venerable cat, but Larry liked it well enough. The cat could give a shit. Larry picked him up and scratched his ears, an act that was greeted with the usual purr that rumbled up from such a depth it was almost inaudible. He ambled into the kitchen, cracked a beer, and pulled out some Auricchio provolone. It was from an Italian importing store in the North End and should have come with a Materials Safety Data Sheet for hazardous substances before being allowed into the country. T.H.E. Cat was fed some dry food to keep him at bay, and Larry made a foray into the dark recesses of the old place. He had moved into town four years ago, after his divorce, and still was not used to this super-cramped life. Of course, the suburbs were scarcely better. The cat had made an easy adjustment, having already slipped into the rarified realm of 75 percent dream time that befitted his advancing years. His youth in the suburbs had been riotous and fulfilling (before that unfortunate ex-tomcat business), so Larry did not feel too guilty about the transplant that allowed no outdoor privileges. This way the cat would keep what was left of his ears, if nothing else. He grabbed his mid-distance hiking pack, which he had carefully stuffed the previous night with everything he felt he might need, latched onto the overnight bag, set both by the door, and made some other last-minute preparations, mostly centered around dental care.

After he finished the beer, he gave T.H.E. a final scratch and locked the door behind him. The stately cat settled in for the evening, feeling the first psychic warnings of hard months of cold weather ahead, even through the thick old masonry walls. Most cats just *know* things like that, like a much smaller number of people do; like Larry did. Larry had already made arrangements with Carol, the woman directly downstairs from him, to take care of his treasured friend. Carol and Larry were more than neighbors, and more than "just friends". Larry hated that phraseology. As though a real friendship were not every bit as important and demanding as any other relationship. Sometimes more important, in the scheme of things. In any event, it was no real secret that they maintained a modest sexual relationship that more than made up for the lack of teenage intensity with friendliness, compatibility, and coziness. Carol was good for him at this stage in his life, sitting as he was on the cusp where late middle age threatens to give way to early old age. Funny how it is possible to keep adding modifiers to put off the change in terminology. Why not late-late-late-late youth?

Guilt of any kind certainly did not enter into the way Larry characterized this relationship. Given the circumstances of his divorce, he could easily make a case that he had been ill-used. Even a casual observer would likely say that, in fact, he did come out way down on the short end. But he had acknowledged even in the depths of that struggle that he would not walk away without shouldering some of the culpability. Nonetheless, even though his ex still loomed large on his horizon as someone of great importance, he saw no reason to march on out of his sexually active years without some sexual activity ongoing. He still rather enjoyed it after all. And Carol was a good-looking woman and fun to have sex with. About ten years younger than Larry she was a widow, trim and graying a bit. 'Prostate' was all she ever would say about the widow part." "Prostate" was all she ever told Larry about that topic. Ugly subject, he imagined, and he did not care to speculate or investigate further.

The very lack of sheet-shredding, feral sexual heat was actually a comfort to Larry, along with the fact that she had no connection with his university at all. His thoughts turned to one of the dangers of his position. Perhaps being a professor in the year 2000, at the turn of the century and millennium, when just looking at an attractive co-ed at a politically incorrect angle could land you in the back alley with the personal effects from your office in an old trash sack and your books and papers in a heap, had dulled what had been a razor edge in his youth. More than his age, such daily exposure to forbidden riches may have rendered him more cautious than he otherwise might have been. "Just like the damn mercury thermometers," he thought. Women of college age burned with the white heat of reproductive readiness and should be protected from slavering dirty old men. But in a kinder, gentler age, if a young woman was in your office crying because she flunked your final, you might at least feel free to close the door without it costing you your job.

But keeping your eyes (hands did not even enter in the equation) to yourself in such an environment took work and skill. The words that worked for him were almost a mantra. He would simply think "There is no fool like an old fool. I can do nothing about being old, but with some care and thought, I can do something about being a fool." By couching the prohibition in this way, the chain of causation started with the idea that he was simply being reasonable and trying to avoid looking like a Real Asshole.

Larry regained the parking garage and stowed the last of his gear. The trusty vehicle awaited its master's touch and chuckled to life. It seemed to be eager to leave this warren for clear air and something new. Again, on the road, he threaded his way through the tangled web of local streets and ultimately eased the armored, camouflaged Űber-Hase out into traffic on the Mass Pike, heading west. His plan was to stop at his ex-wife's house (formerly *their* house, jointly held) in Wellesley for supper, catch a few winks on the couch, and head out in the early hours. He liked driving at night and particularly enjoyed daybreak from behind the wheel. In his waking fantasy dreams, he saw himself as a long-haul trucker. It was nothing he would want to do in the real world (kidney problems and all), but he still looked at the eighteen-wheelers with plates from high, lonesome country, like Wyoming, with a certain wistful envy. No one ought to be that free.

One of his good friends back in Grahamsville, Alton Frasier, had driven the big rigs. He hauled produce all over the country for the best years of his life. A drunk on the wrong side of the road on the outskirts of a small Georgia town put him out of business. The jerk was besotted (blood-alcohol 0.23), witnesses had seen him staggering out of a party, he had been driving at least ninety according to the state police's reconstruction, and he had swerved into Alton's lane. In what was clearly a reasonable attempt at survival, at least hypothetically, Alton had gone into the other lane to avoid him. Not as good in practice as one might have hoped. The drunk swerved back at the last instant and wrapped his Oldsmobile around the front of the giant Peterbilt like an aluminum beer can. There was not much left of the Olds, but the Peterbilt was scarcely scraped.

The problem was that this fine citizen was the cousin of the county assistant DA. Alton had a warm spot in his heart for William Tecumseh Sherman from that point on. Larry figured Alton and the general, who had arguably invented Total War (with a strip of land between Atlanta and Savannah as his laboratory), were comparing stories about Georgia right now. Renal failure took old Alton in '84.

Traffic was abysmally heavy. He mentally checked off the years until he could buy a camp in upstate New Hampshire and kiss Boston goodbye. He liked the town well enough, much better than the Big Apple or the dread LA, for example, but always having to wait for other people in lines or in traffic was starting to grind him down. He had gone to undergraduate school in Manhattan, and the reaction to that experience was to move upstate to the Catskills right after graduation. He had little in the way of marketable skills, with a BS in mathematics, unless he was willing to teach thugs how to add up their drug-sale proceeds, so he thought he might as well be unemployed in a place with some natural beauty and no crowds. Now he was back in a city, serving thirty years to life at an urban university. A few more years and he could go out on phased retirement, or even go emeritus. His research would be at a point where he could come in for a few months out of the year and tinker in the lab, which he could likely keep as long as he had grant support and spend the rest of the time up in the mountains telecommuting and playing with the new numbers he'd generate or writing. At least it was a pleasant fantasy that eased his mind when traffic slowed to the point where old women in walkers were outpacing him.

He was looking forward to seeing his son Karl that evening. His ex-wife, Andrea, had called him brimming with excitement yesterday afternoon to tell him that their wonderful, beautiful, magnificent only child was planning to come down from one of his bivouacs a few miles west of Springfield, Vermont. He had not been home to the Boston area in over a year, and Larry missed him.

Karl was a free spirit. He had gotten a degree in English at the University of Massachusetts in Amherst, and talked of teaching or writing, or both if he could pull that off, but now he was just hanging out. It was a tough time for English majors. The health professions or law did not interest him, and even if he could land a middle-management business position, he would likely rather pound his hands with a hammer. The middle class was disappearing. It was as difficult to make it as a physicist as a Shakespearian actor. No path was easy. In a way, it was liberating. If you did not much want to be a physicist and really loved the idea of besting Sir Lawrence Olivier's rendition of Hamlet, you were at least as likely to make it in the latter as the former occupation. But Karl was doing nothing much at all that Larry could see. He was making lampshades out of parchment, painting on designs, and selling them at craft shows across New England. This was *not* a money tree. He had a girlfriend who was raising herbs for alternative medicine, also something less effective than inventing DOS or Windows as a way to wealth. She raised other herbs as well and had been indicted by an unfriendly prosecutor with limited vision. She had a young child by a former lover, so Larry suspected the charge would be dropped eventually. He had written a letter to the DA himself in support of leniency. He often thought it would be a very good time to legalize pot.

Karl lived in many places across the year. Vermont was his summer haunt, and as close as he would get to calling a home base. Assuming the indictment could be dropped in time, his girlfriend would join him in the next spot down the line. Her child might or might not go along, since the woman had an extended family that took care of her most of the time anyway. When the autumn came on and the days got shorter, Karl would grow restless. By October, when Vermont and the rest of New England was in its finest pelage of fall colors, Karl was usually in Taos, New Mexico, staying with an unsavory crew of men and women—also with no visible means of support beyond a small store that dealt in all manner of used tools, household goods, crafts, dried flowers, old filling station signs, and memorabilia of cowboy days. Among other things, which a

New Mexico grand jury would find as unappealing as did their Vermont counterparts.

Spring would see him head up through the Rockies, across Idaho, and into central Washington state. Here, he would work for apple farmers to prepare the orchards for the summer's growth. He was good with trees, seemed to learn about them quickly, and was handy with a ladder and a chainsaw or pruning shears. Several farmers there knew he was coming and hired him reliably. By early summer, the ancient Volvo would be at the cabin in the central part of Vermont, near a little town called Londonderry. This place was not much in the summer, but it bustled in the winter with the ski season in full swing at the many nearby resorts. Larry was unsure who actually owned the cabin. Presumably someone paid the taxes, or the town fathers would have auctioned it off long since.

It was here that Karl curated the one exception he made to his rejection of material wealth. He was a collector of ship's chronometers. Not replicas or modern electronic units but the real thing, from the age of iron men and wooden ships. These were brass masterpieces, timepieces from the late nineteenth century that sat in jeweled gimbals to neutralize the rolling of the seas. Chronometers represented the finest mechanical escapement timepieces ever made—direct linear descendants of a prototype conceived by a troubled genius who made his first tower clock entirely out of wood. It had wooden bearings, wooden gears, all hand carved with great care and nearly superhuman skill. It was finished and began its first ticking in the eighteenth century. It is still running. This man solved a major problem of his century: how to know your longitude by knowing the time in Greenwich, England, to the second, no matter where you were on the ocean.

Larry admitted to being very impressed with this collection. As a father, though, he was hard pressed not to wonder where the money came from for such amazingly expensive artifacts. He was also given to wonder how these sacred instruments could sit in an empty, unlocked cabin for eight months out of the year and never grow legs. He had a pretty good idea that they would not so disappear. If whoever it was that shed his unseen protective cloak over Karl's worldly goods in his absence could scare off the vile weasels who skulked about in the backwoods of New England looking for camps to break into, the prospect of his being a friend and colleague of sorts of his son was deeply troubling.

It was a great disappointment, but not much of a surprise when he did not see Karl's tottering Volvo sitting out front of the house. Externally, the car was reminiscent of Larry's Rabbit in rampant decrepitude. The difference was that the scruffiness went more than skin deep in the Volvo's case. It left an oily blue fog behind, its valves made a terrible din, it had just enough oil pressure to keep the bearings lightly lubed, and the transmission spit the gearshift out of second after about twenty miles per hour unless you manually held the handle in place.

As a first guess based on the car in question, Larry figured car trouble, but when he got inside, he found that the car had not broken down. His ex-wife, however, had. Andrea was in tears. Even after all the years and all the disappointments, she had never found a way to armor herself against her son's utter lack of filial piety.

"That miserable little shit! Slimy little sack of rodent excrement! Steaming mound of ulcerated sheep spleens!"

Not a bad string, but no more than a six on a scale of one to ten based on her talent. Andrea had used up all the really good expletives on

Karl years before. The most she could do tonight was just derivative of her own best work. Larry slumped against the staircase and listened as the tirade went on for another few minutes. He finally saw a tiny crack in the monolithic wall of invective.

"OK, what the fuck did he do now?"

He said it quickly, so he might take credit for having gotten a complete thought out on the table.

"If I thought you would answer your goddamn work phone, I would have called and saved you the trouble of coming out here. You know, *most* people *answer* their phones. It means someone, possibly someone with important information, wants to talk to you."

It was not true that Larry never answered his phone at work, but he had left work early. This was not true of his apartment, where he really didn't answer the phone. He also had no caller ID or answering machine on that unit. It was for outgoing calls only. Larry V.'s First Law was "If the phone rings and you answer it, the chances are nine out of ten that it will be your problem. If the phone rings and you don't answer it, the chances are nine out of ten that it will be somebody else's problem." Words to ponder gravely and with infinite respect for their unassailable logic. Most of his slowly evolving list of top ten laws worked equally well, in an empirical way. For example, Larry's Fourth Law (up from Sixth, as of December of the previous year, which was particularly foggy) stated, "If you see a car in a parking lot with its lights on, its doors will be locked." It had never failed despite long, hard efforts at data acquisition to falsify it.

"OK, let's dial it back a notch and let me hear it. I can guess. And for once, will you stop being so surprised when he pulls shit like this. I feel really bad when he screws you up like this, don't get me wrong, but he has been doing this nonstop since he was fifteen. And every time, you beat yourself up."

"That creep son of yours called just about the time he ought to have been getting here. He made some lame excuse. He does not lie well. You'd think he would have improved at least a little bit from all the practice he gets. I was not paying much attention by that point. I imagine the pot harvest is in full swing in Vermont. They have to be on the move all the time, keeping the drying racks out of sight, driving out of town to buy baggies, throwing camo over the plantation to fool the chopper jocks. You know the drill."

"Yeah, I know. I used to help you, don't forget. You know that old saw about the acorn and the oak. What's your beef with him following in his beloved mother's footsteps?"

"It was different in those days, the late sixties, early seventies. It was kind of a not-for-profit deal. Christ, we practically gave most of it away. I just wanted to have enough so that people would hang out and party. I liked that, and I liked smoking back then. Whoever Karl is mixed up with is the real thing. These kids are making their living off the shit, and they could do hard time. I can't even guess the volume, but it must be enough to push it to a felony if he gets popped."

"Well, if it's any consolation, as we move into this brand-new decade, century and millennium, I see real progress on getting it legalized."

Larry had clouded emotions about Karl's involvement in the home-grown racket. He was very concerned not only about the law, but about the group he was in with. He had helped Andrea in the old days and had enjoyed it. It was part political in those days. Screw the Man! Lots of things were political during the 'Nam era, and if he could put one in the Man's eye, he was all for it. He had hauled hog manure off into the woods, put up deer fences, watered starters, culled male plants, pulled, dried, and weighed out ounce bags. But he seldom used any of it even back then and had no interest in it at all now. He hoped Karl was not in this too deeply and was smart enough not to haul product around the country and to stay out of any big deals at the higher levels of whatever organization he was recruited by. He was not a high roller, had very modest needs, and would be pretty low in the organization. Just a foot soldier. But that cabin, bloated with priceless chronometers, was never far from Larry's mind.

Andrea ceased rational discourse at that point, and the tirade started back up and went on a bit longer, but Larry was not really listening. Andrea was obviously losing steam. He had long ago found that he could think about almost anything he wanted to when she was on a roll like this, and she never noticed. What he was thinking about during this precise interval of time was the smell of the house. Or, more precisely, what was now lacking in the smell of the house, namely stale cigarette smoke. Andrea's boyfriend, Jean-Marc (he liked to refer to him as Robespierre to annoy her, successfully) was a heavy smoker. Larry hated the way the house smelled when he showed up on his occasional visits. He had always been firm about smoking in this house, and guests knew about this and respected it. They would dutifully wander out into the breezeway to light up, and Larry left a labeled coffee can out there for the butts. Until Robespierre, the house spent many years free of the stench. Now he would get pissed off all over again every time he smelled the ruins of the sweet aroma of the place he used to call home.

He was aware that part of this feeling stemmed from knowing his successor had been around. This was the spoor of his rival. The divorce had been her idea solely, spurred by her having met this guy, but not solely a result of her infidelity. He could have lived with that, after a fashion—maybe even looked the other way so it could go on, but she just did not want to be married to him anymore. He was still in love with Andrea, make no mistake about this, despite what she had done. He would not add "to him," as he knew it was done "for herself", but surely she had taken the active role. The emotions that crushed him when he saw them together were tough to describe, although they were more ancient than civilization itself. Here was *his wife* with this other guy. It was strange to see him in control of her, or at least the two of them in mutual control of each other. He knew that when this man wanted to make love to her, she would comply as she used to when he initiated the act. But he was not as much concerned with the simple act of sex as he was with the underlying and more profound change in her allegiance and loyalty. At least he seldom had to deal with the guy personally. Jean-Marc was not a very big or robust man at all, standing only about five-foot-eight in his stocking feet, and he looked like benching the forty-five-pound bar without any plates on it at all would be a tough job. Larry repped four plates on the bench and squatted more, multiple sessions in any given week. That was a lot of muscle sitting on massive bones that lofted him six-foot-three. Jean-Marc, although convinced by Andrea that Larry was a gentle giant, and though he was not a physical coward, was also one to be reasonably prudent about his personal safety.

The aftermath of cigarette smoking made Larry think that the air had been murdered. By this he did not mean just polluted or damaged; rather, it was as though the air's life-giving essence had been stilled by passing through the burning weed. Pipe smoking did not seem to do this in his mind. He absentmindedly thought about the physics of combustion and wondered if it was not as much a function of the tobacco as of the method by which it burned that made the difference, as cigars had the same perceived effect as cigarettes. He had never smoked. His mother's cigarettes and his stepfather's cigars had made of his life a stinking torment. Car trips were abhorrent, especially in the winter with the windows closed. He had never thought that emulating that sort of behavior was a good idea from the start. Later, he had spent as much time as he could in places up high, where there was not a lot of air at all. Your relationship to air becomes strained up there, and you start to develop an appreciation for how tenuous a hold we have on our source of oxygen. The atmosphere is in the process of *ending* when you get up there! You know in a way that you can't feel down below that the air surrounding our planet is not infinite. Why anyone would willingly scorch their lungs and gradually render them useless was beyond him.

He had felt what it was like to strain for every breath, with each step an almost impossible effort. But then he could come down off the mountain and almost feel as if he were drinking the air like a rich liquid. His mother could not come down off her self-made mountaintop, and she died of a combination of COPD and congestive heart failure, in a manner in which there was no dignity at all. His stepfather had checked out with a massive coronary and spared himself and the rest of the family the grief of the long dying. But the root cause had been the same. Larry's biological father, who died when Larry was only seven, also died of a coronary and, in mute testimony to the total lack of justice we all must deal with, had never smoked at all.

The tearful tirade wound down to its sorry cloaca. Larry had long since realized the very simple truth that as with his own progenitors, he and Andrea were not completely at fault for what Karl had become. But Andrea still beat her breast about it. The popular fad of going so far as to sue your parents, or at least blaming them publicly and humiliating them for what you turned out to be, was beyond ridiculous in his view. There was an instance where kids had murdered their parents and tried to get off scot-free on the grounds that they only did it because their parents had botched the job of raising them properly. People certainly could damage their kids by abuse or neglect, Larry felt that was a given, but he also thought it took a lot more than most parents dished out to create really nasty little shits. Karl may have used Andrea or Larry as templates for what he had become in part. Weighed in the balance he really was not a bad kid. But he was thoughtless and self-absorbed. And that could cut Andrea deeply. She really loved him beyond measure and just wanted to see him once in a while. Karl might have been roughly the same person in another home, another country, or another century. The Mendelian promise and curse of independent assortment of alleles and the victory of nature over nurture sits there over all our deliberations, smiling.

The dinner Andrea had planned was Karl's favorite: Polish stuffed cabbage. Andrea was not Polish. She had learned the recipe from one of the boyfriends she lived with before meeting Larry. She never told Karl that, but Larry knew the fact well. It had never been a problem before, but tonight, for the first time, the source of the culinary delight rankled. He had had his own prior experiences before they met but had never actually lived with anyone, with all that implied. Once in a while he would speculate about what it had been like for her before (about which she told him nothing at all, not even names) and how it was now with her new man. He wondered how it all compared with the considerable portion of their lives they had shared together.

They spoke little over dinner. Its association with Andrea's past aside, Larry really did like stuffed cabbage and even enjoyed the tectonic flatulence it engendered, so he concentrated on his meal. Andrea's colorful outburst had demanded a quiet aftermath. They ate the dinner without taking much pleasure in each other's company, drank a little wine, and Andrea stalked off to what had been their room after a perfunctory cleanup. Larry made it a thorough cleanup, as was his way. A tiny peace offering. He threw his old sleeping bag on the couch and nodded off quickly. As he drifted off, he mused again on the fact that the stale smoky smell really was almost gone. It took a long time for that to happen—weeks, or even months, maybe. As sleep claimed him, he was already consigning this to long-term memory for further thought and consideration.

He had always been able to sleep easily, and the depredations that (late) middle age often made on people's rest patterns had not touched him yet. Even when there were serious unresolved matters at stake, he went to bed and slept, deeply, and without bad dreams. At least without bad dreams that he could remember. He never used an alarm clock. He hated them. He thought that 4:00 A.M. would be about right to be up and around, and that's exactly when he awoke, fresh and alert, like a cat. Not like T.H.E. Cat. That old teddy bear, estimable though he might be in other ways, was still comatose an hour after getting heavily disturbed on his end of the bed when Larry arose. Larry could awaken within seconds of the time he chose, and his mind was already up to speed, prepared for whatever was to come. On this Friday, opening into the weekend, he knew only part of what was to come, the part he had planned himself. He knew his route and his destinations tonight and tomorrow, but that was almost all. The rest would have to sort itself out in its own good time, and he refused to speculate.

He brushed his teeth and let himself out quietly. He started the car and let it roll almost noiselessly down the driveway before engaging the transmission in second gear and heading out. He felt a touch of smugness, thinking that he had not awakened Andrea with his departure.

And he had not, in fact, awakened her. She sat in the dark in the cushioned bedroom window seat, watching him leave. She had not slept all night and so, technically, could not be awakened. She watched the car as it made its almost silent way down the cool predawn street until it was out of sight. Then she went to bed knowing now she could sleep. She would "sleep fast," as her mother always used to say when tucking her in. She needed to be at work at the hospital at 11:00. It was going to be a tough day.

3

Sleep came finally to Andrea after this long, dark night of quiet thought. Her mind had not been racing meaninglessly but had been focused and clear. She'd remained surprisingly free of fatigue through the long hours. She had made a lot of decisions in those hours in the shank end of the night, and there was now some peace in places in her mind that had not seen peace in a long time. This brief visit had precipitated her asking a lot of questions of herself that desperately needed answers and resolution. She had known it would, even longed for its effects. Larry's simple physical and spiritual presence could do that for her still, even after all the troubles they'd had. Karl's turning up missing had not been all that bad a thing in the end, since it gave them a quiet time, even though they spoke little and said nothing of consequence. This curious man's presence had that effect on many others, about whom he knew nothing, so it was not her long relationship with him that made it work. While he had few friends anymore, he was often sought out by people who just seemed to want to talk to him about nothing in particular, and they always came away feeling better for no discernable reason. There was actually an underground network at the university she knew about that clued people into this. This was extremely odd on the face of it, given his outwardly gruff demeanor. And even more oddly, Larry never twigged to why people whom he barely knew would wander into his office to chat and leave after a bit. Perhaps if he knew what his presence meant and what it could do for others, the power, if that was what it was, might leave him. Perhaps he was insulated against that knowledge for that very reason. The magic, for want of a better word, had worked once again for Andrea. Channels opened up in the depths of her spirit, and her mind's eye went with that flow.

For one thing, she now was certain it had been the right thing to do to end her connection with Jean-Marc. That was now an old decision, relatively speaking, but one that she had been uncomfortable with until this very night. She would certainly miss him a lot in many, many ways. It seemed crazy to tell someone a relationship needed to end when it seemed to be going so well and seemed objectively to be a good thing. In contrast, when she had told Larry she wanted a separation, and then eventually that she wanted a divorce, it had not been horribly difficult for her. Ugly? Yes. Messy? Yes. A difficult decision? No. Jean-Marc was already thoroughly in the picture and was occupying a tremendous part of her consciousness at the time. Despite what Larry and others thought, meeting him, and drifting into their affair had not really been the cause of the breakup, just a symptom that her marriage had gone terribly wrong in her view. Larry had taken it very hard, and she now felt great regret at having hurt him so badly. But at the time, she felt they had no reasons left to be together, and she had lots of reasons to bed with her new man. Part of it was Larry's strange melancholy, which had haunted them both since that horrific, tragic day back in the Catskills. They never spoke about it, but he had been fundamentally, almost unbelievably changed afterwards. This omnipresent ghost had finally worn her down, and it seemed as though as Larry aged, he was becoming more deeply under its thrall.

But that was not all of it. She had gotten used to the ghost to some extent. But during the course of any given day, there seemed to be a stultifying staleness that dragged her down. He didn't seem to have a lot of time for her and the things she liked to do. Mentioning this to him got the predictable answer that things were tough at work and the university was driving everyone harder with each ensuing year. He was ill-tempered, withdrawn, and unwilling to work with her to change what was going on between them or even acknowledge it. It seemed to her that he was no longer giving her the part of his life that was her due as his wife of so many years.

What she got from Jean-Marc was a laundry list of things that she never got from Larry in all their years together after his injury. Jean-Marc gave her the little things that she needed so badly, in addition to what she thought of at the time as the big ones. Her choice of what to call "the big things" seemed odd to her now, almost naïve. She had trouble now naming those big things; they had receded and disappeared. As far as the little things, that was easy. He brought her flowers (which she loved), candy (which she did not but never told him), wine, little presents of all sorts. Most importantly, it was obvious that he was always thinking about her and how to please her. Come to think of it, that might number amongst the big things after all. The birthday presents he got her were always small, not spectacularly expensive, but of the highest quality. More importantly, their selection was the result of deep thought about her and what she did and what she liked. It was easy to get used to that sort of attention. But whatever it was that drew her to this interesting, good-looking man at the expense of Larry had been expunged from her psyche as thoroughly as though she had been passed through a white-hot fire and the mineral ashes returned to life with a whole new suite of organic chemicals. There was not the slightest vestige left of how she felt back then.

The thing that clued her in to the problem she had with her relationship with Jean-Marc was that it was very easy to explain the appeal by the simple novelty of it. When you were starting out with someone new, the adrenaline was pumping twenty-four hours a day, every day of the week. It was not too difficult to figure out what someone wanted when you were thinking about them nonstop. It was not that the fun had gone out of it yet. Even though it had been almost five years since they first crossed paths and started their relationship, it still was new by comparison to the decades with Larry. Her new mate had not stopped thinking about her a lot, and the time they spent together remained truly rich and marvelous. What began to trouble her about her behavior was the sheer banality of the process. People could fall in and out of relationships with such ease these days that the fun thing to do was to change partners as soon as the raw rush wore off and then immediately start over with someone else, complete with the requisite untapped fifty-five-gallon, Teflon-lined, stainless-steel drum full of adrenaline. It was a little bit like surfing. In this case, it was not a moving wave on a beach but a standing wave in a river. To stay on top and keep the excitement to a maximum was the goal.

Not to put too fine an edge on it, but Larry could be a pain in the ass. He was always drifting off when she was talking to him. He really believed that she did not notice this. His eyes would glaze over, and she knew he was off somewhere else. He might be on top of Annapurna, or he might be deep in the numerical solution of a nonlinear differential equation that described some damn thing in the atmosphere. It really bothered her that even when she was trying her best to keep him on task with some important matter that needed his attention, he was filtering her out. There are times when you need to be present and accounted for in the face of the enemy. Given a few hours and a spreadsheet, she could have come up with a fairly complete file of such things, this being only a random sampling from the mix. But that did not matter anymore. At all.

There certainly had been lots of excitement with Jean-Marc. The sex was obviously a big part of the game, despite her age. Maybe especially at her age. He asked a great deal of her physically—far more than Larry could ever have imagined doing. In fact, it was a bit much for her, eventually, and at one point she told him that he was taking *Story of O* way too seriously. It actually cooled him off for a while, which at that point was a good thing. For sure, there was no chance she would ever open up to Larry about the things they had done. Unfortunately, she now rather liked some of the things she and Jean-Marc had managed. Problem was, how could she ever try them now with Larry, assuming she decided to try again, without him realizing it was something she was bringing in from outside? He would know that it was the first time *he* had done it, and the first time that *they* had done it, but probably not the first time *she* had done it. Well, Sunday mornings were long and lazy, and maybe she could find a way.

Andrea and Jean-Marc went out a lot, which was something that Larry had hated to do. He really, actively hated not being home at night. He hated the television, and he never turned it on willingly. He liked to sit home and read. To his credit, at least he sometimes read things other than *Physical Review Letters* and such, but his reading a book about society in post–World War II Japan was not the same as going out dancing or to a really nice restaurant—one where you have to dress in fine clothes, make reservations, and spend a whole lot of money. If Larry were to be buried in a suit, Andrea was certain that his corpse would rise up and rend the garments right before the eyes of the horrified mourners. Jean-Marc was as comfortable in a thousand-dollar suit as Larry was in his bathrobe. Come to think of it, Larry had spent an awful lot of time in his bathrobe when he was around the house those days.

The game of comparisons was fruitful back when she was preparing to extirpate Larry from her life and trying to justify it to herself and others, even Larry himself. One list kept getting longer, and the other remained painfully short. Go or stay. Whenever she put Larry up against Jean-Marc, Larry came up the loser. Except in the things that she now knew counted more than all the others. In fact, they mattered so much that putting those other things on the same page, or even marking them down at all, seemed almost obscene.

What started her on the road back was a simple one-hour visit by Larry. That and no more. He said little during that visit, as was his way. But the visit had occurred as she perched on the edge, looking over into the blackness beyond, and it had made all the difference. She had gone in for her usual physical, as usual a year late, and they did all the obligatory tests, plus a few others after a routine examination of her armpits. She was wonderful at denial and always thought they were doing those tests on *her* just because they needed to make another payment on the equipment. She worked in a hospital but was not affiliated with any of the actual health-care delivery as such anymore; she managed the office staff. This meant that the dreary day in, day out flux of sickness and death haunted the halls of other parts of the building. It did not even "smell like a hospital" where she worked.

What they told her was that everything was not OK and might be very far from OK. They gave her a preliminary diagnosis of non-Hodgkin's lymphoma. She had a swollen lymph node in her armpit that looked pretty nasty to the oncologist, who had tsk-tsked his way through that territory. The fact that it did not hurt at all had allowed her to avoid noticing it for quite a while. They would have to do more tests, one being a biopsy. The hospital was way past busy, and it would take two weeks just to get the biopsy on the schedule—even for her, an "insider." The biopsy was duly done, and the result sat in a folder in a file for another agonizing week until the pathologist could pore over the contents. In the meantime, she was spitted over a hot fire. All she could think about was the damn lymph node. She dreamed about it; she saw it in her food she saw giant lymph nodes in the sky, dripping with ugly cells that were dancing to the wrong song. This was the hardest period of time in her whole life. The uncertainty drove her to a very bad place. She would sit down at her desk and try to work, and thoughts of chemotherapy, losing her hair, wasting away, eventually dying would weave themselves into every conscious moment. She feared the hour she would receive the news, wondering if not knowing for a little longer might actually be better. It was like Schrödinger's cat, neither alive nor dead until its box was opened, and the results known to the universe. After all, if she did not know yet, she *could* still get good news. Once you got the bad news, there was no longer any possibility everything would be OK. This sort of logic orbited her head day and night as the slow mills of the medical gods ground their grain exceeding fine.

She did get the news, and the word was good. The node was certainly not cancerous, but it was in bad shape anyway and needed to come out.

It was duly removed, and she spent two nights in the hospital—unusual in this day and age, but she was an "insider," after all. Jean-Marc was at her side throughout all of this time. He was a trooper. He slept in her room both nights and stayed with her at her home when she was released. They had never moved in together, despite their close ties. When she was in the hospital, he brought her flowers; he brought her more accursed candy, which she secretly put in the kidney dish next to her bed, much to the amusement of the night nurse. He could not have done more. But compared to Larry, he did nothing at all.

Larry stopped in once at her house for about an hour during the time she was awaiting the biopsy result. That was all. When he left, everything had changed. She had history with Larry, but that was not what made it happen. History can mean a lot, of course. The comfort of the familiar, the way a hand is always in the right place at the right time, or a playful flip at a lock of hair at a predictable moment. That can mean safety sometimes, but that would not be enough now. What she felt when Larry walked into the room that afternoon was that awesome healing power he had, in fuller measure than she had ever known. It was the one last thing in her "stay" column that she still craved. In her desire to make the stay list zero out, she had tried mightily to push it out of her mind with her partying and dancing and long romantic walks on the beach in Bermuda with Jean-Marc. This day, it came home like an underground rumbling, as of vast currents of water flowing deep beneath the earth. It was not audible but was felt in her soul, and there was immense power there. It buoyed her spirit, it gave her an energy she could not explain, it made her less afraid of the dread results. She had never been afraid of death before, largely because through most of her life she had treated it as irrelevant to her. Life stretched out beyond the horizon, and what waited there did not matter. But this whole damn lymph node business had the word mortality written over it in large letters, and the number of her days was a meaningful tally now that she had crossed over the vanishing point. It surprised her a bit that this energy that flowed between them had not diminished in the slightest, but remembering, for the first time in a long while, who (or what?) Larry might be lessened that surprise greatly.

Having come face-to-face with her own end, now sitting balefully in the real part of her world, made her think about who she might want to face it with, whenever that time came—now or forty years hence. After five years, Larry's list was growing rapidly again, and Jean-Marc's had shrunk to nothing. We all jump off alone, that's a truism, but we can hope that the last face we see is the one we want to see. Larry. "You big fucking geek!" she thought almost audibly. If it could still be worked out, and that was a big *if,* perhaps the two of them together could navigate the terminal pathways of their lives with a certain dignified strength. Plan B was for her to go through a series of lovers like Jean-Marc, trying to use the adrenaline rush to keep out the darkness. Each time she did that, she knew it would be harder; she was not getting any younger, and the darkness would always be there and would always be closing in. For comfort like this she could give up the flowers, and she could definitely give up the candy.

The decision to implement Plan A was a lot easier than the plotting for its execution. First, she had to find the strength to show Jean-Marc out the door. This was tough. He was a really nice guy and clearly enjoyed being with her. She did not want to be cruel, but then she was trying for survival here. Now, she would have to square things with Larry.

Aye, there's the rub. Square things with him. She had cheated on him, dumped him, divorced him, took his house, took half his retirement, precipitated his having to sell his gun collection to pay for the lawyer's bills, and more. He'd had to sell a rifle that had belonged to his father and grandfather before him. This was not going to be easy. She already had a gun dealer working on buying them all back—with some success, actually, despite the draconian laws about gun ownership in what the dealer called "the People's Republic of Massachusetts." What troubled her the most these later days was the anger she had directed at him. Rage would be a better word. There was a lot of healing and forgiveness needed here, and Larry's powers did not extend to healing himself. It would have to come from her, a mere mortal.

For openers, there was the anger. She could never understand where all that rage inside her had come from. It boiled up unbidden as the marriage dissolved around them. She was not by nature an angry or vindictive person, and certainly Larry had never committed any of the sins that could have spawned that bile. He had just been going along, leading his life as he thought to do, with honor. It could certainly not be perceived righteous indignation for years of perceived neglect. It boiled up out of a void inside that she had not known about previously. She had certainly done enough to anger him, including the ultimate treachery of infidelity, but he never rose to anger himself in answer. What she mostly remembered was the rush when she fired what she hoped were mortal shots at him. It was like riding a swift horse, and while riding it, she felt suffused with unlimited power. She felt as though she could, at her will, call down the Hammer of Thor to split the living rock. Powerful stuff, like the excitement and adrenaline pump she felt when riding her lover.

But anger is a Pale Horse, and surrounding it there is always a stench of death and decay.

Larry had taken it all and the pain was plain to see. There were times, and she had to admit this, when she liked seeing her bolts of anger take their hideous toll. The effect on the surface was gratifying, in its way, but somehow she always knew that even her worst shots never hit his very core. Larry had a light deep inside that she could not dim and that infuriated her, driving her to greater heights of rage. Always trying for greater penetration. But now she knew it was a blessing that such a dimming had never happened, even as she also now knew that it could not have happened. Whoever he was, he had a center of gravity even deeper than the planet's core. Larry was a strange man by any standard, and the oddness in his eyes was only the pilot light for deeper fires.

She had seen a picture of him when he was young. In fact, it was the headshot for his freshman college yearbook, crude and hastily shot. But it was quintessential Larry. He was looking just past the cameraman, almost but not quite over his shoulder, and the effect was eerie. It was as though he were looking at something no one else in the room could see. If the cameraman had looked over his shoulder, he would have seen nothing at all. He actually may have done so, thinking for a moment there was a third party behind him. Larry could affect people that way. But, as happened with Shackleton and his men crossing the desolate glaciers and peaks to reach safety, the specter with Larry and the photographer would never answer to the role call no matter how many times the count was taken.

She mused on Karl and what he needed as the dark, lonesome hours of that night ticked by. Karl needed help, and she could not do it alone.

Larry was the man she needed at her side for the job, but he had to come to grips with who his son was and who he might become. Karl was startlingly like Larry, but the father would never admit to that. The clock collection, the running around the country, the beat-up car. Karl adored Larry, but he was afraid to become close, and that was not surprising. It could not happen until Larry did the groundwork. Karl desperately wanted his dad to be proud of him, Andrea knew. But Larry was a tough act to follow when accomplishment was coin of the realm. She and Karl had once been riding together on an errand, and the announcer on the public-radio classical music program was talking about Wilhelm Friedemann Bach. The announcer was pointing out how hard it was for this poor man, really a very talented composer in his own right, to be the son of Johann Sebastian Bach, and a contemporary of Mozart. Karl had said, "That about sums it up for me." Larry was a monolith. What Karl could not let himself believe was that he had the potential to pace the Old Man if he could just see the power there in himself and reach escape velocity. She would need to get Larry on board for this. The foolishness Karl was involved in now, as frightening and annoying as it was, would be no more substantial than a cloud. This was another good reason for implementing Plan A.

She had heard about this woman Carol who lived downstairs from Larry in his building. Andrea had eyes and ears that kept tabs on matters relating to him. She would have to deal with that soon. This was hard too. She had had the fun of over four years of great sex with a new partner. Now Larry was belatedly doing the same thing, and she hesitated to ask him to call that off. And Larry was a stickler for the balance pans that blind Justice held in her hand. He was certainly not doing this for revenge, just for the joy of the relationship. And she could not forget that Carol was not a stick figure. She was a living, breathing person with her own stake in the matter. Andrea saw a healthy relationship that she was now thinking about breaking up for her own gain. Funny: now she of all people was beginning to feel twinges of jealousy. That jealousy would have to be removed from the mix, even if it took therapy to do it. But she would not be dissuaded. If it came down to a head-to-head matchup, she would win, of course. She knew Larry like Casals knew the neck of a cello, and she also knew that despite everything, he loved her still, with an unabated power. But a frontal assault like that was not fair—it would make her a bully in the harshest sense of the word, and she would not do it that way.

What she might do was see if they could go on as three. Carol was a wild card in that game. Andrea could live with a threesome, considering the stakes. She thought about the idea of "sharing" Larry with Carol as objectively as she could. It seemed not to bother her as much as she thought it might. If your partner has ever had another lover or lovers, that partner is always shared for all time. No one ever forgets previous lovers if those relationships were meaningful, and they migrate to the sheets with you every night and mingle with you and your current partner. It is only a question of time and space, and the word "current" becomes meaningless. She would contrive to meet Carol and begin to see how that landscape looked in the light of day.

Larry had asked her several times to come visit him at his apartment. She had said no every time. It was kind of a code that they both acknowledged but never spoke of. She was not sure how it had come about. He was making the tacit assumption that if she ever came down into

Cambridge and stopped in at his apartment, it would mean that there was a sea change in the offing, and that she might be ready to talk again about their relationship, or what remained of it. They had not spoken of this in years. She supposed that if he returned to what had been their house, it would now be her territory and she could put up deep and impregnable defenses. At his place, the roles would be reversed, but Larry would not put up any defenses there. The next time he asked her to stop by, and he would, she would say yes.

4

The gas tanks were full and would suffice for the whole trip to the Catskills and back. In normal usage, if he did not use the car around town too much, he would not need gas for a couple of months. He had put in two custom oversized tanks when he did the major modifications to the car, shoehorning them in. He occasionally stopped at full-serve pumps just to check out the look on the kids' faces when they pumped thirty gallons or more into a decrepit Rabbit. We all need to have a little fun now and again, thought Larry. But it sure compromised his luggage-storage space. Fortunately, he always traveled light and alone.

The traffic heading into the city was already heavy, but the outbound lanes were mercifully clear. With luck, he would dodge the traffic bullet as he went through Worcester. Then, as he casually scanned his rearview mirror, he saw a truly wondrous thing. There were two cars practically in an embrace, coming up behind him at more than eighty miles per hour. The first car went on past Larry and ripped off into the night. The second fell in behind him for a bit. Larry was going almost that fast himself, trusting the Mass Pike troopers to be looking at the inbound lanes where their prey was concentrated. There were three lanes to drive in. Why did this unknown and constitutively unknowable individual want to tailgate him when the road was utterly empty? But, of course, this was the legendary "Boston driving," despite their being well clear of the city limits, whereby it was usual to see cars in the far-left lane of multilane divided highways swerve precipitously across all the other lanes of traffic to catch an exit, starting with less than a few measly yards of slack. He had never gotten used to it, even after all these years. He had learned to drive in Upstate New York and became impressive at aggressive driving in his own right in New York City, where he had spent four years as an undergraduate in the early sixties. There were rules there that one followed in the murderous game of daily automotive mayhem, much like the rules devised by the Marquess of Queensbury. He had the equivalent of a black belt in urban driving, from a tough dojo. But nothing prepared him for the chaos of Boston and its surroundings, where there were no rules at all. There were a few guidelines. For example: don't make eye contact, just pull out; or, even if you have just muscled a little old lady off the road, run a red light, and sideswiped a baby carriage, always assume the others around you are at fault, honk your horn, and give them the finger.

The driver behind him, strangely, seemed to need another vehicle in the space just forward of his hood. Baby geese are like that and will imprint on anything that might be Mom during a short phase of their post-hatching development. This person apparently had similarly imprinted on a moving vehicle at some point in his life and could not seem to drive all by himself without tailgating. Larry was going just a bit too slowly to satisfy him (Larry assumed male gender without proof), and the novelty of having a different companion quickly wore off. The car careened off around Larry's right, the driver using the breakdown lane to pass, even though there were completely empty lanes to the left, gunned off into the gray predawn, and caught his earlier companion after a brisk chase at a speed that must have neared a hundred miles per hour. The two sped off into the darkness bumper to bumper, each meeting some strange, metaphorically erotic need in the other. Given that one followed the other, he speculated about the roles they were playing against this scenario, but that took him into some very weird areas that he did not like visiting, and he broke the train of thought.

To purge the disturbing thought, Larry wistfully conjured up images of the sparsely traveled back roads of northern New Hampshire. "Live Free or Die." It said so right on the license plate. That sounded pretty good right at that point. Thoughts of golden parachutes for older faculty with bloated salaries (like his, he thought honestly) occupied his mind for a while. He still had work to do, though, and it kept him at the anvil. What Larry did was important to him. It was why he went to school for all those years, why he put up with the political machinations of incompetent administrators. He had no illusions that he was going to help humanity directly with what he did. That was for applied scientists and engineers, or MD/PhD medical researchers funded by NIH. What he did was to look as far beyond what was known as he could look and bring back ways of seeing the physical world that were new and might lead on to other discoveries. Knowing more precisely how storms started sure seemed likely to be useful down the line.

Larry was still good at that. His mind's eye had not dimmed and his energy level, while not as high as it had been when he first started and had tenure on his mind, was still prodigious by any standard. He wanted to fill in the gaps on how storms formed in the atmosphere, among other things. He was not directly concerned with the now critical studies on the causes of global warming that were the underlying cause. Rather, he looked toward deeper explanations for how mildly troubled air sitting over the ocean in late August could organize itself into a giant killer hurricane. Or why the American Midwest was scoured by tornadoes. These dynamic monsters spontaneously coalesced and formed highly organized systems that utilized and dissipated energy. They were much like life itself in that regard. Entropy is extraordinarily low in a living organism, but at the overall expense of higher entropy in the universe. As for the "monster" part, one of his go-to examples was the Great Red Spot of Jupiter. This is literally a storm several times larger than the Earth itself, with an apparent lifetime best measured in centuries. The universe was filled with storms. And with life. The evolving hypotheses and theories still awaited a master's hand to bring them to fruition. And Larry was one of the great masters. He would quit when it was time to quit, before he was deadwood, stealing his salary and hanging on by a thread called tenure.

He had purchased a bagel and some cream cheese the day before to get him a few miles down the road. He deftly opened the package with his right hand and managed to spread a couple of clots of the cheese on the bagel halves without taking his eyes off the road for more than a few seconds. When he left on a long trip, it was important to him to put miles behind him early. Fiddling around incessantly before leaving drove him nuts. He would rather buy a new toothbrush when he arrived at his destination than make one more trip back for the one he already had if it lay forgotten in the bathroom. He usually planned ahead and did a good job of being ready to leave, so it was fairly easy to get a running start. He almost did not survive Karl's childhood. Leaving for a weekend with a young son was not efficient *at all.* Stopping for breakfast with less than fifty miles or so behind him would be unacceptable, especially on this trip. This trip in particular. He finished the snack and worked his way into a mindset to keep the miles flowing by unnoticed. He shut down the public-radio news station that he had switched to a while back and put a CD of *The Goldberg Variations* into the player and let the master's music flow over him.

Larry had personal heroes whom he consulted regularly. Johann Sebastian Bach was at the top of the short list. In another age, the man might have been a great physicist or mathematician. Even the simplest of his works were filled with great passion. They were wonderful to listen to, of course, but to the mathematician, they were all this and much more. They were examples of the very stuff and substance of what music is. The Baroque age was one of great rigidity in its music. Everything had to fit perfectly, and the scales were always the same—nothing in between the cracks, as was heard in later times. Rhythms were precise and measured. To the modern listener, it still resonated deeply. Bach's work had been transmogrified into jazz, rock, new age, almost everything. The amazing result was that it always worked, subject of course to the taste and skill of the person doing the transcription.

Larry had pondered this often. He craved an explanation that could satisfy the rational part of his mind as well as the aesthetic. Perhaps a unification theorem that would bridge the two. The metaphor that ran through his thoughts most often had its origin in fluid dynamics. This worked acceptably for Larry, a man who had written one of the best texts on the subject. Probably there were few to whom this would be in any way useful to emulate, but he was never going to write a treatise on Bach, so he figured he could damned well use any metaphor he wanted if it helped move him in the right direction. He conceived of a vast store of fluid energy, waiting, ready to be set free. Music was its conduit. Each branch of music had its own way of releasing its energy, but the amount of power it could carry determined its greatness for him. The better the conduit, the more pure power could be unleashed. Bach's music was a pipeline, with a quiet, smooth, inexorable flow that dwarfed that of all but those who were his near equals. Larry thought in calculus, and the calculus was the mathematics of flow and dynamic movement. There had to be a connection there.

Larry was never judgmental about music. He liked many kinds, understood the mechanics, and knew the history of a fair proportion of these. He always judged quality within a given type by the amount of this mysterious, metaphorical power he felt surging when he listened. It did frustrate him in a way, since it could never be measured objectively, and for a scientist to conceive of an entire system that could never be hooked to a meter was an irony that amused him. There were others.

He had one CD in his case that he hauled out and contemplated deeply. He would save this one for the trip home. Somehow he knew he would need it then, so he would hold off. The disk had had a cover picture of a young woman—a child, really. Small, thin, of exceptional demeanor. She was attractive in a way that transcended but did not deny sexuality. And that was certainly part of the compelling scene. She held a violin, the details of which could not be easily picked out from the picture. He frankly missed the old album covers from the vinyl days. His vinyl collection was massive and mostly in good shape. A few of the rock and blues albums from his halcyon days were wondrously worn. He often recalled his Lightning Hopkins album *Fast Life Woman* that he found one nauseous, head-pounding morning sitting on a cheap (now ruined) turntable in the fraternity commons room. It looked as if it could be used in a radial arm saw to cut cement block. It had been coated evenly with beer and then, in some unknown cataclysm of the late-night tail end of the session, covered with a fine rain of broken beer bottle fragments. Being a mathematics major, he knew without thinking about it much that the tiny fragments must have resulted from a truly titanic collision. The bigger the fragments, the lower the impact velocity. But his head thudded on, uncaring. The ad hoc adhesive had dried, bonding the equally ad hoc abrasive to the disk. By careful washing he managed to remove the industrial abrasive coating, ultimately saving all but the title cut in playable condition. He imagined he could get it on CD now, though any number of mental notes to do so had gone unanswered. But his thoughts turned now to the pictures on those old albums, which were large and demanded attention. R. Crumb's cover for Janis and Big Brother, the strange demigod on Leonard Bernstein's recording of *Le sacre du printemps,* the urine-covered monolith on *Who's Next?* All now reduced to tiny miniatures. He would very much like to have a full-size copy of that picture of the young violinist.

It was hard for him to separate the cover of the magnificent recording he was now contemplating from the sounds within. J. S. Bach, as usual. The piece on the disk that really got his juices going was the second partita for unaccompanied violin, which ends with the magnificent (he had heard it called "huge") chaconne. People who seldom listen to classical music have often heard this piece, and it sticks with them. Hearing it was a spiritual event for him every time. Spiritual in the deepest, broadest sense of that word. All music affected him, but this piece was for him almost too much to bear sometimes. He did not listen to it too often, for fear that the effect would wear off. But in reality he suspected it could not, in the same way that for the faithful, the reading of a favorite psalm would always bring comfort. It would be hard for him to tell anyone why or how this happened, although he had half-formed ideas drifting like specters in his mind. The music pushed him close to an unseen but very real barrier of sorts, and seemed to show him the way through, if he could just listen hard enough and well enough and could read the message that was tantalizingly close to the surface. The barrier was like the one he felt coming down on him from above, the one that kept his body from the blinding heights—the heights he might once have scaled but could never again master in these later years. Maybe they were one and the same, just different manifestations.

The process fascinated him on a rational level. He asked himself, almost as one might work through a catechism, a series of questions. What, for example, was the source of this map of the escape route? Here was a very young woman, holding a chunk of ancient wood with strings under tension. A bow with hair. Nothing much. A man dead these centuries who made little black marks with ink on lined paper. What was the Way that these people followed? It was far more than technique, or knowledge, or skill. The maker of the violin transcended his materials to produce something magnificent because of the superiority of the sound his instruments could produce. His life had been devoted to the Way of the Violin, or the instrument would never have been cherished for so long. The young woman knew and followed the Way of the Musician, the path to greatness that appeared in her even as a child. And the composer, the monolith of the baroque, of all music ever, who ended his days writing a work for keyboard that could be appreciated as well by a mathematician as by a pianist. A work that may not even have been meant to be played. Each had become a master in the truest sense, not because of raw accomplishment but because each had come to understand what they were doing in a way that was at once magnificent and pure. The power of all three masters at work on this recording was immense, almost inhuman. When put together in one spot at one time, a keen-edged tool sprang into existence, capable of attacking the frustrating barrier, maybe breaching it. If he could only find the hidden directions implicit and hanging in the air, he fantasized it might be his to use.

It might be a question of resonance, he reasoned. Of course, reason was the *last* thing he ought to be using in this quest, but it was the tool he used best. And, startlingly to himself, he could use reason with some success on things that were spiritual. Resonance was an eerie thing even to those who worked with it daily on a mathematical basis. Resonance brought down the Tacoma Narrows Bridge, and the engineers who designed it never saw it coming. Resonance drove events at scales from the super galactic to sub-atomic particles. Electrons could talk to each other across parsecs and the speed of light meant nothing. But he had no equations that he could write and solve, no quantities to put in a spreadsheet, nothing but the feelings he got when that chaconne was ringing in his ears.

He returned the CD case to its padded carrier. The most haunting thing about the cover picture was that the violinist was not looking directly at the camera. She was looking over the photographer's shoulder just a bit, as if at something beyond that the cameraman could not see. Larry often wondered what that might be, and his favorite idea was that it was the shade of Johann Sebastian Bach, a stein of good German lager in one hand and his amber-hued clay pipe in the other, winking at her from beyond time.

The sun was thinking about rising by this time. He switched CDs to a copy of a Dave Van Ronk album and considered his options for a real breakfast as "Lazarus" boomed out with its strange drone. The bagel was beginning to wear off, and his stomach was growling. The normal time at which he ate his morning meal was upon him, and the stomach clock that drove his physiological day was as accurate as the other onboard timers. He wanted to clear Auburn, the point at which the north-south traffic passing through Worcester joined the Pike. People heading for Hartford and New York City would be clogging the interchange soon, getting on for the short run west to the next exit at Stockbridge to grab 84 south. That exit would do fine. He made it a point never to eat at any of the franchised establishments on the Mass Pike, or any other turnpike that they bestrode. He had once been making a run back home from Albany on a bitter night after a seminar at SUNY. The heater in the VW bug he had at the time was a joke. All he wanted was a nice hot bowl of chili to drive back the cold. He pulled into one of these chrome-and-plastic eateries and ordered his chili with a hot cup of coffee. What he got was execrable on a biblical scale. He could stand his spoon up in it, and it would not budge. It was the consistency of modeling clay, and the tiny bit he was actually able to bring himself to try nearly gagged him. The coffee was cold and tasted as though the grounds were still in it. What made the whole incident worthwhile was the man sitting two stools down at the counter. The expression on his face was one of amazement, disgust, conspiratorial friendliness, and a host of other emotions in measure too small to label but still adding nicely to the whole ensemble. It was a look that a great stage actor might work years to perfect and still fail. Larry started to laugh, the man did too, and everyone had a great time except for the poor waitress behind the counter, who saw no humor in the situation at all. From her dour look, perhaps she saw no humor in anything.

The sun was well up when Larry rolled up to the exit he wanted. He liked this time of day on the road. There were still some cars heading east with their headlights on. He always felt he was in a brotherhood with them, since it meant they too had been up before the dawn. He imagined that at least a few of them had been driving all night. He liked to do that when he was young too, but now that he was no longer young, he felt the need of a good night's sleep almost every night. The caffeine surge was not enough to drive off the nods, and once, forced to drive well into the night to get home for a class the next morning, he had been awakened by the dread feel of the right front tire rumbling on the gravel of the shoulder. This near miss left him wary of pushing on too far into the night's tail end. Getting up early cut the pie equally well and would suffice.

He paid his toll and nosed into local traffic, following a road marked by a sign with a knife and fork, along with a gas pump, a bed, and a big letter H. He had once thought this was to save space, or perhaps to guide foreign tourists. He now had the firm conviction, based on a stint teaching freshman physics, that this was for the legions of Americans who could not read the words *gas, food,* or *lodging*. The strip along the feeder road was typical and without merit. It had the usual cheap furniture store, a bank, three gas stations, two rival motels, and an aging diner. This would do just nicely. He had his usual desire for food that was not on his normal allowed list. Travelling did that to him. He could go for weeks with low-fat foods, lots of grains, vegetables, fruits, all the good stuff. Then, when he got on the road, the craving for sausage, home fries, eggs over easy, and sometimes a chunk of steak or even corned beef hash was too much to resist. The coffee would not be emasculated colored water either. Caffeine was on his to-do list just then. Lunch would be equally serious within its own genre, and grease and salt would once again triumph.

The restaurant was crowded, and he spotted the last opening, grabbing a stool at the counter. "We who are about to form arterial plaque salute you!" he thought. He ordered his greasy repast with a certain contrary joy, but he did tack on a nice big glass of grapefruit juice so he could feel at least a little good about what he was about to consume. This was an entire serving of fruit, after all, according to the FDA. When it arrived, he jumped in with messianic fervor. It had been a long time.

The man who sat down next to him after the space cleared looked a bit disheveled, in the manner of traveling salesmen who live in motels and cars for months before a stretch of home. While he awaited his own wondrous fare, he struck up a conversation with Larry, perhaps thinking him, correctly, the better of his two possible counter companions to talk to. Larry, of course, based on long custom, listened carefully. The salesman seemed to be interested in conveying considerable information about where he had been and what he had been up to. It turned out that he was from Waltham and was on the way home after a long swing through northern and western New York State. He was peddling a moderately successful line of software written specifically for the accounting needs of small manufacturing businesses. They would have materials, inventory, payrolls, taxes, worker's comp, all the usual, but each of these businesses would have their own special additional needs. This is where this tiny company could help.

"But don't the monsters just wipe you off the face of the earth?" asked Larry, helpfully.

"If you stay really small," he noted, "you can get a pretty good business going, and the big pigfuckers will leave you alone. Just stay under their radar. If you grow past a certain size, you start to rattle their cages and you get squashed."

"How do they pull that off?" Larry was genuinely interested, as computers and software were his life's blood, although he rarely bought anything other than compilers and word processing systems. And Larry *hated* the "big pigfuckers," really a lot.

"Usually, they buy you out. Most of these small businesses are not public, so there is no hostile takeover or anything like that. They are owned by individuals or families, and the thought of getting one big check and hitting the beaches in the Yucatan is hard to resist after a lifetime of busting your chops."

"I guess the end is they just merge the product lines, keep the name, and send any residual work overseas, right?"

"Check. Every time."

The man's food arrived, but his consumption thereof was not an impediment to his dialogue.

"You must have a pretty rough time trying to convince small-business people that you are going to be around for more than the next month or two. You can get pretty heavily invested in a database, what with all your records in there. What do you do about that?"

"We just use a commonly available database under everything we do. All their old records can be imported. The important thing is how you massage them. You need to get them the reports they need done the way they want them. We just write macros to query whatever database they can import into. We also tell them that if we go tits up, they will still have the database to interface with another system. It's kind of ghoulish planning for your own demise, but it keeps them happy."

"You can't sell over the *net*? What keeps you out on the road?"

"Yeah, we do most of the actual sales over the net. They buy, download, and we send them a software key to activate, but we need to get out amongst the multitudes and press the flesh too. You still need to sell. I bring along demos, set them up, and show them how we can customize the program for their individual business right on the spot. The big guys don't do that. They can't. They make the programs so huge that you have everything but the kitchen sink, and then you need to pare it down and do the customizing yourself. If you can figure out how. We do all that, and we don't have a phone tree on our customer service line."

"You look like you'll be glad to get home. How long you been out?"

"Three weeks. New York is not a bad gig, but from Syracuse west, it starts to look like the Midwest." There was a certain dark look about his eyes that told Larry a lot.

"I get the impression you don't like that part of the world all that much."

"Nope, and I'll tell you why. It was two jobs back. I was selling stainless steel cookware to restaurants and hotels. Not a bad job, but the company went under. Anyway, I had an old company van that was on its last legs. Fucking back was full of pots and pans that made an awful racket clanking around all the time. It's a wonder I'm not fucking deaf from that shit. I worked for them on toward the time when the boss and his secretary got physical and split with a whole bunch of the company funds.

Left his old lady holding the bag. It was a good, working business, but he was the one who knew what was what, and she ultimately had to fold her hand. That accursed van did not get repaired or even serviced particularly well at this stage of folding up. It lost oil pressure and threw a connecting rod as I was heading back to Philly. I was in western Nebraska when it went. I conned the company into wiring me some money, managed to get a motor from a wreck that fit, but it wasn't in much better shape than the one that died. I put an oil pressure gauge in to keep tabs on it so I would not get stuck again. I would have just left that piece of shit right where it quit running if it had. Full right to the roof with stainless steel stock pots and all.

"I ran it the rest of the way home at forty miles an hour, running fifty-weight nondetergent oil and two cans of STP in her. Try that sometime under all that huge goddamn sky out there. *Forty* fucking miles a fucking hour! I watched the oil pressure gauge like a hawk, maybe more than I was looking at the road. Shit, how often do you need to look at the road out there anyway? There aren't any hills or turns. And you're going forty! Any faster than that and the oil pressure would start to drop. I'd have to slow it down to thirty for a few minutes to let it cool down and wait to pick up those few psi. Nebraska is big. It took me three days to cross, what with one thing and another. I have trouble sleeping nights anymore. Must be of an age, I guess. Sometimes I wake up and think I'm still in Nebraska."

Larry told his companion to have a safe trip in to Beantown, paid his check, wandered out to the parking lot, started the Rabbit, uncharacteristically checked its (aftermarket) oil pressure gauge as it idled smoothly, and got back on the Pike.

5

He could have jumped onto I 84, run down through Hartford, Connecticut, across the river near Newburg, and then on through the Shawangunk Mountains to Ellenville. The valley there was deep. The Rondout creek that runs through it heads north to join the Hudson near Kingston. Water falling to the east of the high ridge would take a far different course. It was like a miniature continental divide. One raindrop could go either way at the last instant before hitting the ground. The continental divide and other places like it had always fascinated him. Now, in his work, he was dealing with bifurcations like this daily. The tiniest alteration could yield huge consequences.

The world was filled with places like that—far more than most people would ever realize. Physics, chemistry, and geology were not the only disciplines that studied such odd places. Among many others, history was rife with examples. "For want of a nail, the shoe was lost . . ." The stand of the Twentieth Maine under the command of the green colonel Joshua Chamberlain at Little Round Top, holding the Union left at Gettysburg, could be the type specimen. This was a pivotal action that was embedded in one of the most pivotal battles of the Civil War. The men that charged down the hill and routed the Alabama regiment were no more gallant than countless others on both sides. They were no braver than the Alabamians, under Oates, who were tired and at the end of a thin red line themselves. Those gray-clad warriors fought like the very devil to take that hill. And they lost, and Pickett lost too, and Lee went home forever. What fascinated Larry was the way in which their actions were amplified by chance. If they had not done what they did, had not held the position, the possibility exists that the Union line would have crumbled from left to right, routed as it had been so many times before, leaving the field to the Confederates, deep in the state of Pennsylvania with nothing but empty road between them and Washington. History was full of such examples in the affairs of humankind. It was not just in physics and meteorology that chaotic systems were turning up. The position of one man could change history for all time, the velocity of one atom could make the path of an entire planet unpredictable, the tiniest movement of air could send a drop of water to different oceans, a continent apart. Pure chance set the course of the Chicxulub meteor, sending it on its way to devastate the earth so it could be reborn with those tiny little upstart mammals in charge, instead of the mighty dinosaurs.

Larry was in more control of what he was doing than the planets. He wanted to head down to the Catskills via the route he had first taken as a child, old NY 32. His parents had decided on an outing to the mountains, and instead of going to the nearby Helderbergs, just outside Albany, they wanted a change of pace. The Helderberg Mountains were not without their own presence. The reservoir for the city, called the Alcove, was situated in these mountains. The name Alcove conjured up images of water running deep in the living rock. They could be easily seen west of town on clear days. They were tall enough to be harbingers of winter, becoming snow covered well before the city itself was visited. They had gone on countless Sunday afternoon picnics in the summer, and long drives in the fall and winter up in those modest hills. Larry remembered every one of those occasions, and the love of his family revisited him. One time in particular took center stage.

The family left early in the day for the drive to the Catskills, avoiding the new thruway that Governor Dewey had built (Dewey's Folly, they called it for a while . . .), choosing instead a winding country highway that brought them into the mountains proper through a notch at the town of Palenville. The village had been a tannery town centuries before. The Catskills had been heavily forested with hemlock, and the bark was needed for the tanning process. Palen had been a prosperous tanner in those days, and the town was named after him. To Larry's mind, the name evoked images of even greater antiquity. The root of the close-sounding word that led him in this direction was *paleo,* as in paleontology.

On the way down from Albany, they passed a small mountain that had an aging hotel on the top. In the heyday of the Catskills as a summer haven for the rich, the hotel had been a famous resort. Now it was in ruin. There was an old cog railway bed that led to the top from the east. It had concrete trestles that spanned ravines and was a good hiking route to the top. A road had been built at some point, and it was accessible by automobile, but as a young man he had returned and first made the climb up the railroad bed. Walking along the concrete trestles, many feet over the deep ravines, was part of the fun. He loved the exposure to the heights. The hotel building itself had been in very unstable shape when he got there, or he would have taken the risk and explored further. The roof was caving in, and the floors were rotted out, so he looked in judiciously from the broken windows, and tried to imagine what the place might have been like before its demise. His imagination was still fired by ruins and old buildings. The acres and acres of old brick mills in Lowell, near his adopted home in Massachusetts, was another place that he would have liked to explore. Arson claimed the remains of the hotel a few years after he made his pilgrimage. The locals found it quite a good show when it burned.

He recalled an adventure years later on a canoe trip in New Hampshire, down from Lake Wentworth to Winnipesaukee. The river went down through woods and came out in an old mill town. The water was moving swiftly at this point. As they came around a bend, he saw ahead an old, abandoned mill. The river was bound right into the building. They gingerly went with it, just inside, and saw the water disappearing deep into the bowels of the ancient structure. The roaring gave them warning, and they backpaddled out easily and portaged around. Larry always wanted to go back and look again to see this wondrous work of harnessed water.

He was trying to recapture some of the feelings he had when he first saw this ancient range of mountains. He had little to go on but his feelings in this highly speculative venture he was involved in. The Hudson Valley region is amongst the longest settled in the country, and it has countless legends of the surrounding hills, the story of Rip Van Winkle being only the most famous. As a young child, Larry was told that thunder was the sound of Henry Hudson and his men bowling, and he had believed this to be so. Despite a knowledge of storms—their origins, physics, and mechanisms—that likely equaled that of any living person, perhaps he still did. The Catskills were much more imposing than the Helderbergs and were filled with deep mysterious places. The woods were all second growth, the first growth of forest over almost the entire area having been sacrificed to the tanneries. What was left was harvested for lumber or firewood. What grew in these mountains now was a mix of hardwoods, with some conifers at higher elevations. Almost anything marketable was quickly snapped up by the few remaining gypsy loggers. Hemlock was still prized, not for tanning but for its legendary durability in the face of moisture. You could lay a sill on the ground, right on wet grass, and build a barn on it. No foundation was needed. It would last the life of the builder and beyond, just sitting there. It was not a strong wood, but if used in its full dimensions, instead of the pathetic scrim that lumber yards laughingly call a two-by-four, it served well. It was well-known that you needed to nail it up green, or it would turn into a pile of airplane propellers as it dried, even if "stuck" in a proper pile. You ended up covered with fragrant sap at the end of the day. There were a lot of fine houses and outbuildings here, crafted of this timber, that had stood the test of more than a century.

He recalled an incident during that first trip that would stay with him for his whole life, perhaps had shaped his life in ways he could not fathom. He had been sitting in the back seat of the old Ford, looking out the window, when he spotted a waterfall, nearly hidden in the foliage. He commented on it, but his father stopped for nothing but gasoline until his preset destination was reached. This included the hygiene needs of the other occupants of the car. It was always a good idea to stop in the bathroom before getting into the car when dear old Dad was at the helm, which was normally the configuration. Larry had made careful plans to look at it again on the way back home, but despite his best efforts, failed to spot it. He was bitterly disappointed. Flowing water, especially water moving over rocks and dams, most particularly into caves, fascinated him, as was the case with most kids. But it was way more than that for Larry, because he could actually *feel* the movement deep in his soul.

This little waterfall returned to him in his dreams countless times, although with decreasing regularity as he aged. It had been many years since he'd had the dream. It was a dream dominated by a sense of great loss. He would be in a place in the deep forest, clearly the Catskills, and there would be wonders to see. It would be a place of great peace and safety. It could only be reached through a portal from someplace familiar, perhaps under his own kitchen table. In the beginning of the dream, he could find the entryway with ease, passing back and forth from his room, or the kitchen, or wherever the door was located, into the deep woods. As the dream wore on, it became more and more difficult to find, and the dream ended with the door lost forever. The melancholy could last through his whole waking day. In this way he knew about Xanadu first-hand, and he knew about the Lake of the Coheeries, and a certain ward-robe. Perhaps it was a common dream, he did not know. He had never asked anyone, and no one had volunteered the information. The dream had started again recently, just before his invitation arrived. It had its old intensity and clarity, and he was certain it was one facet of the compul-sion he was under to be on the summit of Peekamoose Mountain on the twenty-second of September as requested in that invitation.

He had lost other places in the real world over the years. He hoped the place he called his "cold spot" would not become numbered among the places he had lost. One particularly strange example of a lost place was Brickyard Road. He had gone shooting there as a teenager with his best friend. His friend's mother had dropped them off on a dark fall afternoon at the end of said Brickyard Road, along with a couple of boxes of .22 shells and a little Mossberg bolt-action rifle. This was an excellent first rifle for a youngster. It was a slick little weapon, with a fore stock that pulled down. You could pretend you had a submachine gun. At the end of the road, there was an abandoned brick factory, complete with ruined kiln and acres of deep woods, with a little lake deep in the forest. They shot up their shells during a couple of hours of exploring and headed back. He never found the place again. He still looked sometimes when he went back to the area to visit his sister and her family in Schenectady. Even though he was armed with the best topological maps and a GPS, and after spending hours of questioning people in the area, the place never deigned to reappear to him on the face of the earth. But the cold spot had been visited many times, and he knew right where it was.

When he first moved to the town of Claryville, he resolved to do some serious exploring, acting on his undiminished fascination with the area. It was on one such aimless jaunt that he found the place that is always cold. He did a lot of this exploring on his Triumph motorcycle and would never have found this spot if he had been in a car. The bike was almost a part of his body in those days. He still had it and was in the process of a full ground-up restoration. Offers of large sums of money fell on deaf ears.

He had told many people about the place but would never tell them precisely how to find it. This was not necessarily out of any secretiveness but because he thought that for this place to have the right effect, someone would have to discover it for themselves in much the same way he had. Roughly, it was on the road that runs around the east spur of Peekamoose Mountain, on the way from the Ashokan Reservoir area to Grahamsville. He found it one hot July day. He was cruising along, carving lazy turns on the twisting road, enjoying the almost sexual pleasure that only a fast, good-handling bike can offer, when he dropped into a deep hollow. Suddenly, he was freezing cold. Not as in the cool of a shady ravine, but really January cold. The sensation was eerie. He was not a believer in ghosts and such but was not immune to the hard-wired, primitive fear of the unknown. He was glad enough to sprint through the spot to the sun and muggy warmth on the other side. He cranked the throttle and went on to other spots where summer was still in charge of things.

It was some time until circumstances brought him that way again. It was another warm day, and this time he had a car, which he parked in a small refuge a little way from the spot—oddly, from his own perspective, leaving the keys in the ignition. Perhaps the portable refuge of a car vs. a bike gave him enough security to stop and explore. The road ran along a steep part of the mountain, and there was a rock cliff on one side and a sharp drop on the other. In the bottom of the dip, he noticed a peculiar arrangement of rock slabs on the other side of the guard rail that rimmed the drop-off. He climbed over the rail and saw that there was a set of steps leading down over the edge. They were of undressed stone and had been set into the bank by a master. The stairs clung to the slope without a hint of having moved in the long years that they had lain there. They must have been there since colonial times. He had seen similar craftsmanship in stone walls around the state. The walls stood unaffected by the frosts that heaved and buckled them every winter, as though they were held together by some unknown adhesive, and yet there was no mortar in them anywhere. A quick glance at such a wall would make one think that each stone had been cut to fit, with paper-thin cracks between, but they were untouched by chisel or hammer. It was the patience and skill of the craftsman who took a random collection of rock, left in broken heaps by the last glacier's retreat, and turned it into an enduring place of great order.

He followed the steps down and found a small cave in the rock that could not be seen from the road or even by a pedestrian on the shoulder. The cave was very shallow but was clearly the source of the cold air that was filling the hollow. There was a frigid breeze coming out of the opening. He followed the cave in for a few feet and came to a dead end. The air was coming out of a hole in the rock that was about a foot in diameter. It was rimmed with solid ice, although this was August. Despite certain deep-seated misgivings, he reached in as deeply as he could with one arm, to be greeted by a deathly cold. The air was below freezing. There is great order in the crystals of ice, and there was great order in the steps that the highway builders had miraculously left untouched. Tiny fortresses making a rude gesture against entropy.

He could never find out any more about this cave. None of the old-timers he talked to knew about its history, but they pointed out that there were trappers and mountain people who lived up in the high country in the old days. Perhaps the steps had been set there so the cave was easily accessible from the horse-and-foot trail that preceded the road. It certainly would have made a good place to store a deer carcass or other game. There was no geological mystery. There were ice caves in the nearby Shawangunk Mountains that were frozen all year round. For a few dollars, one could visit them. No doubt this was an outlet of another such formation in the side of Peekamoose Mountain. But knowing this fact in no way alleviated the curiosity that had festered in Larry for all the years since he first explored the place. Who were the people who used the cave so long ago, and what might you find if you could only, like Alice, get small enough to fit through that tiny hole and follow the icy wind to its subterranean source?

As Larry passed through the farm country north of the mountains, he happened to notice a large field that had been only partially hayed. The farmer had taken the sensible precaution of not mowing the whole area at once. This probably meant he did not have a huge tractor and mighty hay baler, likely being a hobby farmer with a few head of beef critters, or dairy goats, or horses. He had mowed at least six or seven swaths in from the outer edge, working in towards the center. He must have raked and baled this portion and figured to go back and work up the rest when he could. This was usually done when the weather was unsettled and rain was possible before the hay could make up. At some point, one simply has to start mowing even if the weather is unsettled, or there will be no chance at getting any hay in at all. The entire past summer had been very rainy, Larry knew very well, of course, so it was no surprise when he saw windrows of unbaled hay lost in the second growth. It was a huge field, and the loss of even these few swaths must have amounted to hundreds of bales. The farmer had not gone back to spread the ruined hay out of the windrows with the tedder, nor obviously had he baled up the remaining hay to get it off the field. Organic gardeners, landscapers, and highway departments often bought spoiled hay as mulch. Larry wondered what problems might have befallen the farmer that would have made him leave the windrows to complicate next year's haying, and why he had not gone back to get the rest of the field. There were unpleasant implications to the scenarios which arose unbidden to his mind, but he hoped it was just because the barn was already full of nice dry, green June-cut clover hay for his herd.

As he passed the field, he noticed something curious thing in the uncut portion. A spot of color caught his eye, and he quickly identified it as a bunch of balloons tied together. They were rubber helium balloons, no longer capable of flight, resting on the yellowing timothy heads. They were at least a hundred yards out in the grass, and since there was no disturbance in the surrounding un mowed region, he assumed they had gotten there on their own. Helium leaks rather quickly through rubber balloons, and they lose buoyancy with time. Larry, in the same way that he knew what to wear for his trip without consulting the weather report, knew what the winds at all altitudes had been doing for the last several days. This is by way of saying that being able to absorb this information was an undocumented feature of the sub-rational part of his mind. These voyagers could have been aloft for several days, and with the winds at their most probable altitude, he made an educated guess at their point of origin. He wondered if there had been any agricultural fairs in the last few days in the Peace River Country region of Alberta, and his mind drifted off to faraway places for the next few miles.

He headed down to the Ashokan Reservoir before cutting into the mountains. He wanted to stop at the memorial for J. Waldo Smith, who had been the engineer whose genius had been behind the system of dams, reservoirs, aqueducts, and tunnels that kept New York City in drinking water. And water to flush toilets, and water to . . . well, he thought he would try to keep from thinking in that vein. He was not much of a fan of this man who had altered the mountains so gravely, but he liked the spot. He had found it on one of his journeys of discovery. There was a small drive going into a copse of trees. As he neared the center, he saw that all the trees were planted in such a fashion that they radiated away from the center of the grove. At the focus of all this vegetation was a strange stone tower. The plaque described the man and his works. What really fascinated him was the iron door at the base of the tower. It was securely bolted, but there was a barred window in it. If you put your mouth close to the opening and spoke in a loud voice, the cavernous interior would return the sound of your voice transmogrified into the voice of a mountain god.

He had mixed feelings about this reservoir, and all the other works that made New York City possible by dint of supplying its water. There were certainly marvels aplenty to ponder. The tunnels, for example, run deep in the rock, and are large enough to drive a car through. At one point there is a tunnel that drops seven hundred feet vertically, passes underneath the deep Rondout Creek valley near the town of Ellenville, and then rises six hundred feet back up on the other side. The image of a huge moving column of water dropping vertically through those dizzying heights in the dark beneath the mountains can be very unsettling.

There had been heartache associated with the reservoirs. Farms and homes had been lost that had been old when the Revolutionary War was fought. Larry remembered a particular boat-launching site. It was still permitted to keep a rowboat on the reservoir for fishing if you did not move it in from another body of water. One excellent site for putting in was on the highway that had run down the valley in the old days. The crews had left it alone when the valley was prepared for the flooding. It was still paved and the traffic control lines painted on it survived the years. Larry never failed to get a strange, indescribable emotion as he looked at the road disappearing beneath the dark, mysterious water. Eben Friedland, the man he was planning to visit and stay with that night, had been born in Eureka, a tiny hamlet on the Rondout Creek. It had been swallowed by the reservoir that bore the name of the river. The local folks always called it the Lackawack, the name another lost town.

One year, while he had lived in Claryville so long ago, there had been a drought. The Rondout was all but emptied by the thirsty toilets of New York. He had gone down with others to see the old bridge at Eureka. You could still see the cellar holes. The crews had moved a few houses, and demolished and burned the rest, so at least the ghosts of Eureka were kept to a minimum. Eben had not gone to look. There was a tune Larry always hummed when he thought of the burning and the upheaval of the reservoir's coming. He had an old album that was still playable, featuring Pete Seeger and some cohorts, called *Indian Summer*—now long forgotten. It was an instrumental soundtrack for a movie, also long forgotten, about the wrenching change that the reservoirs brought to the mountains and their people. He also thought of "Ashokan Farewell," a traditional lament written in later times, as a theme for a documentary on the Civil War that he had particularly enjoyed.

Larry reached his goal. A dark and autumnal melancholy seeped into the marrow of his bones as his mind's eye wound down a lost road toward those dark waters and what might yet lie beneath them. Perhaps lost lives, perhaps lost souls. Larry was going home.

6

The rest of his trip seemed to pass quickly now that he was in his zone. He had a light lunch, this despite his earlier resolve to pump his LDL numbers back up to something scary again. He made his two allotted stops to see first Waldo, not forgetting to yell into his ghostly iron-barred window, and then the strange doorway into eternal ice. These brief halts furthered his attempts to slip back in both time and space. It was his hope that when whatever awaited him up on the mountain arrived, he could be as ready as possible given the near total unknown quantity that sat at its core. He wanted to give a good account of himself, as he knew he must.

But there was time yet before that, and he was good at filling apprehensive times such as this one with thoughts and actions that were positive, no matter how rocky things ahead looked. He pretty much *had* to be. It had not always been so; this was definitely an acquired trait in his case. There was harsh history behind that. He had had a dreadful experience at the dentist as a young child. He now had only snippets of memories about the experience. There was blood, shouting, broken baby teeth on a towel. His mother rushing in. Not much else, which was a blessing. He could not remember the pain. The dentist had actually ended up spending the remaining dregs of his life in a home for the criminally insane for abusing patients. He had had terminal syphilis, and it had eaten him up. Those were the good old days of medicine. This was the sort of thing people never believed, despite Larry's reputation for utter truthfulness, until he showed them photocopies of the newspaper clippings about the trial that he had patiently unearthed from the microfiche at the old *Knickerbocker News* morgue, now at a local Albany library. The last evening paper in the state, he guessed, now in oblivion with so many others. And the morning papers were joining them as well, one by one, as reading anything at all substantive and not on a phone faded from the world.

His mother had taken to avoiding telling him when dental appointments were coming up. He would stop sleeping nights until the appointment was over if she gave him any warning, so she would just show up one day at his school, grab him, and haul him off to his doom. This had the advantage of keeping his anxiety in check, but at the cost of his never knowing when that other evil shoe would fall. If he had not just *been* to the dentist, there was the ugly possibility that at *any time* his mother's yellow Pontiac would be sitting out there in the school parking lot.

Since those dark days, he had developed considerable skill in dealing with approaching ugliness of any sort. When his colleagues were tearing out their hair and lamenting about the upcoming semester and the return of the undergraduates, he would be calmly getting lots of work done and cheerfully pointing out to them that "it is still August; what's the problem?" He called the incoming hordes the "marabunta," a corruption of an Indigenous name for army ants that he remembered from an old movie about the Amazon starring Charlton Heston.

He pulled into Eban's driveway and cut the Rabbit's motor. He unwound himself stiffly from the car's confines and wandered toward the sound of an ancient diesel that was moaning and grunting behind the hay barn. He would not have gone to the house first in any event, since this would have been a grievous insult up here in the hill country. Except at dinner hour—noon sharp, that is—to go to a working man's set of buildings in a rural area, and to go to the house first while there was light in the sky, just might help garner you an enemy for life. The presumption was that if there was daylight, the man would be out working in his barn, fields, sawmill, smithy, whatever. It seemed to be a lessening problem in younger generations.

Eban was a man in his late seventies now. He lived alone—his wife of nearly fifty years had recently died. Their several children were all long gone from the area to places that boasted actual economies. He had been a dairy farmer in Grahamsville for all his life, in a place that did not have much to offer for a farmer of any sort. It boasted bony soil, what there was of it; steep hills everywhere; and frosts in June and August. Despite this, Eban had pushed on with determination against all odds, had managed to find enough fields to hay and plant to ensilage corn to keep his modest but sufficient herd through the winter. He survived at this because he owned his land and paid cash when he needed equipment. He was a proponent of appropriate technology before that became trendy. He knew, without a fancy government consultant to tell him, that you could not make much money for yourself to keep when you paid out almost all you made to the bank in debt service. But make no mistake, the road Eban walked his whole life was a very hard road.

Eban still clung to the entire farm, not wanting to see it fall to developers, whom he loathed, while his rangy old body drew breath. Certainly, he had put enough of himself into it over the years. He hoped that someday he would pass peacefully in his sleep, right in the bed and room that had been his for so long. He had dwelt there ever since the painful move from Eureka. He figured he would be found by a neighbor who might notice he had not been out and about for a day or so. A practical man in all things, he additionally hoped that it would be winter so any smell might be kept to a minimum. The thought of drawing his last breath in a hospital or nursing home after all the years of falling asleep to the same window, dresser, bed, print of *The Last Supper,* and almost totally faded pictures of his parents drew a bleakness from the depths of his soul that he could not abide. It was at times like these that his mind's eye saw trailers and double-wides marring the fields he had tended so carefully. He would shake himself like a dog and cast it all out and find something better to occupy his thoughts.

Larry found him out back running his wood splitter. He had been prepared for any eventuality and expected something like this, especially as summer was ending. He already had on his steel-toed work boots, having laced them on when he got back to the car after visiting the ice cave. He had his hearing protectors and his heavy leather work gloves close at hand and donned them. He hated to appear as a wimp, but constant loud noises really made him irritable, and he did want to protect what was left of his hearing. Woods work, with poorly muffled crawler motors and chainsaws howling those many years ago—before OSHA had mandated such fussiness as protective gear—had taken some chunks out, and he did not want any more to go. Music was way too important to him.

Without saying a word, Larry grabbed a chunk of rock maple from the pile, walked up to the splitter, and set it down on the bed. Eban nodded briefly and only barely perceptibly in acknowledgment and hit the valve handle. With a deep chuckle, the old diesel motor in the tractor kicked up a notch and the ram sent the wood against the tall, wicked-looking wedge. With a groan, the wood broke apart. It was already dry, Eban having cut it to length and piled it last winter, so it made a satisfying crunch.

Larry loved splitting wood with hydraulics. He had heated his home in Claryville with wood for as long as he lived there and was particularly fond of wood heat, but the splitting had been miserable at first. He'd used an old axe, supplemented eary on with a set of wedges and a sledgehammer. Hours of frustrating labor would yield a small pile of split wood and a couple of wedges buried in a particularly evil chunk. He never cut good trees for firewood, always ratty-looking old maples, elms, dying beeches, anything that had no other possible value. As a consequence, splitting was a character-and-body-building exercise. Until, that is, the blessed day he borrowed a hydraulic splitter. He especially liked to attack ratty crotch sections of elm, the worst wood of all to split, as it would not so much split as explode. He loved to take the meanest ones and hoard them all till the end to savor the experience. Sometimes they ended up looking like giant brass pot scrubbers, crushed by the titanic force of the liquid moving through the galleries of the arm.

Eban's splitter was homebuilt. This was not to say it was not excellent. Eban was a master welder, and every joint in the rig had that border of arc weld that is often described as a *row of dimes,* a sign of perfect control of the moving arc and rod. The body of the unit was an old chunk of building I beam; the wedge was a nondescript piece of steel, built up from chunks of tool steel that had been ground to an edge. The hydraulic ram itself was salvaged from a worn-out Case bucket loader that had been used by the crew that serviced the reservoirs and their surrounding roads.

Larry was pleased to see that it had been carefully rebuilt and did not leak hydraulic fluid all over the ground. Eban might not have been too concerned with the EPA's crankiness about mixing hydrocarbons into the soil, but he did not like to waste hydraulic fluid, and did not much fancy having it all over his firewood when he hauled it into the house. The splitter lacked its own source of power for a pump system but rather relied on the old John Deere tractor's own, through umbilical hoses. Larry also noted that these were almost new. A needle-thin spray of hot fluid from a pinhole leak when the line was under pressure was a dangerous weapon. Eban believed deeply in using enough power on any task, and the diesel motor of his farm tractor, old as it was, delivered enough to slice a piece of wood in half sideways, let alone split it along the grain.

The John Deere looked to be still capable of independent motion, but its farming days were long in the past. Larry remembered a story his mother read to him as a child. It involved a John Henry–like battle between the new diesel-powered excavators and an old steam shovel. In the final face-off, the steam shovel had won on guts alone, but its operator had dug himself into the basement hole with no way out. The building's owners, swayed by public opinion, had left it there and transmogrified its boiler into a heating plant rather than dismantling it. The shovel's operator had gotten the job of tending the boiler. Eban's old war horse was in its furnace days now.

Larry fell right into the rhythm of the work. He was well aware of the code of such matters, which was graven in granite. If the ram stopped going back and forth other than to reverse itself, he would lose a *lot* of points. He made sure that there was always a piece of unsplit wood on the bed, and that the apron that surrounded the wedge end of the beam was always emptied of split pieces. This involved a complex juggling of fresh chunks, pieces that needed splitting a second time, and pieces ready for the pile. Eban managed the pieces on the bed, which was a full-time task for him from this point on. Small round chunks that were thin enough to be ready for the stove needed no splitting, and in the middle of all this, Larry had to find time to heave these onto the finished pile. The work ethic in the country is funny. There are rules you need to know and follow precisely, or you could be considered in some way defective. He remembered once when Eban, his son Vrest, and Larry had been teamed up working the splitter. Splitting was easiest with three people: one to split, one to bring fresh wood, and one to take off the freshly split chunks and heave them on the pile. Vrest was pulling the wood off, and he was "riding" the chunks through to save that bit of a second. This means maintaining contact with the pieces as they travel past the wedge, normally not as dangerous a practice as it seems at first blush. This time, however, a particularly nasty crotch chunk had taken a bad turn and the open split had snapped shut around his thumb, driven by all the force of the ram. The tip of his thumb had been squashed like a grape, the nail in shreds, but he never flinched or even looked at the wound, let alone tending to it, until they broke for dinner. He kept on without losing a beat. To have stopped things, even long enough to jump up and down and curse, would have broken the timing of the crew. You just did not *do* that. A working crew is timed like a motor, with camshafts, pistons, and valves. If one part quits, the whole unit jumps time and you have a mess. Larry had been impressed with this. He never once let a crew jump time when he worked, and he would not even now that he was writing journal articles and lecturing somnolent students full-time for a living.

The smell of the diesel exhaust, hot hydraulic fluid, dried sap in the freshly split wood, and the sound of the motor as the governor reacted to the loading and unloading of the hydraulic cylinder began to have a hypnotic effect. Of the two, the smells were probably the more compelling. Smells are processed in an ancient part of the human brain. The front part, now associated with our vaunted intelligence, was once allocated almost entirely to processing the chemicals found in the water of our fishy ancestors. Everything else was built on top. Smells provoke some of our most intense memories. For Larry, it reminded him of the Case bulldozer he ran back when he worked in the woods here for Jimmy Blandsford. The afternoon was hazy and warm; the work was hard but not taxing, despite the need for a bit of planning to keep up. He slipped away to another time, decades gone, to when his life went through its seismic change. He did not visit here often. It is said humans can put pain away in the past. If this were not so, women would never have a second child, nor would anyone run a second marathon. But this pain never went away.

7

With a flip that bespoke much practice, he tossed the empty into the back of the pickup. It joined its colleagues in the half-melted snow, nestled against the toolbox. For reasons that defied both statistics and physics, none of the bottles were broken. The patch of snow was getting smaller; it was April after all, and there were other hard objects to offer a less-than-soft landing. A chainsaw, cans of gas and oil, two lengths of patched three-eighths log chain, a peavey, a pulp hook, the head from the motor that had preceded the one currently powering the truck, a rotting cardboard box full of valves from the selfsame head, a crankshaft from a different motor, and two shovels, one with a recently broken handle, made a partial list of the contents of the rusting bed. A piece of plywood, still bearing traces of concrete indicating its former life as part of a form, was all that kept these contents from passing down to the road below and into History.

Larry grabbed another cold sixteen-ounce bar bottle from the battered cooler and popped the cap off with his harness buckle. He did not like canned beer and always had that buckle handy. In a pinch, one could stop the truck and use the metal bumper as an anvil for this task, but this was the sort of thing he felt cops might notice. This ad hoc bottle opener had been with him for years now and was polished to a fine sheen from all that time in his pocket. He pondered the attachments we form with inanimate objects as he began work on the newly available beverage. This chunk of metal that he had adapted for a task not part of its original design was almost a part of him at this point, more so than even a prosthesis could be. This was not solely because of the countless beers he had opened with it but also because he had carried it on so many of his adventures. It had been in his pocket on the summits of Cotopaxi, Assiniboine, Grossglockner, McKinley, Aconcagua, and more. It, like he, had survived a dunking in the Rapid River in Maine, a close encounter with a bear in Glacier National Park, and a barely controlled fall of seventy feet while on belay in the Canyonlands of Utah when a piece of red rock gave way beneath him. How could you explain to someone who did not feel any attachment to such a thing that there was a bond that could be forged to this oddly shaped piece of mild steel. People treasure wedding rings and such. Why not a harness buckle that you use to open beer bottles, when it is a travelling companion of such constancy?

This was only his second beer. He would pace himself. He was starting to worry just a bit about the constabulary around the area. A few recent highway deaths involving alcohol had prompted a crackdown on drinking and driving, and he was not too anxious to lose his license. He had become a target of some suspicion among the local cops anyway. He was of uncommon height, had a thick beard down to mid chest level and a ponytail nearly down to his waist. This was not a good time to look like that, what with daily pictures of antiwar demonstrators burning American flags and spitting on soldiers returning from Vietnam. But being an outlaw was never easy, and he was willing to pay the price. Few citizens ever seemed interested in messing with him anyway, so it was seldom a problem for him in particular, but cops were a different story.

He really needed this beer. The events of the day had left him shaken and depressed. It was his hand on the throttle of the Case when the shit hit the fan, even if he was not in any way to blame for what had happened. Knowing that on a rational level did not absolve him from the guilt that washed over him in waves. They had been working a sizeable hemlock stand on the side of Slide Mountain for about three weeks now, ever since the snow had melted enough to get the crawler in. Jimmy was anxious to get the hemlock done with and move on to the stand of ash beyond. He was a gypsy logger but knew enough not to ruin several thousand feet of hemlock just to get to the ash, which would fetch a much better price. The baseball bat factory up over the mountain was hungry for that ash, so the temptation must have been great to haul the hardwood logs through the hemlock stand, potentially ruining a fair share of softwood for future harvesting as the cables and chains dragged against the trunks. Everything Jimmy saw was haloed with dollar signs, and a built-in calculator was always working to maximize his gain. He apparently had the hemlock promised to a local yard as dimension lumber.

Larry ran the crawler. He was a natural with hydraulics and could do just about anything with a bulldozer blade, forklift tine, or backhoe bucket that he could do with his hands. He had gotten the job by picking up an egg in a tall-stemmed wine glass with a backhoe bucket, and then placing it carefully in the hand of the startled Jimmy Blandsford. He was hired on the spot, with no haggling on wages. Karl was the young man that Jimmy had recently hired, mostly to help Larry directly with his assorted tasks. Karl's job at this point was to set the choker chains on the logs that Jimmy had carefully chosen, felled in the right direction, and limbed. Each chain had a nearly circular hook at one end, with a slot to allow the chain to be inserted. This rigging could be put around the log quickly, and the chain would slip through the slot in the hook, securely holding the log when it was pulled tight. The other end of the chain would be fed through a keyhole-shaped piece of metal called a harp. The chain would lock into the narrow part of the keyhole. The harp was fastened to a ring called a slide that ran freely along the cable from the bulldozer's winch. As the winch reeled in the cable, all the trees attached to their harps and slides would collect at the end of the cable and be pulled in close to the tractor, ready to be twitched. The load was then hauled to the yard area, where Larry's next job was either to load the logs onto the truck or stack them with another older crawler equipped with a high-lift loader.

This particular day, Karl had set the chains, harps, and slides on four large hemlock logs, and Larry started to pull the load together. The trees were all already near the end of the line, and he had let out almost the entire length of cable on the winch, as he could get no closer—even on tracks. The run back to the load was perfectly straight, which was slightly unusual. Normally, deep in the woods like this, there was at least one stump or tree to wind the cable around as you pulled up the load. But Larry had done it this way many times with no problem. There was no reasonable explanation for what happened next that Larry could come up with then, but in later life he might easily have written equations to model it. It did happen, so it was clearly possible, but vanishingly improbable and impossible are interchangeable terms out at this end of the curve.

The cable pulled up and lifted off the ground, making an unbroken run back to the logs. Karl was walking along the cable, as he usually did, and was a few feet away from it as it started to pull up. The logs were now bouncing around as they drew together at the end. Nothing about what he was doing was either unusual or in any way more dangerous than anything else you do minute by minute working as a logger. Larry was watching the steel line as he worked the handle that controlled the winch clutch. He was not thinking about much of anything, certainly nothing that he could remember later. Without warning, a strange commotion began in the cable, for all the world like it was being shaken by powerful hands randomly all along its length. At a point near the gathering load, all the unconnected movement coalesced into one sharp peak. Unlike the wave you might start in a taught clothesline by plucking it like a guitar string, it extended only above the line of the cable. There was no "down" part at all. In a heartbeat, the strange wave snapped down the cable at a breathtaking velocity. It hit the winch at the other end, almost picking up the crawler, and in doing so, expended its energy. In its trip down the line, it neatly and almost surgically cut off Karl's left arm, which he had randomly dangled over the cable, about three inches below the elbow.

Karl looked down in disbelief at the stump. There was something about this that seemed important to him, but he was just not sure what it was as yet. Things were clearly different than they had been a second before, and he knew he needed to do something, but the unreality of it all was too much to handle. He took one step toward Larry, with a quizzical grin on his face, and then began shrieking uncontrollably when the reality set in. Larry got to him in perhaps one more second, running as fast as his long legs could move him over the rough ground of the scarred forest floor. He grabbed Karl in a giant bear hug, pinning his arms against his sides. At the same time, he yelled for Jimmy, who was already moving in their direction as fast as he could manage.

The hug had the amazing effect of calming Karl almost instantly. There is something hardwired in our brains that protects us when an injury like this occurs. Instead of running off into the woods howling and pumping out the last of his life's blood, Karl quickly grabbed the stump just above the wound and compressed it with his other hand. Larry's presence infused him with a calm that was surprising to all three. In later years, he would speak almost reverentially of Larry's actions in these critical moments. He would never even think of blaming Larry—a "dumb flatlander" to many, if they remembered him at all—for the accident. Once, several years down the line, he broke a man's nose in a bar fight for suggesting such a thing.

Jimmy arrived in a moment and sized up the situation quickly. He ran to the crawler and grabbed the first aid kit. It was not enough for handling this level of mess, but it did contain a piece of line that he could use for a tourniquet. He tied the cord around the arm just above the elbow and signaled Larry to release Karl from his steel grip.

Jimmy, as calmly as he could, said "Get him in my pickup; it's faster than yours. I'll get the arm."

"Right."

Nothing more was said nor needed to be said. Karl was by now going into shock and was not a part of the conversation any longer. It was amazing he had lasted as long as he did. The truck was about a quarter mile back down the mountain at the point where they had stopped plowing the snow with Jimmy's truck during the winter. Larry, who was enormously strong even for his size, carried the smaller man down the path the crawler had left coming in and put him in the cab. The footing was treacherous in the melting snow, but he did not stumble. Jimmy found a plastic garbage bag in his truck and ran back for the arm. He put in some snow from one of the remaining drifts that looked at least moderately clean, still, and packed it around the severed limb. He was not squeamish about this at all; the need to get the limb cooled quickly was uppermost on his mind. He had heard something about this on TV once, and fortunately, it had stuck. Perhaps, given his line of work, he had made a point to stick it in a place where it could be retrieved at need.

The trip to the hospital in Liberty, about twenty minutes away, was done in the absence of any talk at all. Jimmy drove at a pace that, remarkably, exceeded even his usual insane velocity, and Larry sat with his arm around Karl. Karl just looked out the window with a dull gray expression, devoid of pain or anxiety. At the hospital, both pieces of Karl were duly handed over to the emergency room people, and that was the last they had to do. The letdown was incredible and surprising. They went from having Karl's life literally in their hands to being excess baggage in about a minute. No one even much wanted to know the details of the accident at this point. They just needed to know what had been done with the limb and how long it had been since the accident. A decision was made that reattachment was an excellent choice, and a light plane was arranged to take Karl to a hospital in New York City where the work could be done. And that was that.

Larry and Jimmy rode back to the work site in silence once again.

Jimmy said "Put the place to bed, will you please? I have to go talk to his folks. I don't figure they are going to be too happy about this, and they don't like me much from up front. They don't have shit for money, and I have no idea where they are going to get the bucks to pay for Karl's medical bills."

"You mean you don't have insurance on him?"

"Fuck no! He works thirty-five hours a week. You never wondered why he quits an hour earlier than you do every day? It's all I can do to keep your ass covered. I'll kick in what I can out of my own pocket, but I been payin' him 'green' fuckin' money. He don't pay taxes or any of the rest of that shit that I know about, and I don't pay any goddamn insurance.

"Why do you pay it for me? You do, don't you?" Larry was getting a bit uneasy at this point.

"Yeah, but you're worth it. I knew I'd never get you if I didn't. I have been in this business all my life, and I never saw anyone who could run hydraulics like you."

"OK, so what happens when Karl tells the nice people at the hospital about the accident, and the state comes down on you like a D9 Cat falling out of the sky? Your ass will be sitting in a big bottle of formaldehyde on some bureaucrat's desk in Washington, like some kinda trophy. He'll show it to his kids. 'Look, Gerald, look what Daddy did! He chopped this guy's ass off and put it in this bottle.'"

"No fucking way. Karl ain't gonna say shit. He'll tell them he's a private subcontractor."

"You didn't say a thing all the way over to Liberty. How the hell are you and he gonna get your stories straight? They'll ream you and clean you."

"You don't get it, do you? Out here we're born knowing how to survive the shit that Albany and Washington dump on us. There *is* no story to get straight. You just don't say shit. You don't want to pay taxes and social security, you want a job, you learn the rules. And you shut your mouth when the suits come around asking questions."

Larry said nothing more on the subject. He didn't wonder further how Karl and his folks were going to pay for the hours of delicate surgery. They probably weren't going to pay anything at all. They lived in a crumbling trailer in Neversink, had minimum-wage jobs when they worked at all, and had long since learned how to work the system. The Empire State would end up picking up the freight on this one. Reattaching a limb was not an outpatient procedure. Mountain people had their own way of doing things. It usually worked, but sometimes it seemed a bit harsher than it really had to be.

Larry started the crawler, winched in the load, hauled it back to the yard, and finished loading the truck with as many of the hemlock logs as he could get on it. It was badly overloaded, and if the state guys spotted it, it would mean a fine. The state guys would not spot it. When Jimmy came back, his wife would drop him off. He would check the chains on the load, pull down the road they had built into the stand last year, and disappear into thin air. Jimmy knew how to get from every timber stand in this part of the state back to his small mill by back roads that the state guys would never see, even from the air. That was how you stayed in business, how you got from day to day and paid the bank a little bit and paid your ex-wife some child support once in a while, and the way you had enough money to eat, and the way you bought a new snowmobile or a new motor for your bass-fishing boat. This was survival. Larry was learning about that. Larry knew just how much weight you could put on the old log truck before the springs would break or the rear end would vomit out a greasy pile of gears, seals, and ninety-weight lubricant. He was learning how to survive too, and he was a quick study.

8

He headed the truck down the road toward Grahamsville and drained the second beer. He hesitated only an instant before cracking another. Screw the neo prohibitionists. And he recalled he would need more beer home as well. He had just been through the town twice, and now he had to go again, but he had not been in a position to stop either time. Grahamsville had a good grocery store, but he would need to stop at the little bar in Claryville on his way back to pick up brew. Grahamsville was dry. Funny thing about that too. There had been a genuine type-specimen gin mill in town years ago. There was a knife fight and a murder that precipitated the puffed-up outrage of the citizenry. The townspeople had voted the place dry, and it had never gone wet in all the years since. A fair fraction of the good burghers of this tiny hamlet were as stout a crew of serious drinkers as he had ever met. The new folks moving in only added to the locale's stature in that regard. He knew of a colony of bikers in town who had a regular illegal delivery from a distributor in Liberty that was the largest single drop on his route, larger than any of the bars or mom-and-pop stores.

As he came down out of the hills into town, he noticed the power station, as he always did. That structure continually amused and intrigued him. If anyone came into town from the west, they would follow the course of a nice little mountain stream. It emptied into the reservoir on the east edge of the town center. There sat the power plant, and the uninitiated might think that the creek was powering the generators. One look at the sheer volume of water would dispel this naïve notion, but the question arose about where this unexpectedly large amount of water was coming from. In fact, it was travelling down a huge pipeline from another reservoir to the west. It traveled for miles through this subterranean main, drifting along in calm laminar fashion. Larry always fancied the water must be surprised to be precipitated out of the peaceful darkness into the tumultuous chaos of the turbine and the gate to daylight and the roar of the cascade down to the reservoir's edge.

The reason he wanted extra groceries and beer loomed overhead. Larry always knew what the weather was going to do, and all day the circuitry in his brain that carried this information was buzzing with the news of snow in the offing. Lots of snow. The fact that it was early April was not going to change his mind about this at all. The weather report on the radio continued to speak calmly about some rain showers, maybe flurries up high and chilly weather and clearing to follow. Larry knew better. He felt the shifting patterns of the winds aloft and knew where the cold air and moisture were as certainly as the positions of his limbs being monitored by his cerebellum. The milky sky above was just one visible piece in the puzzle. Although Larry was unaware of this fact, the locals knew of this talent, and without saying anything, the other customers in the store noted his purchases with heightened interest. The old-timers here seemed to have something of this talent themselves, and they too had been uneasy. Larry's actions confirmed what they suspected. They had survived in this harsh part of the world for a long time without weather on the radio. He did not go over the line, but bought canned goods, some flashlight batteries, a box of candles, some dried beans, extra milk, eggs, bacon, and some flour. Within an hour, there was a rush on at the store that racked up nearly $1,000 for the cheerful proprietor.

As he left the store, Larry saw an ancient truck pull up. The operator was one of the people who was behind the biblical beer delivery. The truck was a wondrous thing, even by Larry's high standards. It was a Diamond T bread truck, a defunct model with the name of a defunct bakery on the side: DUGAN'S. There had been fifty or so for sale down in Monticello a few years ago, but he had been too slow to get down there and score one of his own. The truck, powered by a massive Hercules motor, showed a rating listed on a panel on its side for the ridiculous maximum payload of 750 pounds. This was likely to save registration fees, but the more truthful plate on the frame put on by the manufacturer had it listed for two tons. Larry marveled at the giant multileaf springs, and what he could see of the differential without actually crawling underneath warmed his heart; it was huge. The Dugan's people must have done something really stupid to end up going out of business. They certainly knew how to pick trucks.

He stopped to say hi to the driver, whose name he must once have known. He was an ambling bear of a man, at least as hairy as Larry himself. They had met at a wild party at the top of Pepacton Hollow where a rich Long Island tax accountant had a huge spread. The accountant was notorious for these parties, which could last a week or more. Larry did recall that this man he now faced had once been referred to as "Dr. Leather" by the people up on the hill, but he was seldom called that. He also knew the derivation of that curious, ominous name. The man, unbelievably, had a doctorate in biology. Added to this, his wife made leather goods and sold them at the resort hotels in Liberty and

Woodbourne. In fact, Larry had once stopped in to pick up a deerskin handbag for Andrea. She had a creepy place for a workshop, down in the clammy basement of the shack they lived in. She laughingly called the business Leather from the Crypt, but its real name was Erda, after the Teutonic earth mother. They must listen to Wagner. Funny kind of bikers, but the real thing for all of that.

He was relieved that as near as he could tell, Dr. Leather did not remember his name either, so names were dispensed with by unspoken agreement. He knew the man worked as a helper for a local electrician and asked, "Still working for old What's-His-Name, the one lives over by the chicken farm?"

"You mean Hal? Nah, I'm starting my own woodworking business. I figure if I'm going to eat roadkill and milkweed pods, I might as well be my own boss. Besides, the guy is the cheapest man I ever worked for in my life. Last winter tore it for me. Hal takes on some plumbing in addition to electrical. We were putting in a bathroom on an addition, and Hal had all this old, salvaged shit copper pipe. It was black, must have been through a fire or something. I was standing knee deep in freezing mud, spending most of my time cleaning off black corrosion so I could sweat the joints. None of 'em leaked, but it took two hours before I could feel my feet again."

"Hard chance working for a jerk like that."

"No, it's not like that. I owe Hal. He gave me a job when I first came out here to live. I thought I had a lab tech job in Alaska and was just waiting out my time, but that pigfucker Nixon took a meat axe to the NIH budget. Prick. So here we were, no job, no money, no prospects. Working for Hal seemed pretty good at the time. And really, Hal's OK if you can get past the green teeth. I just got sick of electrical work on old houses, hanging around in filthy crawlspaces, you know. I was working on running some wire in a crawlspace once and realized my head had been resting on a mummified dead cat for ten minutes. Seems like kitchen cabinets and furniture would have to be cleaner, at least."

"Picking up some supplies?" Larry asked, by way of easing out of the conversation and getting on with the rest of his waning afternoon. Asking an inane question was as good a way as any. He thought he might do him the favor of suggesting he get a bit more food than usual, maybe some batteries. He was not worried at all about the man's beer supply. Larry did not advertise his talent for meteorology often, but he rather liked this man for some reason and thought (incorrectly) that he was good at hiding the source of his weather information.

"Yeah, gonna snow like a son of a whore, so I thought I'd get enough to last a few days. Later, man."

Larry looked a bit surprised. He realized that Dr. Leather must listen to the weather report on the same odd channel he did.

"Yeah, keep her between the banks. Nice truck! Give me first refusal if you want to sell it."

Larry wearily headed back out of town towards Claryville for the last time that day. Andrea would be home from her shift in the business office at the hospital in Liberty. He had not been able to talk with her when he and Jimmy had brought Karl in after the accident. She actually preferred that he not pop into the office unannounced. What with his height and yeti-like appearance, she liked to prep people in advance when he was coming by as a matter of courtesy, so they did not spill their coffee when they looked up and saw him looming.

Andrea had moved out of her apartment in Liberty and in with Larry last fall, acknowledging the obvious fact that they were a couple that was becoming permanent. It was still a bit new for him, having to concern himself with another person's presence. If he wanted to go off for the evening and have a few beers with one of his far-flung groups of friends, he now needed to call and announce this fact. And he had to be prepared to abandon the plan if need be. For example, if Andrea had planned a meal, then it became a trade-off whether the fun he would have would balance the guilt, and with passing time, he was more and more likely to head back home. All in all, it was pretty fair trade, and Andrea never suffocated him, nor he her. He was not sure about marriage yet, but having an old lady was working out. They had a lot of fun together, and he had not realized how sharing a living space with someone you loved could put a spin on matters that had no direct connection with your living arrangement. But Larry had rough edges that needed work, and there was no getting around that. He was willing to tackle them with her, but he often did not know where to start. They both figured it was a work in progress, with genuinely solid reasons for putting in the time.

Larry headed the truck up the Claryville road and started the long climb out of the valley. He stopped at the bar and picked up two cases of tall-neck bottles of his brand. There was definitely something in it for the owners of the place to keep plenty of this particular substance on hand with Larry living close by. There was almost no traffic beyond that point except those who lived there. It was a dead-end road unless you had a trail bike or an exceptional four-wheel-drive vehicle. For all practical purposes, the road ended at Teson's.

Tesons was a mansion built by a wealthy marine trader at the end of the nineteenth century. It was not being lived in but was maintained by a caretaker who was paid by the family. The house sat in a narrow hollow with sharply rising ridges on both sides. A small brook ran past the house, and Slide Mountain loomed to the northeast. Larry always visualized this place enshrouded by mist, though he knew it was not always misty when he was there. He once parked in a small clearing just past the house for a climb up Slide on a bright October day. The summit had about four inches of fresh powdery snow, and it was like paying an early social call on winter to welcome it in. That was the first time he saw the place. That was a memorable climb, even for a man of Larry's experience. One can never pick what will stick in the memory.

The house was magnificent. It was three stories tall, with multiple chimneys. It had porches, wings, towers, all the things an inveterate romantic would need to fire a gothic imagination. Inside, it was at least as imposing. Larry once got a full tour of the place. The uncle of one of his beer-drinking buddies was the caretaker, and he knew when he was going to be up there and suggested a visit. The old man was proud of the place and knew its every nook and cranny as well as the history behind it.

The caretaker's father had worked on the house, and he remembered when it was being built. The basement was crafted of huge boulders that had been set in place whole and dressed by hand. You could see the rough marks of the mason's chisels on the rock. The floors were of exotic hardwoods and the walls had elaborate wainscot panels. There were fireplaces in every room, with rough stone mantels. The hearth in the main hall was of great size, wide enough to take an eight-foot log. The main chimney was an edifice unto itself. It consisted of huge blocks of undressed stone that had been hauled up by oxen pulling log sledges on a temporary earth ramp. In the main hall, fit for a mediaeval lord, there was a portrait of the man who had commissioned this masterpiece. He was wearing a full Japanese kimono.

This curious man had spent considerable time in Japan and was fascinated with its culture and art. When he returned home and started the house, he wanted to bring as much of this culture back with him as he could. He commissioned a Japanese garden to be built on the grounds. This garden was to occupy several acres straddling the little brook that coursed through the valley. He brought from Japan more than one hundred workers and designers, who stayed for over a year to construct the garden. One hesitates to use the word *landscape* for such an undertaking. Landscaping is what you see around condos and split-level ranch houses. What these people were doing was part of an ancient and highly traditional Japanese art, akin to calligraphy, raku pottery, or swordsmanship. It is a Do, or Way, in the Zen sense. In Japan, flower arranging is considered a martial art.

When the garden was done, it was of considerable interest to Japanese who followed such matters, because of the exotic (to them) location and the unprecedented assemblage of respected practitioners who had created it. It was judged to be one of the best examples of the traditional Japanese garden in the world. Larry had a suspicion that this was in no small measure a result of some synergy between the gardeners and the Catskills themselves. This is easy to believe, in light of a singular event that occurred decades after the garden was completed. A major flood came through the valley and did serious damage to the garden. Rocks were moved, bridges destroyed, even the course of the brook changed in places within the garden's boundaries. But this was not the tragedy it might seem at first telling. The garden was not obliterated, or even terribly ruined—only altered. Japanese who came to inspect the garden after the flood were struck by its exquisite beauty. It was never "restored", since it was now closer to the perfection the builders had envisioned but could not achieve without the mountain's help; they termed it wabi-sabi. The garden was still studied by those who find such things enlightening.

He pulled into the driveway of his—now *their*—cabin and began to unload the groceries and beer. Andrea, a tall, slim young woman with long, dark hair, met him halfway back from the truck, squeezed his arm on her way past, and grabbed another part of the load. Two trips for each of them finished the job, and that included Larry's chainsaw, which he did not want to get buried. Larry went back and turned the truck around facing out toward the road, as there was a gentle downslope from the road to the house. Facing the truck out would facilitate ramming through a snow berm. He never liked the downslope much, preferring to be up from the road, but had gotten used to it in the two years he had been there. The property was priced right, and the small inheritance from his aunt could only go so far. He had built the place himself and had done a creditable, if not brilliant or artistic, job of the affair.

Andrea was already cooking, having herself stopped at a store in Liberty after leaving work. They would not want for food. She was using the perishables up first. Larry went out several more times for firewood, gleaned from the dwindling woodpile in the shed.

"How's Karl?" he asked her. "You hear anything from New York? Did the plane get off OK?"

"Not much to report. The ER crew stabilized him fine; he was in shock, which you knew, but thanks to you and Jimmy, he did not lose nearly as much blood as they thought he had. What the hell happened out there, anyway? Ransome said he couldn't have done as clean a job with a scalpel and a bone saw."

"Goddamndest thing I ever saw."

Larry related the story with appropriate detail and embellishment. Not that it took a lot of dressing up. It was a strange enough story already. Larry still puzzled about what he had seen—or thought he had seen. He still felt it could not happen the way it did. Many years would pass, and many journal articles on nonlinear phenomena would be digested, before he would have an inkling about what he saw, but he would still never believe it could have happened the way it did.

"I am still working with it being my fault. I can't stop beating myself up about it, I feel really shitty. It was me that was hauling the load. I know I did nothing unusual, dangerous, or careless, but it still comes down to the guy on the crawler. But it couldn't happen! There was no way. I have twitched thousands of logs for Jimmy and never saw a wave like that in a cable. But Karl is down in the Big Apple hurting bad.

"Jimmy wasn't watching when it actually took place. I told him about what I saw, and he didn't seem too surprised. He's been around woods work a lot longer than I have. I'll ask if he's ever heard of anything even remotely like this at some point. He's seen a lot more twitches than I have."

Andrea wisely moved the talk in another direction. "Why so much firewood? It's been pretty warm the last few days."

"Snow's on the way, and a lot, I figger. It'll be windy as hell and pretty cold by morning. Next few days won't feel much like April."

"I just listened to the weather report about half an hour ago and they called for a few showers and clearing by morning. You listen to a different station?"

"Yeah, I pick it up with my fillings."

Now seemed as good a time as any for a little revelation about himself.

"I just always seem to know what the weather is going to do for a little while ahead. Sometimes it's a long ways ahead, sometimes just a little while. It's pretty hard to explain. I don't tell many people about it, but now I'm telling you. It's pretty personal and actually kind of weird. I never really worked out what to think about it, so I usually *don't* think about it."

"You think it's some kind of extrasensory perception shit? I thought you were a scientist and a skeptic."

"Yeah, I am a skeptic. But it just works. For what it's worth, I don't think it's extrasensory. It's nothing paranormal, Twilight Zone or something. Maybe it's just another way of putting together what everyone else sees and feels. Didn't you notice the milky sky today? The wind started to shift around to the northeast around 1:00 and now it has teeth. Go stick your head outside and feel it. You can *feel* the power in the rush of air. It's like there is a fist in it. Anyone can see and feel that much. As we were coming in, you could even smell the snow. Me, I just don't have to think about it, you know, say to myself that the milky sky is a cloud shield from a storm, or that the northeasterly flow means low pressure moving in, or that the dampness means moisture coming in from the ocean. I probably just integrate all that without verbalizing it, and it goes straight into the same place where we all process heat and cold.

"But what I can't yet explain is how I can sense the forces that drive the events. When things are moving, even things I can't see, I feel them.

Like the waterworks under these mountains. I always know when I am crossing one, and I sort of feel all of them all the time to one extent or another. I could probably map them for you on the back of an envelope. I can even feel a strange movement under the floor of the forest—maybe just water traveling in root systems, but I'm not really sure about that. You get used to it. I don't think I'm alone." He did not mention his encounter with the Dugan's truck driver that afternoon. He had not sorted that out yet. He thought he would pay the man a visit and ask him as casually as possible if he knew where any of the water tunnels were. The answer might mean a lot.

"I am trying to remember if my grandfather ever told me any stories about weather seers on the rez."

Andrea treasured the fourth of her that was Iroquois. She never wore it on her sleeve, although it might have meant a competitive edge in scholarships or in job hunting. She just loved it for what it was, a link to the past, to who she was. It made her feel a bit special and keeping that to herself seemed right.

"Your grandfather was a CPA in Massena all his life. He probably listened to the radio like everyone else."

"He grew up on the reservation. He had a lot of great stories. I used to love to go up there when I was a little girl and listen to him spin them out. He could go on for hours, sitting there smoking his pipe. I still love the smell of pipe tobacco. He had stories about the Catskills too. Always said they formed one of the pillars that hold up the world. He never told me what the other ones were. I've never found out." She made a mental note to add this item to the long list of research projects she planned to do one day on her genealogy and the history of her tribe.

"I would have liked to meet him."

"Yeah, you two would have gotten along great. I did a lot of growing up when I was with him. He always seemed to be at the center of himself. I can't explain it better than that. He was a man in balance and harmony. Even living in town away from where he grew up never took that away from him. He visited the old folks on the rez some, and I got to go myself a few times. I was too young to learn what I could and should have, but it made a big impression on me."

Andrea served up the rich stew she had concocted from simple ingredients, just beef, carrots, potatoes, and onions. There was little seasoning other than salt, pepper, and a bay leaf. She was an excellent cook, but she kept her dishes to a spare minimum of ingredients. Perhaps that was what made everything so hearty and delicious. Larry opened a beer and checked out the morning paper. He always read it in the evening, a habit born of heading off to work early and not having any time to sit and lounge over a cup of coffee, plus he grew up reading an evening paper back home in Albany.

Andrea cleaned up the dishes and thought absently about negotiating a new rule: if you cook, you don't have to clean up. Seemed like a good deal to her, and Larry, who always homed in on the justice of things, would approve. The dishes were making a bit more noise than usual as she pondered how to bring this up without precipitating any sort of altercation. Larry noticed the increase in volume, dropped his paper, and started to help. She figured this was a good sign.

As she looked out the window over the sink, she noticed that snow was beginning to fall. The driveway was already white, and the light from the house down the road was no longer visible. She went over to throw another chunk of wood in the stove and shivered a bit, even though it was warm in the dwelling. There are more ways than one for cold to cross a wall, and maybe even different *kinds* of cold. It was down to twenty-eight degrees outside, and the wind was moaning out of the northeast. She glanced over at Larry and gave him a quizzical look. He was busy with putting the leftover stew in the refrigerator and did not notice. Who *was* this guy, really?

Morning dawned, gray and dreary. The power had gone off in the night, and they had to conserve water for cooking and minimal hygiene like brushing teeth. Fortunately, Larry had built an outhouse against such misadventures, and a cold butt just made the fire and warmth of the house that much more wonderful. The portable radio had moderately good batteries, and they got the "new" weather report calling for another six to eight inches before it would taper off. Andrea looked at Larry with an upraised eyebrow, an implicit question on her face.

"Two feet" was all he said, and she knew it would be so.

The day passed in the sort of comfort that comes only in a snowstorm. Larry had never lived in the South, and he doubted if there was anything like this to be had huddled around an air conditioner when the temperature outside crested one hundred degrees and kept on going up, with humidity in the meaningless range. He conceded it was all in where you came from and how you were raised. The metaphors were different for Southerners, that was all. This climate was his.

He and Andrea sat with legs absentmindedly touching, occasionally rubbing, each about the same distance from the stove, each lost in a book. The wind was a constant presence that was felt more than heard in the small building. There was certainly no work for them today, or maybe tomorrow either. If there is magic in the world, snow is certainly of it.

Storms like this in April were not unheard of here, especially up in the higher valleys, and Claryville's location was certainly the type specimen for a high valley. But this was unusual in its intensity. At least the new snow would be gone in a few days. Larry and Andrea both liked the winter and enjoyed the occasional days off that storms spawned, but the earth was already awakening to spring, and this had set the calendar back. There had been all the dark reddish colors coming out from under the snow, and in the lowlands, daffodils were already coming up. Most of all, they liked the smell. Each season has smells, and for Andrea, especially, spring smells were the best. The leaves and mulch that had rotted under the snow all winter were now coming out from under the drifts and the sun was driving their smells into the warming air. That was all gone for now, buried under nearly two feet of new powdery snow. The cold, icy smell of winter was back for a spell, but it was like the spray one puts on the window at Christmas to make your living room look like a Currier and Ives print, or maybe a scene from Dickens. A couple of swipes with a wet rag and it would be spring again.

Larry liked to savor the curious and singular days in any month that either presaged the one to come or recalled the one past. October was the month that usually offered the most numerous of these. On any given October day, you could feel like it was high summer, early fall, or even late fall. And in these mountains, there were days that were downright wintry in this most changeable of months. This day was at least two months in the past, maybe three. The storm would have been a credit to January. He would be back to work in a few days, even if the snow lingered in the heights. He needed the rest after the accident, and he would take the time off and be glad of it. He thought he should call the hospital as soon as the phone was back in service to check up on Karl, but other than that, he posted himself no daily duty roster.

The old oil lamps gave off a faint smell like a diesel engine and the fire hissed away. They were down to the wood that had been at the bottom of the pile all winter and had not dried well. The book fell from his hands, but he did not notice as he dozed with his left leg entangled in Andrea's. She had long ago let her science fiction paperback show Larry's the way to the cabin floor.

9

With a start, Larry noticed that he had just handed the last chunk of wood to Eban, who processed it with the same clockwork regularity as all the others. Larry mused that when you are working hard, the last piece should always come as a surprise. If you spend all your time thinking about getting to the last piece, you are not working at peak efficiency on the those that go before. He stripped off his gloves and hearing protectors as Eban throttled back the old tractor motor. He ran the shaft all the way back into the cylinder to protect its wear surface from rust and shut the rig down. The silence was foreign, almost unwelcome.

"So, b'Jeez, how's my old neighbor been doin'?" Eban's huge old mitt dwarfed even Larry's considerable hand. It was as hard and leathery as ever. Eban seemed not to have quit work entirely. Even if he had, those hands would never soften. They had spent too much time fastened to unyielding rocks and ancient equipment to lose the memory of the sixty years of farm labor. "Much obliged for the help."

"Good to see ya, Eb, you old fart. I see you haven't slowed down too awful much."

"Well, I guess maybe a little. This ain't no real winter's wood here. I had an oil furnace put in when Mother got so sick. I had to tend to her so constant that I didn't have time for feedin' the fire, let alone workin' up the woodpile. 'Sides, when she got so bad at the end, I was afraid she'd wander into the stove."

So that's what it had been. Larry had wondered. That was probably all he would hear about the loss of Martha, Eban's wife of a long lifetime. Alzheimer's was not the best choice if you wanted to die in a dignified manner. Tuberculosis, in fiction only, of course, was the top of the heap for theatrical operatic endings wherein you could still sing an aria in your last minutes that would knock the dentures out of spectators in the back row. You could look really sharp at the end. Puccini would not have had Mimi die of Alzheimer's.

"You know, I was always cold when we had that damn furnace as the only heat. You could never get really warm. I used to wander around the house lookin' for a warm spot. I'd walk by the stove in the parlor, and it was almost like it was suckin' heat out of the room, sittin' there all cold and dark like it 'twas. I just put up enough wood these days to keep the kitchen stove goin' all the time, and on really cold nights when I'm in the parlor watching a movie, I fire up the old station agent in there. Feels like old times when Mother and the young 'uns was around. Come on, let's take a walk around the place. You haven't been down this way since I sold the herd."

Eban and Larry walked around the old farm. It was a marginal farm at the best of times, but well-run for all of that. This was not the rolling dairy country of the western part of the state, but it had supported farms and human activity for a long time. Those who chose to build and work here were a breed apart, survivors. The old buildings were still in fair shape. The house and original barn were old when Eban had started working the place. Eban had always believed in good roofing, and these structures would last until the generation beyond the next, but the chances that anyone would farm this place again were slim to none.

Larry was lost in memories. He had helped Eban during the haying season for a few years, and the place was like a second home. Now the hay barn stood empty. It was the oldest outbuilding in the set, probably older than the house. Farmers back in the day tended to build their barns first, and then the houses. Practical priorities were important when you were living on the edge. It was an old post-and-beam structure, poised on the side of a hill. You just can't waste level ground on buildings where it is so precious. The rear of the structure was at ground level, but the front faced downhill, and the main floor was about eight feet above grade on that side. There was an earthen ramp with a little bridge going to the mow door. It must have taken a lot of work to build it that way, but the lay of the land was inexorable in its demands. The cavernous opening smelled only vaguely of hay now, and it was old dusty hay at that. The roof was lost in high, dark shadows, like the vaulting of a cathedral. Larry remembered when it was full to bursting with fresh green-gold bales that had the most wonderful odor there was on the planet. There was almost infinite satisfaction in going out to the barn on a rainy day after the hay was in. You could hear the drops beating on the roof and sit smugly in your dry haven surrounded by the winter's stores.

It wasn't hay until it was under the shingles. It was frustrating to look out at a field full of nice dry hay as the clouds piled up in the west. Most of the work was already done. You limed, fertilized, mowed, tedded, raked, and finally baled. All was for naught if the rains came before it was under the shingles. Helplessness is one of the hardest emotions to deal with. They had never lost a bale while Larry was working there unless it was a result of equipment failure. Balers in particular were catalysts for some of the most inventive profanity this side of the New York

City waterfront. Other farmers started to watch to see when Eban would hook up his number-five John Deere sickle bar to the mowing tractor and would follow suit. Eban, of course, always asked Larry when to mow.

The much newer attached cattle barn was equally desolate. The milking equipment was long gone. Stainless steel bulk tanks, pumps, tubing, and compressors held their value well and represented a considerable investment that could be recouped when a farm quit its working days. The smell of manure and silage had faded years ago. There was just a moldy smell from the concrete half walls. The stanchions were all still in place, as were the mangers and feed troughs, items of little worth hereabouts these days. The silo that had been on the end opposite the hay barn was also gone, sold when the milk-handling things went. The chicken house stood open, the tool shed was almost empty, and the corn crib had collapsed, a victim of rotten sills. You don't fix what you don't need, and raising a corn crop to be picked and dried instead of chopped and ensiled was never very practical, even when the farm was in full swing. At least the fields were kept up. Another farmer was haying them now. He was making huge six-foot-by-six-foot round bales that you could just leave out all winter. He recalled someone in town using an old Allis Chalmers Rotobaler, which made small cylindrical bales that resisted rain. He figured that was what gave them the idea. Still, it did not seem right to make up your hay and leave it out in the field all winter. Most dairy farmers didn't even make hay anymore, instead chopping the grass green and ensiling it. Only horse breeders and stable owners ever called for small bales of good dust-free June-cut hay anymore.

Drying hay for the winter was a mystical thing for Larry. He used to keep pigs years ago when he lived in Claryville and had salted the meat to pull out water and cure it, smoked it over apple wood, and finally air-dried it further for storage. Andrea had raised garden herbs and dried them in the sun. Sunflower seeds were dried for the birds. Firewood had to be seasoned to burn. He felt a kinship with the bees, who collected nectar and let it thicken and dry to honey. Water was the source of life, but it was also the medium that took everything that had been alive back around again, like the River Styx. Water meant rot and decay. Usually that was the correct order of things, but if you wanted to feed yourself and your animals in the iron months of winter, you needed to hold the water at bay for a while. Eban's good galvanized, painted, rolled-steel roofs were one manifestation of this effort.

As they walked up through the yellowed early autumn fields, Larry spotted a small copse of young trees in the next field up the hill. It had to be relatively recent, because he clearly remembered mowing this field, and it was not there in the early seventies. And even if his memory had failed him in this, there were no older trees, as one often saw in small ravines or swales that were either never cleared or left to return to nature's will because they were only marginally productive. Old fields returned to primal forest slowly when abandoned. There was a succession of growth. Often, the real forest moved in from the edges tentatively, perhaps fearing the pain of the axe. But the opportunists, like the alders and poplars, were always quick to move to the task, yielding ground to the climax trees only grudgingly.

"So, what's that shit about?" Larry queried. He was curious about this wart on the face of a field he knew so well.

"That shit is about gettin' angry and not figgerin' things out," replied Eban.

"Sounds like we ought to take a short walk up there. I am guessing there is a real good story attached to this one."

"Well, b' Jeez, I guess probably so."

They began the detour up to the tiny glade, across the stubble left after the second cutting of hay. Second cuttings were always a shot in the dark at best. You could fertilize all you wanted to and watch the weather forecasts like a hawk, but you still could end up losing the whole deal. The grass was beautifully green, full of protein, and delicious. But the days were short in late August and into September, and you need light to make hay. Sun. Go ahead and cut, but unlike June and August, the sun was late arriving and early leaving, heading south, and hay dried slowly. And nothing ever smelled like hay cut in late June and preserved quickly by a sun that seemed like it would never leave the middle of the sky.

They arrived at the copse in a few minutes, neither man bothered in the least by the uphill side trip. Fields in the Catskills often had alarming angles.

"So, what the fuck? Looks like a mower/conditioner down in that mess!"

"Yup. Just right. Belonged to Merle Crouch. Still does, I s'pose. Funny guy. Angriest man I ever knew. Don't speak with him much anymore, but he's probably just as angry as ever. Nothing ever worked right for him, and when it did, he figgered it was a fluke. He ran a dairy farm over t'other side of Thunder Hill, up near that pile of cars Raymond had. Asked if he could take the hay off my fields when I quit the business. Told him OK, s'long as he kept the fields up, fertilizin' and mindin' the shit growin' in round the edges. Worked OK for a coupla years. He'd come in and spread lime and some 10-10-10 just on time. Mowed early, got a second cutting, and kept the brush down. I didn't give it a second thought. Then the fourth year, he was out mowing the second crop in late August like usual and I heard the most god-awful ruckus up here. Now, I ain't so good of hearin'. Run them chain saws and corn choppers too long to hear much more'n the TV turned up real loud and the deer poachers uncorkin' out back. But I heard him shoutin' right enough, all the way down t' the house.

"Thought he was in trouble. I recall when Mel Eck's son got caught up in a corn chopper and lost his right arm and half a shoulder. I was drivin' truck behind him and had to stop the chopper. Asshole left the tractor's PTO in gear when he jumped off to clear the intake. Lived, but he never was the same. Father never got over it neither. Anyway, I jumped in the old truck and ran on up, figgerin' I'd need to throw a body in the back, maybe. There was Merle, pounding on the mower with a sledgehammer, screaming like the hounds of hell. Scary, kinda. I thought he was goin' ta vapor lock on me right there. 'Member, there's a big ol' chunk a ledge right here, and I allus used to go round it. Course, we mowed with a number-five John Deere sickle bar, as you know—you run it a bunch. Some folks are number'n a pounded thumb. He just lifted his machine high's it would go and left the cutters running. Musta figgered he had enough clearance, and just kept on goin'. I guess it was just too much work to let what's really there get in his way. Musta' thought he was livin' right at the foot of the cross an' Jesus hisself would protect him.

"So, the cutters clipped the living rock. Any fool would have seen that comin'. And of course, Merle figgered he wasn't no fool, so he didn't figger it. Bastid never figgered out much of anything. If you were to take the time to poke through all that alder, you'd find a good charge of tool steel chunks and pieces of cast iron from the gear casings.

"And then he just fuckin' left the rig. Unhooked it from his three-point, pulled the PTO shaft off, and left. All the time keepin' up a real good dialog between him and his creator. I figgered he'd go home, have couple of beers, wind down, and come back for it. It could have been fixed, prob'ly. But he never did. It was a personal thing between him and his bad luck. And his bad luck won. Took me two years to find a new guy to keep the fields clear. Meantime, the shit started growing up around the mower, and I ain't goin' ta move it. Phil just mows around it ever' year, and ever' year the trees grow thicker and older. I speck it won't be too many years before the whole place goes back to the woods. Don't bother me none. I'm done with it—done with farmin', done with life, nearabouts. But the woods owned it before anyone. I just have a lot of trouble getting' straight how they did it back in them days. Up at dawn, work all day with oxen, axes, and bucksaws. Just how the hell do you clear a field like this with tools like that? I worked hard all my days, but I don't know how anyone could work that hard."

The tour brought them back to the house, past the small kitchen garden. Eban maintained just a small vestige of the huge and wonderful one he had tended back in the day. Larry guessed he still raised at least fifty times as many tomatoes as he needed and was not disappointed when they detoured through the patch. Eban tossed him one that had escaped the frosts by dint of a sheet of heavy builder's plastic that sat at the ready nearby. It was delicious. Another thing Larry missed was real tomatoes from the little raised-bed garden behind his house. He corrected himself: *not* his house in Wellesley. He would not even think of buying the little receptacles of pink oatmeal they called tomatoes in the stores but frequented the farmers' stands down at Haymarket near Fanueil Hall when real tomatoes were in season. This one was not a summer tomato, though. Tomatoes picked this late had a slight bitterness to them. Not at all bad, but he could tell they had ripened during cold nights. He wished he had been here a month ago. He would have helped Eban with his surplus of tomatoes. He could live on them.

The rest of the garden was pretty much gone from the heavy frosts. There was still some Swiss chard and some Brussels sprouts, both of which took frosts and got strong on them. The beans were dead, along with the cucumbers and peppers. A pumpkin or two lurked under the dead canopy of leaves. Eban cut some chard, asked Larry to pocket some more tomatoes, and they headed inside. The sun was getting low, and there was a chill creeping out of the shadows. The mulling fire in the kitchen stove felt pretty good when they got inside. Larry had worked up a good sweat, and his clothes were soaked through. Eban showed him where his room was, upstairs in the southwest of the house, and Larry went back out for his pack.

"I don't suppose you'd want a beer, there, perfesser?" Eban queried as Larry went back towards the stairway.

"Eb', I'm drier'n a popcorn fart. I figger I'll know what to do with it when I get my hands on it." The number of beers they had shared over the years might best be tallied using scientific notation.

He changed quickly into dry clothes and laid the sweaty ones out to dry. He would wear them for the climb tomorrow when he'd get them just as wet all over again. All his time on the trail had ingrained very practical habits. You could not wash clothing very handily on the move.

Once in a while, shirts and shorts could be rinsed in a stream, but mostly you took them off, dried them out, and put them on again the next day. But socks especially needed to be washed regularly. They would start to feel like plastic wrap after a few days otherwise and suffocate your feet. Blisters were not far down the road when that happened. Wearing smelly clothing was just something you got used to on the trail. That and no showers. You can't really smell yourself, he found out, unless you really work at it. He put on his soft-soled campsite moccasins and went back down to see what Eban was up to.

Eban had a cold beer out and open for Larry when he walked into the kitchen, and another of his own that he was working on. Larry would have brought some along, but the custom of hospitality here was such that this was not proper. The host got the beer, and that was that. Eban was fussing over the dinner, which smelled wonderful. It was sitting on the back of the ancient stove in a cast-iron Dutch oven, bubbling away slowly, emitting the smell of chicken, parsley, celery, thyme, and other wondrous flavorings. Eban was taking a cup of broth out of the pot. He set it aside to cool. The cup was about two thirds full of broth, and the balance was clear golden chicken fat. He cleaned the chard and cut off the big ribs, put a big pot of water on the hot part of wood stove surface to boil, and sat down with his beer.

"Harder'n hell to get a real fowl nowadays. Friggin' egg farmers give 'em all kinds a poison to make 'em lay, and they ain't fit fer cats. I know a fella keeps a few chickens fer himself and friends. They get used up fer layin' and he gives me a call. I heard you was coming, I called him right off. Can't make decent chicken 'n' dumplings with store-bought chicken. Ain't got no flavor."

"Grahamsville doesn't seem to have changed too much since I was here last. Lots more houses, but not much commercial development."

"This whole place has turned into a suburb of the City. Most people don't make their livin' here anymore. The timber's all gone, you never could make nothin' farmin', what the hell else is there? You need one hardware store, one lumber yard, one market, one restaurant. That comes up to just a couple local families. A few folks drive truck, like my brother did for most of his life, a few sell real estate. Things is quiet."

"I didn't get over to Liberty, probably won't. How's the resort business doing?"

"Gone. It was already startin' to fade when you was here. Those guys with the black outfits still own a bungalow colony here and there, but that's 'bout it. There's some sort of pagoda over on Old Broadhead Road now. Everything else is pretty much history."

Larry remembered the bungalow colonies and resorts well. It always puzzled him. The people that frequented the resorts and the local folks, even those who had migrated up from the City, never commingled. It was like they were invisible to one another. He once read a story about a world that was so crowded that it was habitable by the populace only in shifts, and you could never leave your shift. The people on the off shifts were never seen or heard by the on shift; they were in cold storage. It was much like that. The resort people depended on the locals for food, repairs, and so forth, but never for social interaction. They never actually dealt with them. The resorts were islands, universes that were self-contained and impregnable. The people would arrive in Cadillacs or Lincolns—movable fortresses, proofed against the outside world—and disappear inside the compounds. Larry had never met one of them.

The bungalow colonies were already on the skids when Larry was there years ago. He remembered the ruins in the woods. There was always a huge central building called a "casino," a separate residence of the owner, and the rest of the structures, the bulk, would consist of a series of small, self-sufficient cabins, with refrigerators and small stoves. A friend of his had bought a colony on a quit-claim deed after a foreclosure. The stove and refrigerator in Larry's cabin in Claryville had come from there. He had had a wonderful time exploring the place. His friend had the casino bulldozed, and Larry still mourned the huge commercial gas kitchen stove and bread oven that had fallen into the basement. The floor was so rotten that there was no way to salvage them without risking life and limb. He still had occasional flashes of regret about that. What he might have done with them was not the issue—just their loss down in the subterranean tomb, with the ashes of the burned building sitting on them. These places could be very creepy. There were often swimming pools with trees growing out of their cracked bottoms, handball courts in the same condition, mysterious outbuildings falling to compost. He could never get enough of exploring abandoned buildings.

"Too many goddamn houses around here to suit me now," said Eban wistfully. He would never move again.

"You're talking to the wrong guy for sympathy. Try living in the Boston area for a while and tell me that again. But I do remember it was a lot more peaceful back when I lived here."

It had been. Seeing the new housing and roads was annoying. He wanted everything to be the same as he remembered it. But watching this kind of "progress" always irked Larry. It was like dawn creeping up on you on the most wonderful romantic night of your life, when everything was magical. When the dawn comes, all the magic goes away. Seeing the remote places eaten by civilization gave him that same feeling. He remembered one of his rare acid trips, when he had spent an entire evening looking at a knothole. It coruscated with all the spectral might of the sun itself, viewed through a prism. When he came down off the trip, it was just a knothole. He wondered if there were any places left on earth where Wild still flowed pure. Probably not. Even the moon was littered with human trash.

Another round of beers came out of the refrigerator. Eban checked the cooling broth and found it still too hot for his purposes.

"Those bikers ever leave Old Broadhead Road?" asked Larry. He had a momentary flash of an ancient bread truck that he still coveted.

"Yup, right after you did, maybe six months or so later. I can't remember the guy's name who owned it, right off."

"All I can think of is a name they called him once in a while: Dr. Leather."

"I couldn't even remember that. Been too long. He was down a few years ago for Alton's funeral. They were pretty close for a while. Hit it off real well. I never saw much of him myself. Funny thing, I overheard him talking to one of Alton's kids at the wake. Seems he moved up to Maine. Damned if he ain't a professor or something up there somewhere, just like you. Way he told it, he just wandered in the front door of the place and asked for a job and got it. That was the gist, anyways."

Larry privately dismissed this as even a remote possibility. He knew the guy had a PhD from the rumors around town, but things just did not work that way in academe. You needed to go through a few iterations as a postdoc, and then grovel your way into a job. There were so few jobs for regular faculty that he was continually surprised when anyone at all applied to his department's graduate program. Masochists, mostly, these days, but then he had gotten a job, and there were few other things he would want to do with his time. He thought, hope springs eternal. Even with all his great successes over the years, he would not want to be out looking for work right now. He would make a point of finding out that biker's name and learning the real facts about how he got that job. There must have been more to it than that. And the man interested him for other reasons.

"How's your boy doing? Vrest still in one piece?"

"That damn kid! I sent him to school to learn computer programming. I couldn't let him take this place over. That kid could hurt himself sleeping in bed at night." Larry remembered the incident with the wood splitter. "He couldn't get the drinkin' under control and had 'bout four nasty car accidents. Finally, New York, in its wisdom, took away his license pretty much for good. The worst one, he almost lost his leg. I went down there to the hospital, must have been three or four A.M. Hank Ordway, the state cop on duty, called me. Thought I oughta know what's up. The doc told me he needed my permission to operate. I asked him what he was gonna do, and he told me he hadda cut off his leg. I grabbed him by the wrist real hard and told him he might better figure out some other way of fixin' him up if he wanted to be able to operate on anybody else down the line. Bastard listened, did some harder figgerin', and saved his leg. I apologized later, but he agreed I'd done just good." Larry considered what *real hard* might feel like from those huge spring-steel hands.

"Where is he living now? I thought I'd stop in if I have time on Sunday."

"He's pretty far off for that. He moved up near Lake Erie. Good fishin' up there. I always liked the country myself. I put him onto it. We used to go ice fishin' up there a lot. I once figgered on retiring up there, but when Mother got so sick, between the workin' time I lost and the friggin' medical bills they squeezed me for, I'm lucky to be able to stay on here. I s'pose my days here are numbered anyway. Hope I die before I get too feeble to split m' own wood."

"What's he doing up there, computer work?"

"Naah, the school was a fraud. Anaway, now all that work's bein' done in Calcutta or some damn place, I hear on the news. He's working in a hardware store. His wife works too. They do OK, I guess. I got a coupla grandkids off 'em. I went up to see them last winter. Damndest thing happened. He handed me this chunk of stainless steel, 'bout eighteen inches long, ast me if I knew what 'twas. I said I never see sech a object before. Turns out it was the pin from his leg from that accident. Friggin' thing pulled loose. He was settin' eatin' breakfast one day and felt this lump in his hip. He went in and they made a little cut and pulled it out. Leg must be OK, he ain't fell down or nothin'. Still limps bad."

By now the broth from the chicken had cooled. Eban put some baking powder and salt in it and stirred in flour until he had a thick batter. He opened the Dutch oven and spooned that batter over the chicken, closing the lid tight. He checked the clock over the sink and made mental note of when a half hour would have elapsed. He tossed the chard into the pot with a chunk of salt pork and got another round of beers.

"You learned how to cook; I see." Eban had always said he "usually kept a woman around" for that, but Larry was not going to tease him on this matter. He thought Martha's death was probably too fresh and painful for that. But Eban was surprisingly open about it. It must have hurt the tough old farmer badly for it to show at all. He was all mountain man.

"Before she got so bad, she wrote down all her receipts. She never forgive her grandma for takin' all hers to the grave with her. The old lady lived to damn near a hunnert. Seems like she had enough time to pass 'em along. I 'member her grandma's ginger snaps myself. They were the best I ever had. She never wrote her receipts down, and never told anyone how to do it. She was just mean sometimes and wanted people to miss her, I figger. Funny way to do it. Now all we think about her is that she took her receipts to the grave with her. I learned a few basic things from Martha when she was clear, and then I hadda do all the cookin' after she got feeble-minded. Got lots of practice. Seemed like, fer a while, she'd git a little more chipper when I made things I remembered her likin'. That was all I could do. There at the end, when she was finally in the home, she didn't even recognize me. Couldn't talk nary 'tall. She finally forgot how to eat. I told 'em to let her go in peace, stop feedin' her with that goddamn tube 'n' all. When I finally got angry enough, and scairt the rotten little shits enough, they let her pass. I still had to sign some kinda release. Ever body wants to cover their ass. I told 'em if they didn't let her go on easy, I'd have to come in and shoot her. Would have too."

About this raw fact Larry had not the slimmest shred of a doubt.

Eban's mental alarm dinged and he served up the food. Chicken and dumplings, chard with salt pork, butter, and vinegar, and sliced tomatoes. An honest meal of excellent food for the last day of summer. It did not feel much like summer as the rest of the house started to cool. The kitchen remained warm and cheery. The dumplings were the best Larry had ever tasted. The flavor of the broth permeated them to their very centers, and they could not have been more tender. He remembered them from when Martha used to cook them herself. A large woman, full of life, and as honest and friendly as it was possible to imagine. She was a real farm wife from the old mold. She worked hard, raised the kids, could milk and bale hay with any man, and still cooked the best farm food there ever was.

This was the cooking that Larry loved above all others. He liked ethnic food of all sorts, but the frilly stuff in restaurants now, like artichoke pizza with cheese made from water buffalo milk, was just so much foolishness, he thought. When the nights started to come early and frosts rolled in from the north, you needed *food.* Eban had survived a lifetime of salt pork, beef stew, pies, roasts, and potatoes cooked in the old-fashioned manner. He worked it all off every day of his life. If all you did was sit at a terminal all day, maybe you did need to count grams of fat. Larry certainly did, and he worked out regularly. But if you got up when the sun was just a rumor to milk sixty head of cattle, feed them, clean the barn, haul more hay down from the mow, trot endless wheelbarrow loads of silage out for the afternoon's feeding, eat a big dinner, go out and haul firewood and sawlogs out of your woodlot with a tractor all afternoon, eat a light supper, and then go out to milk again, all when the temperature crested at five above at 3:00 in the afternoon, you didn't really need to worry about your coronary arteries as much as city folk.

The meal over and enough cleaning up done that honor be served, Larry and Eban settled back in their chairs. Eban rummaged around for one of his corncob pipes. He still puffed his pipes a bit. Larry liked the smell of most pipe tobacco and was not at all dismayed to see one come out. Eban had tried a briar only once and had never tried one again. He smoked his corncobs until they were nothing but char. This one was on its last legs. These pipes usually burned out when the bottom went. The maker put a paper seal on the bottom to keep air from coming in and burning the soft inner cob material, but sooner or later this would be breached. Ever observant, Eban would take note and start putting Christmas or Easter seals on the bottom to keep the pipe airtight. This would prolong the life of the pipe until the upper part finally disintegrated.

"Any excitement 'round here? Good gossip? People caught in the wrong beds?"

"Well, had a murder."

"Jeez, second one this century. Time for you to move further from the City."

"Nah, was local folks. Born 'n' raised right in Grahamsville. Frank Osgood's the one got kilt. Tony DeKeeto popped him. Those two was born hating each other. They was hating each other *before* they was born. They was hatin' each other before this planet was goin' round the sun, I think."

"I remember the names, but not much else. Never met either of 'em, I don't think."

"Goddamn lucky fer you."

"They get in a brawl or something?"

"Yeah, lots of times, but that's not what got one of 'em kilt. They pounded on each other in bars for years. Was pretty odd how it happened. Tony was driving the plow truck for the town then, and we'd had a pretty snowy winter. You probably don't remember, but Frank lived up on Thunder Hill. Town plows that. Seems Tony took a shine to Frank's mailbox that winter. Kept putting down that wing and clipping it right off clean to the ground. Every time it snowed, Tony would clip 'er off."

Larry had spent enough time putting his own mailbox back to sympathize. He never quite got around to thinking there was any malevolence involved, but it could have gone either way.

"Anyway, one time Frank had enough. His brother was the foreman for the power company's pole crew and had keys to all the equipment. They got post hole diggers that won't take shit offn' no frost we get around here. If some drunk cowboy takes off a pole in his Blazer 'bout two A.M. some Sunday mornin' in January, they still gotta put in a new pole. Anyway, he gets his brother in on it. Soon's we got a nice spell of weather, Frank and his brother take the post auger up on Thunder Hill and put down two post holes, mebbee six feet down, one on either side of the mailbox, lined up just right, if you see where this is goin'. His brother had a couple scrap poles that had been pulled on accounta bein' too old. They cut 'em down enough to handle from the butt end, put 'em in the ground, backfilled, and Frank ran his hose out and soaked the fill. Colder'n hell, and it froze down harder 'n' quicker than shit. He trimmed the tops down to the height of the berm, shoveled a bunch of snow to hide 'em, and waited. Next snow, along comes old Tony in the plow truck, runnin' her as fast as she'd turn a wheel, wing down. Headed right for Frank's mailbox like usual. When he hit that friggin' post it took the wing off like it was never there, swung the truck around and off the road on the far side, into the ditch real permanent-like.

"Tony got out of the truck and didn't say shit. He could see Frank up in his house lookin' out, and knew he'd been had. He walked down a ways to his cousin's trailer and called for his wife to come get 'im. He never called the town folks at all. It was Tony's truck you see. He was contractin' out the plowing. His wife drove them home and Tony got his

30-06 deer rifle and loaded 'er up. Grabbed two full boxes of 160-grain soft points too. Headed back up the hill. Busted in on Frank and shot him dead between the eyes. Kept on shootin'. Frank's wife was screamin' so the neighbors could hear, but Tony's wife'd already called the staties, worryin' about what her asshole husband was up to. Bastard used up every bullet he had on Frank by the time the cops got there. He didn't just pump them in fast. That's the really strange thing. There were the neighbors, waitin' on the cops, listenin'. He'd shoot a round, then wait a couple of minutes, then fire again. Kep' it up until both boxes were empty. Went quietly enough when the staties got there. He's in some home somewhere. With Frank dead, he don't seem to have much to care about anymore. Ain't said hardly a word since. Even his wife don't visit him no more."

Larry had nothing to say.

"You know what pisses me off about that whole thing? The rifle. It was a Winchester model 70, made in the late fifties. Now, *that* is a rifle. No plastic on that one, action slicker than a wet cock. I imagine it sits there in some evidence locker somewhere. I'd bust in and get it if I thought I could get away with it. Damn shame."

Larry agreed and thought of the lost weapons from his own erstwhile collection with infinite sadness.

"How's your daughter Suzie?" Eban had not mentioned her.

His face darkened, and Larry regretted the question. "Cancer. They been treating her reg'lar, but it don't look too good. All her hair's fell out, and she don't weigh a hunnert pound."

"I'm sorry." What else could he say? The matter dropped instantly.

They sat in silence for a space of a few minutes waiting until the earlier mood resurfaced, but it was slow coming back. Eban asked after Andrea next, and that did nothing to dispel the darkening mood. Larry told him enough to keep him up-to-date. No holding back, but there were things he could not speak of, even with this friend of his that he trusted more than any other human on the planet. But Eban chewed on things for a while without speaking, seeming to fill in missing details on his own as he went.

"She'll be back."

"What makes you say that? She's screwing this French guy, she ripped me off for everything I valued, she has half my retirement so I'll have to work 'til I keel over dead in some godforsaken lecture hall to keep from starving. Why is she coming back? Would I even want her back?" Larry was on the edge of getting testy.

Eban was quiet for a spell more and loaded another cob, the first having so much carbon cake in it that it would hold only a tiny amount of tobacco. "I remember you two real good from the old days. Just a feeling."

As crusty as he was, and as unlikely as it would seem to anyone looking in from the outside, Eban had a feel for people the way Larry had a feel for the weather. Larry would think about this opinion very seriously in the time ahead. That sense was why Eban had taken Larry under his wing when he first arrived. Larry had been looking for work, and Eban offered him his first part-time job. They had done a lot of beer drinking and hell raising back then, despite the age difference. After Larry started working for Jimmy Blandsford full time, they still kept up the friendship. In Larry, Eban saw a person who had an intrinsic value beyond his ability to work hard, his honesty, and his openness. He could not quite put his finger on it, but it always seemed to him that there needed to be a Larry. As though just his presence, even if all he ever did was hang out in his cabin up in Claryville, was a worthwhile, even necessary thing. When he and Andrea got together, the two of them in their union made the feeling more intense. The two of them apart had a wrongness to it that Eban did not feel could be stable. He was certain that there were ties between the two that could never be broken, nor even weakened. It was as though these ties were even now beginning to realign themselves and pull. These bonds might even be utterly independent of the two people to whom they were attached.

Eban threw more wood in the stove and sat back down. He began to doze, and Larry was none too awake himself. They went off to their rooms quietly. Larry's room was downright cold. Eban would not dream of turning on the furnace until either the first snow or Thanksgiving, whichever came first. There were thick wool blankets and a down comforter on the bed. He burrowed deeply into this stack of insulation and was quickly on the edge of sleep. As he drifted toward unconsciousness, he pondered Eban's prediction about Andrea and their getting back together. He could hope, he supposed. There would be a lot of fixing up that needed to be done, and he could not initiate it, though he desperately wanted it to happen. He would see what she would do in the coming winter and would again ask her to visit him at his apartment. He thought she should meet Carol, that that could even be a healthy thing for all of them. But as he was on the knife-edge of sleep, with only the very last tiny bit of consciousness remaining, his thoughts were not of Andrea but of an ash tree in a grove north of town.

10

The Pettibone forklift that Jimmy kept in his sawmill yard was way past its prime. Larry had to tie the number-two spark plug wire with twine about half an inch from the plug tip to get that cylinder to fire properly. The added distance seemed to heat up the spark and kept the plug from fouling from the oil that blew past the ruined piston rings. With the wind right, the oil smoke would almost keep Larry from even seeing the logs as he unloaded them from the truck and stacked them on and near the brow of the mill. He kept a gallon can of recycled forty-weight oil hand at all times and had to check the level every couple of hours of running time. This was the last batch of hemlock from their current lot. Jimmy had decided to finish cutting it and then saw it up before it started to discolor. After the freak spring snow, the weather stayed cold for another few days but then rocketed up into the fifties and sixties. The mud left behind when the snow melted kept them out of the woods and even kept them from using the sawmill for a week or so. The baseball bat factory would always be happy to get clear ash, and cutting the hemlock into dimension lumber seemed a good option for a number of reasons. The stuff was already almost all sold right off the mill, and the rest would move soon enough—before it started to dry. They would stack anything left with stickers, just to keep it from molding. Building season was already underway, and folks liked green rough-cut hemlock around this part of the country if they were building for themselves. It did make for interesting carpentry. Sheetrocking over these rough-cut studs was an especial treat, but most folks bought extra spackling compound and slathered it on by the trowelful. Wallpaper and stucco paint could cover a lot of sins.

Jimmy had been in town getting some minor parts for the good woods crawler that was sitting up in the lot, and he was just pulling in when Larry got the last of the logs on the brow. Jimmy started the old diesel to let it warm up. Larry grabbed a peavey and wrestled the first log onto the carriage. It was surprising to some locals that Larry was the head sawyer of this outfit now. Jimmy owned the mill and had run it skillfully for years. But it was no surprise at all once they watched Larry run the stick for just a few minutes. It was almost as though he could see deep into the tree to plan his cuts. Time after time, he would make what looked like a false pass, wasting wood, only to reveal a chunk with a rotten spot or some other fault that would ruin it for a dimension cut. The damaged slab would still yield a couple of small four-quarter boards, so even that waste was minimized. He would go back to cutting the eight-quarter stuff, two-by-fours, -sixes, -eights, etc. Jimmy knew a good thing when he saw it. Larry could get up to 10 percent more lumber out of a log than anyone that Jimmy had ever seen, and he had been around this business all his life. It seemed sometimes that the tree was cooperating with Larry, giving up its wood gladly in exchange for something that was not at all obvious.

Larry was not far away from learning firsthand what that something was. He would learn that there was a *lot* more to trees and forests than cellulose and chlorophyll. Forests are communities, and the individuals speak with one another in remarkable ways. His preternatural sense of flow beneath his feet did not enter into the equation yet. But it most certainly would.

The obnoxious clatter of the cold diesel gave way to a solid thump, signaling that the motor had warmed up enough. Larry started the first log through, taking off a slab of bark and a small bit of sapwood. He perused the cut for a few seconds as the log returned on the carriage, and when it arrived, he worked the controls that advanced the wood into the blade. Then he sent it through again. Quickly, boards with live edges started to pile up. He worked his way through the log, and then Jimmy passed him back the boards and dimension stock for trimming. As the slab wood came off, Jimmy grabbed the sticks and threw them on the burning pile. The finished lumber was trimmed with a small power circular saw to remove the rough ends and went onto the forks of the ancient Pettibone. The wood built up quickly, and the team worked together smoothly, with no false moves.

The dinner hour came, and the motor was shut down. It was so old, and its compression was so low, that it was a good idea to let its lubricating oil cool down for an hour or so at midday. A newer diesel would have been left idling. Larry grabbed his dinner pail and looked to see what Andrea had included. She was in a sprouts phase. She loved them, and made them herself by the bushel. Larry liked them well enough but had gotten a bit tired of them by now. At the best of times, a sprout sandwich on organic whole wheat bread was poor, thin fare for a person doing this sort of work. He was relieved that he had been spared health for today in favor of some actual sustenance and found Genoa salami with provolone in a nice big crusty hard roll. There was a bag of carrot sticks, some celery, a nice green pepper all cut up, so he should not miss out on his veggies entirely, and some toll house cookies. His thermos was filled with hot tea. She had decided he drank too much coffee and had convinced him to limit himself to a couple of cups in the morning. Tea was fine by him. Andrea knew her stuff and stocked up on strong black Darjeeling, delicate oolong, and Japanese green teas when they visited the City. He had never even heard of green tea before she introduced him to it.

Jimmy had his dinner out by now as well, and it consisted of four bologna sandwiches on white bread with mayonnaise. He had two bottles of soda in a cooler, and a bag of candy bars. Larry had gotten used to Jimmy's dietary habits but was still somewhat revolted by the mayo on the bologna. Larry and mayo had had a bad encounter once. He used to like it before that. At least, while Jimmy was eating, he was not smoking. Jimmy could maintain a haze of cigarette smoke that would fill the woods. He seemed never to be without one going, although one might assume sleeping, bathing, and sex would be times of abstinence, even lacking evidence to this effect. He could do physically difficult work, involving both hands and great effort, and still keep one lit. He could even light a replacement without losing a beat while pulling boards off the mill or limbing a felled tree with a chain saw. He favored unfiltered smokes, ones that would ensure the maximum delivery of tar and nicotine to his lungs and thence to his bloodstream and nervous system beyond. Larry guessed he must be at about three packs a day, based on informal observation.

He had a deep rumble in his chest all the time, which was drowned out by a high-pitched wheeze emanating from a point higher in his ruined respiratory tract. When he awoke in the morning, he would cough nonstop for about ten minutes, hacking up large rafts of dark brown phlegm. When he got the coughing under control, he was in shape to light his first cigarette of the day, and this would instantly stop the urge to cough in a most paradoxical way. Jimmy would not have thought in those terms. If he thought about it at all, it was just to note that the smoking must be good for him, since it stopped the coughing. It did not stop the wheezing, or the deep-down rumbling, though. Nothing stopped that.

Jimmy was a curious and surprisingly complex man. He was brash, opinionated, cruel, dangerous, tough to do business with, but utterly honest. As long as you knew what you were doing with Jimmy, you could count on him to be straight with you. You just needed to be sure you knew the rules of the game. If you agreed on a price for lumber and told him what you wanted, you got it. Always. No one ever accused him of shorting them or giving them poor-quality materials. He always paid his bills, and he always expected payment of others' debts. The devil was in the details—in this case, in the bargaining. If Jimmy saw a for sale sign with a price on it affixed to something he wanted, that was nothing more than an indication that the owner was interested in selling this object. The asking price was not only negotiable, it was largely irrelevant. It was a good idea to keep your eyeteeth well hidden in your mouth when dealing with Jimmy, or he would have them. But, once a deal was struck, you could walk on it like the solid granite of the continent itself.

Jimmy was born in Grahamsville and had lived there all his life. His family had been there since the first settlers came. He was not what a romantic historian might want to see filling this role. But Jimmy nonetheless represented a family that had been well settled in when the French and Indian War was being fought not far to the north. The Hudson River

Valley and its surroundings had seen Europeans about as long as any other part of the country could claim. He lived in a dilapidated trailer on rented land. He owned little in a town in which his ancient family had owned much for nearly two centuries. The property where his mill sat was his own, as he preferred to pay a mortgage on these four acres of otherwise useless land rather than his homesite. He would have put his trailer there, as he had no concerns about living next to an industrial site, but there were concerns about the septic system he would need. This close to the New York City water supply, septic systems had to be more than deep holes filled with rocks designed to get the sewage into the aquifer as soon as possible. He had looked it over carefully, and there was no way to avoid having a leach field come out under areas that would need to have log piles or truck traffic. So he rented a spot elsewhere.

His trailer sat on cement blocks and had the obligatory insulated water pipe with heating tape coming up from the ground. The sewer pipes and electrical line were equally exposed. Silver duct tape was much in evidence in Jimmy's world. A ruined color TV sat out on a heap with other equally nonfunctional appliances and unrecognizable junk. There was a clothesline strung randomly among some small trees. A dilapidated Ford station wagon sat rusting on blocks in the dooryard, wheels pulled. The hood was disconnected from its mounts and lay casually draped over the empty engine compartment.

A fifty-five-gallon drum, one end cut out with a torch, lay on its side, staked to the ground nearby by welded-on chunks of reinforcing rod. In it could be found a dog as scruffy as Jimmy himself. He was securely chained to an iron stake, and the limits of his whole world could be seen in the patch of bare ground, worn six inches below grade in places, by his ceaseless pacing. Beyond lay weeds, thick and rank. The dog never left his chain as the days and years of his life trudged on. He walked this perimeter, forever looking for a magic place at the edge of the world where the rules would change. The collar would part, and he would run in a straight line for miles through the woods. The running would be effortless. He would almost float and never tire. And he would never come back to his cold steel tomb. But the collar was of stout leather, and the chain was welded link, and the iron rod was an inch thick and driven in four feet, and the chain was attached at either end with heavy split links, hammered shut. There was nothing in his eyes. They were cold, dead eyes.

Guilt for the decline of the Blandsford fortunes did not reside at Jimmy's doorstep. Jimmy was way too sharp a businessman for that. His grandfather had been the last of the prosperous and respectable segment of the line, and he was the cause of the downturn. He had been a lumber dealer for many years, following one of the family's two or three usual trades. He had a good wholesale business going at the beginning of the twentieth century. He had sufficient means to survive the Depression in comfort, which was rare anywhere in those days. He and his family were considered wealthy by local standards. But he was a gambler, and it was something he was born with, a deep part of what he was and who he became. Some people can gamble a bit and handle it well, but Asa Blandsford was not among that rare company. There were few opportunities for doing much damage to his family's welfare when he was a young man, but as the influence of New York City began to be felt in the area, what with better roads and the advent of automobiles, the chances for putting a few dollars down on one thing or another multiplied. And the few dollars became all of his fortune.

If you had been able to talk to Asa about his problem at all, which would have been unlikely (he was a very private man), you would have been puzzled, unless you were a gambler yourself. It was not winning or losing that mattered—although winning was a lot better than losing, since it meant you could gamble longer. Rather, he entered an altered state when he had more than he could afford riding on the outcome of an event over which he had no control at all. It was addictive, and suffice it to say, it cost the Blandsford their situation. Jimmy's father, Melvin, started his working life running a chainsaw in the woods for "the other guy." His two brothers and sister left for places where good work was easier to find. Jimmy seldom heard from his aunt and surviving uncle, except for the joyless exchange of Christmas cards. One card came from his aunt in Albuquerque, and the other, from his uncle, had an address in central Oregon. He had seen neither one in a quarter of a century and had not attended his other uncle's funeral in 1964. Fort Lauderdale was the other side of the planet as far as Jimmy was concerned.

Jimmy grew up even poorer than his father. Melvin died in a car wreck when he was ten, and times got real hard after that. This occurred in the days when blood alcohol was not always checked, even after a fatal accident, but witnesses said he had made it through most of a fifth of cheap bar rye, each shot chased with a draft beer, before heading home. No one had any reason for concern, or would even have thought to ask Melvin for his keys. You did not *do* that sort of thing in those halcyon days. He was actually in better shape than usual for a Saturday night, they thought. After all, he made it out to his vehicle without help. At least he only took himself out of the running. Himself and a power pole. Everyone knew exactly when Melvin died, because all their electric clocks stopped at about 1:17 A.M., the exact number depending on how close their clocks were set to the real time, and most were up and around before the road and utility crews got things put back in shape so they could register this mortal fact.

School was a cruel joke to Jimmy. The local school officials did everything in their power to make sure he left at his earliest convenience. Even in the liberal mainstreaming mania of the end of the twentieth century, the most died-in-the-wool activist would have been very glad to see him go. At some point, it is permissible to give something up as a lost cause. Jimmy was a lost cause when it came to algebra, history, social studies, English, science, you name it. He was a cruel bully on top of everything else. He had been in the hands of what passed for juvenile authorities in his day many times for seriously injuring other students. Finally, reason prevailed and he was sent packing. He had beaten up one young boy with brass knuckles, knocking out all his front teeth, damaging one eye to the point where it was barely salvageable, and breaking both his thumbs. He was never brought to justice for this. There is far too little justice that sticks to people like Jimmy; certainly not enough to go around.

Putting his years of scholarly endeavor behind him was a good move for Jimmy. He started out his career in the woods immediately and built himself a niche. Whatever else you might say about Jimmy, the man could work. He was strong, tough, and resilient. He studied each task in woods work carefully and worked until he mastered it. He had an eerie economy of motion. There were few around who could limb a tree with a chainsaw in fewer moves. He never seemed to be hurrying, never impatient. Others might rare and bore and jump around, but Jimmy was always the one who got the job done first, with little waste. When he felled a tree, it always went where he chose, missing other valuable trees nearby and with its butt end pointed towards the twitch line. By the time he was in his middle thirties, Jimmy had his own operation. He had parlayed very little but his own talent into a sawmill, a lumber truck, a good woods crawler, and all the other things he needed to make a living on the rugged land in the Catskills. In a way, he had made substantial progress toward restoring the family, although the untutored observer might not see this immediately.

Jimmy was married and had two young children. He was in his late forties at this point but had married a younger woman. His wife, Anne, a frighteningly skinny, wiry woman, was as tough as Jimmy. She had to be. But Jimmy was actually a reasonable husband and father. He was kind to his family and, against all predictions, never abusive in any way. But life in the mountains was no picnic. When you live by what you can do on your own in a day, you get a wonderful feeling of independence. That joy is tempered by the long spells when you aim for the rabbits in the road when you are driving around and keep a skinning knife and a few garbage bags handy in the back seat. Roadkill is not too bad when it's fresh. It is always iffy to take a chance on the stuff you do not kill yourself. When you live by your wits in the mountains, you find that a deer killed in July is about the best tasting meat there is, much better than in November when they are eating pretty poor fare. You also know that the sound of a .22 long rifle does not carry very far, and that this modest cartridge is sufficient to kill a deer if you hit it between the eyes squarely. And it is likely true that you can never pin down the direction of a single shot. Two, yes; one, no. You also learn all these little tricks at a young age.

Jimmy liked his draft beer, and he still liked his fights. Saturday night would find him at the Best Little Bar by a Dam Site, right near the Lackawack reservoir dam. The place was a pretty good bet for a fight every few weeks, and Jimmy seldom lost. Usually, he would pick on folks just passing though from other towns. There were only two or three people locally who could whip Jimmy regularly. One of these men lived in a sea of old cars over behind Thunder Hill. He had over four thousand of them, including some of great worth. Despite sitting on this young fortune in collectible cars, he and his family of a wife and eighteen children were on the edge, just like everyone else up in these hills. He often removed engine blocks by reaching into the compartment and picking them up by hand. Jimmy liked a challenge but was not stupid. He did not fight this man if he could avoid it.

Jimmy finished his dinner and, while he was still eating the candy bars, lit up his postprandial cigarette. Larry had strategically monitored the wind direction before sitting down and was upwind. This, of course, in no way eased his mild nausea watching Jimmy eat candy bars while smoking, but he had gotten somewhat inured to this barbarity and was not more moved this time than at any other to say anything to his boss about his personal habits.

"Gonna get back to the ash next week?" he asked, not really all that curious. He was just figuring the differential in times from his house to the mill vs. to the cutting. The latter was a bit closer.

"I reckon. They want that ash at the bat factory big time, and that shit ain't doing anyone any good up there on the stump. Not many folks cuttin' ash these days. Ain't much good shit left in these parts. I drove up there the other day to tinker on the good Johnny Deere, and the mud's pretty well dried up. Been a dry May, and June's looking the same. We oughta clear the place out in a couple weeks, and get it roughed out to balks for the mill by the first of July. I got me some of the nicest cherry I ever see lined up a ways past you on the Oliverea Road. That project's pretty big. Some of it ain't so well situated, so it could get slow some of the time. It's worth the effort. You should see some of those boles. Beauties. Should take us 'til early fall, and then we can mill it up for Boyertown. Maybe take a few weeks in November to relax, wait for things to freeze up nice. I need some deer meat for the freezer."

The cherry was exclusively destined for caskets. Cherry was, to Larry's mind, the most beautiful wood there was. If it was finished off with hand-rubbed linseed oil instead of polyurethane, it was deeply grainy, with an iridescent, almost three-dimensional look. He thought that making coffins out of the stuff and burying it in the ground was bordering on the criminal, but when choosing a casket for his own mother years hence, he would find it curiously appealing.

"Since when did you ever wait for hunting season to fill your freezer with long-legged rabbit?"

"Since the fucking game warden spends most of his time on the job looking at me through binoculars. Why *me,* for chrissake? I figger he's looking at us right now." Jimmy raised the middle finger of his right hand in the ancient salute and yelled in no direction in particular, "Pigfucker! People gotta eat."

"I kind of like to hunt in November myself anyway. I mean I drop 'em when I need 'em too, just like you. And the game warden doesn't know shit about me, unlike you, apparently. I just like getting out in the woods that time of year. The leaves are all down and everything's just sittin' around waiting for the snow. It's what I'm used to. I remember my dad used to take us out driving in the country that time of year. I have good memories about that. I even like the smell of that time of year." Smell, of course, was irrelevant to Jimmy, who was no longer able even to smell his own cigarette smoke.

"Yeah, well, my dad used to lean out the bathroom window with that old .300 Savage of his and pop them. That's what I remember as a little kid. Used to put apples and a salt lick out there where he could watch them even when he was takin' a dump. We never had a screen on that window. He probably shot it out killing a deer. We were lucky we had glass in it. At least he would open the window before cutting loose."

The image of Jimmy's father standing there with his pants down around his ankles, blasting away with a heavy-caliber weapon, amused Larry, and he chuckled quietly while picking up his lunch things.

"How much ash we got up there?"

"I contracted for the whole lot with an estimate of twenty thousand feet actual yield. They agreed on that number, and we should get at least that much." Of course, Jimmy's dealings were legendary. Larry had not cruised the part of the lot with the ash on it, but he was starting to get a knack for looking at trees and estimating how much processed wood each would yield. He figured if they got less than twice that he would have to reassess his estimate of Jimmy's skill. The people who owned the lot lived in Westchester County somewhere and had bought the woodlot on speculation more for the real estate value. They would probably subdivide it eventually and make the heavy money that way. The trees were totally irrelevant to them, just rank growth in the way of the builders. It amounted to nearly three hundred acres, and they had never walked more than a few of those, near the road. They relied on the estimates of the surveyor on how many lots could be carved out of it under the local subdivision laws.

At this important point in time, Larry was entirely indifferent about the lot and its trees. If Jimmy was able to get a good return on his money, it was none of Larry's concern. The people knew Jimmy's reputation and had made the deal with their eyes open. All the prospect of cutting that lot meant to him at this particular instant was that he was likely to stay employed that much later into the winter before going on "rocking chair money." The state subsidy of seasonal work known as "unemployment" was the only thing that made it possible for Larry and others like him to live in the area at all. Trees were there to be cut down and milled into useful things.

Larry rather liked the openness. He rather liked the openness of clear cuts, to tell the truth. In the typical Northeastern mixed forest, the trees stood thickly crowded together, and unless you were on the very top of an open ridge or meadow, you could not see anything of the scenery at all. He enjoyed his trips to the Southwest, where you could see mountains a hundred miles away from almost anywhere. Open sky was haunting and beautiful. This was also a big part of why Larry always wanted to climb to the high places of the world. If you were not on the actual top of the mountain, your view was always limited. If you were a hundred feet below the top of Everest, you could see only half of the world below, the very mountain you were ascending blocking the rest.

Larry fired up the mill and went back to cutting planking, two-by-fours, two-by-sixes, and other less common sizes, depending on what Jimmy thought he would need to complete an order under the constraints of what Larry could see in the log. The warm late-spring day wore on pleasantly, and even the blackflies were mercifully scarce. When they came to a good stopping point, Larry and Jimmy started making up orders to deliver. Jimmy piled the loads on the truck according to his own system, a bit like building a load of loose hay in the old days. He knew where each customer's pile stopped and the next one's began. He would take the load out after supper that night. People got cranky if they had to deal with hemlock when it was starting to dry. By late in the day tomorrow, a fair share of this lumber would already be nailed in place, starting to dry as straight and true as any kiln-dried, surfaced, and nosed spruce or fir boards around. You just had to allow for the shrinkage.

"Looks like we're gonna get them boards on-site before they start to look like bananas this time." A blown head gasket on the workhorse truck had caused some trouble a while back. It was nothing Jimmy couldn't handle in short order, and everyone ended up happy, but incidents like that can cost you and keep you looking over your shoulder.

"Yeah, the skins of the bananas, you mean. I talked with everyone on the list, and they'll all be home to help unload tonight, so no need to show up later." Occasionally, Jimmy asked Larry to come back out to help.

Jimmy had two cold six-packs of half-quart cans in a cooler in the back of his truck. He cracked a couple and handed one over to Larry, who accepted it with a grateful nod. Canned beer was better than no beer on a hot June afternoon. It was a *lot* better. The cold, bitter liquid hit the back of his throat, and he could almost hear the hiss. The task of getting himself around the pint actually kept Jimmy from lighting another cigarette for an interval of several minutes. Larry was surprised. He imagined that Jimmy's blood must be dark brown, sort of the color of tobacco juice expectorated by a chewer into a cuspidor.

Jimmy really liked Larry. He had few friends, and Larry was not really among them, but still he always liked talking to him. Over the time they had worked together, he had told him things about his life and family that he had never told anyone. No one was more surprised than Jimmy. Larry did not notice, of course. Jimmy was on a long list of people who talked to Larry. Sometimes, even strangers would end up telling him about their problems. And, of course, Larry would not notice.

Larry had been doing this for so long that it became the natural way of life for him. He no longer got excited when attractive young women struck up conversations. At first he had made the reasonable assumption that they must be looking to get some sort of physical relationship started. He quickly found that they felt, unaccountably, that he would be a good person to listen to them. They never seemed to think he would surreptitiously slip a hand on their thigh or do any of the other crude things men did to signal interest in putting part of their anatomy into their assorted orifices. The trust these women put in him was both flattering and valuable enough to him that he eventually became unable to proceed with a physical relationship with a woman unless she made it completely obvious what was on her mind. "OK, Larry, now this is what is going to happen next: we are both going to take off our clothes and . . ." was the level of forthrightness that he required. Andrea had resorted to this, finally, after spending some time worrying about Larry's sexual orientation. She had taken her usual route in vain. Her body English had gotten practically obscene when she finally gave up subtleties and just took off her shirt and grabbed him. That worked just fine, first time out.

"Suppose Karl's gonna be able to use that arm again?" Larry asked, not expecting an answer. It had been successfully reattached, but the prognosis for function was as yet unknown. Larry still found the subject painful. He had talked with the injured man just once after they transported him home from the City. He did not appear bitter at all and went out of his way to assure Larry that he bore him no ill will. In fact, he let Larry know in no uncertain terms that he credited his fast action with saving his life in the seconds after the accident. He could shed no more light on the nature of the mishap, though. He had seen the strange loop of cable coming at him and was unable to do anything about it. It was just moving too fast. No one he talked to could imagine what had caused it, and no one had ever heard of such a thing happening.

"I was over there yesterday after work for a few minutes. He's got feeling back in the thumb and forefinger. Can't move 'em none, but he knows they're there. I gotta figger that's a good sign. He's takin' it pretty well. He thinks he's got it worked out that he can get a job runnin' a forklift for his uncle in Monticello, the one that has got the buildin' supply place on the highway. Man can do that with one arm, no problem. If he gets some use back, that would be better yet. Pretty good work. Steady too. Poor fucker. That whole business has me spooked, kind of, and I don't spook easy." Which was both the truth and a considerable understatement at the same time. "Funny, I get this feeling up there like maybe we just shouldn't be there at all, trespassing, maybe. Weird. Got that even before Karl's accident. Nothin' to it, I suppose. These old hills get creepy sometimes."

Jimmy fired up the truck and headed out for home and supper. The nights were short this time of year, and afterwards he would spend a few hours making his rounds—delivering the loads and drinking a beer or two with each customer along the way. Not a bad way to spend a purple evening in the first week of June. There was the promise of full summer on the way; the nights were still cool, the days not yet too hot. The mountains could almost seem like a friendly place to live sometimes.

11

The day dawned in oppressive heat. The sun was mired in reddish soup, and there was no dew on the rank grass. It was the first day of the second half of June, and summer was suddenly really here. Larry was barely hungry, but he forced himself to eat some cold cereal and a half a cantaloupe. He was sitting in his undershorts and nothing else when Andrea wandered by in her office getup. He could never figure out how she could look so cool and collected all the time. He was already covered in a sticky coating of greasy sweat. The single cup of coffee had been a mistake, but he had found years ago that skipping it meant a headache that aspirin would never touch. He iced down the tea she had kindly brewed for him and put it in the thermos for his lunch.

Andrea was late and left with only a perfunctory "See Ya!" Larry would be late too if he dawdled any more. His enthusiasm for spending half the day on a bulldozer and the other half with heavy log chains in his hands was about as low as enthusiasm ever got for him. Jimmy had not hired anyone to replace Karl, and Larry was setting the chains on the logs, twitching them to the yard, stacking them, and doing any final trimming that was needed. He was coming home more tired than he could imagine at night, but he felt his body, already strong, acclimating to the increased load.

He grabbed the lunch that Andrea had made for him and closed up the house. He hated to shut the windows, because it would be stifling that afternoon, and he would have to run the attic fan for an hour or so to make it livable, but he knew that there would be heavy thundershowers that day and wanted to keep the place dry. He caught the grumble of thunder to the north as he jumped into the rusty truck. “A miss,” he thought, “running on past. Be near noon before ours gets here.” A tiny smile flashed across his face. Even though he had been able to feel weather for his whole life, he still got a spark of self-satisfaction when he was right. He hoped he could be forgiven for this immodest thought. He had removed much of the winter traction ballast from the old truck, and it was riding somewhat higher than it had been. He and Andrea had had a “discussion” about where said ballast should spend the summer, and it was now off in the woods, just out of sight from the house and yard.

The yard was looking rather better than it did when he was tending to it himself, he noted. He had not spent much time planting flowers, tending rather toward things that one might eat. Andrea, however, liked flowers even more than vegetables, and the place was a riot of color. The June heat had fired a mighty burst of growth, and he had to admit he did like the looks a lot better than engine blocks, drums filled with used crankcase oil, and a Jawa motorcycle that lacked a seat, tank, and right front fork. The bike was, he pleaded, a “collector’s item,” but he had lost that argument, along with a few others. The place did look better. His 650 cc Triumph twin was almost new, far more scenic, and fully functional. It was, unbeknownst to Larry, already on its own long journey into being a genuine collector’s item.

Larry pulled into the yard a few minutes early and backed into a dry area near the log truck. This was a habit he had learned unconsciously from his boss, who never drove into a parking spot frontwards. It was something that rural people just did. It meant you could see where you were going when you headed out onto the main road, and this was handy. But it also meant that if you had to leave in a hurry, you would save a few seconds that might make a difference if something unpleasant was in the works. Someone flashing a revolver in a bar fight would be just one example of something unpleasant. One thing struck him almost immediately as strange. The feeling of unrest that he always got in a forest, that there was a powerful surging just under the ground, was unaccountably stronger than usual. In fact, it was a lot stronger than usual. While it was certainly odd, he attached no great significance to it. It was probably just something to do with an anomaly in the water being picked up by the roots. Nothing at all . . .

Jimmy had hauled a load of ash out last night and subsequently returned the truck to be refilled. They had just started cutting the ash, but it was piling up fast. There was a good stock of logs heaped in the yard, and one truckload a day was not keeping up with the cutting. Ash was easy wood to cut. It was straight grained, held its hinge when felled, and was easy to limb. The butts of the trees were all clear of heart rot and promised a good return for time spent.

Ash was nice wood for specific purposes, but Larry found it utterly uninteresting visually. He loved the deep reds and yellows of cherry, the striking grain of the oaks, and the rich patterns of hard maple. But ash was bone white, with a deep, regular brownish grain pattern. The summer wood was hard, like ivory, but the spring wood was spongy. Brown ash, he had heard, had such a pronounced spongy spring layer that when the logs were soaked and pounded with mallets, the layers of hard summer wood could be stripped off and used for weaving baskets and pack frames. Native tribes in the north country, Maine and beyond, once made a living at this trade, going off to summer encampments in swamps where this species grew to weave until the cold weather brought the cycle of their enterprise to an end for the year. White ash had many uses besides baseball bats, Larry knew. It was tough and more flexible than any other common variety of hardwood. Handles for hammers and hoes, tillers, paddles, and oars for boats were of ash when strength was at issue. It was not as strong as oak or hickory but was much lighter.

But none of this was on Larry's mind this morning. He was just interested in getting the stuff in a heap in the yard and getting on to the next job. He checked the levels of engine oil, hydraulic fluid, and diesel fuel in the crawler. The fuel was low, and he topped it off. One tank usually lasted the day. Larry never ran equipment at full throttle. Jimmy was always complaining about that for some reason, probably impatience, but Larry always got more wood twitched in a day than Jimmy could, infuriatingly, and things didn't break all the time. Larry felt that any piece of equipment has a sweet spot, a rate where everything works together perfectly. Oil travels through the unseen galleries to the bearings at the right temperature and in full quantity; valve trains follow their accustomed rounds at the right time, never disputing territorial space with the heads of the pistons; gears stay within their design tolerances for torque. This feel for the equipment's comfort zone sets the good operators in one camp and the Jimmys of the world in the other. At least the latter camp keeps the parts businesses humming as they rare and bore their way through life. Doctors get part of the take too, since they tend to drive their bodies the same way they drive their machinery.

A couple of pumps of grease for each roller and idler wheel, and the same for the odd fitting here and there, and he fired up the motor. It clattered and rattled for a while but quickly smoothed out. Jimmy took exceptionally good care of this one piece of equipment, as it was the very heart of his operation. Maintenance was done well, by the book, and on schedule. Larry hopped on and set off to finish a crude road that he had started late yesterday. He looked over the lay of the land and saw a reasonable path that avoided most of the of the immovable rocks, all the ledge, muddy swales, and the worst of the rhododendron thickets. This plant was the bane of the area, making walking in the woods sometimes impossible in areas. He felt like mowing it down with his blade just for the sheer joy of it but had no time for fun. He dropped the blade and began clearing off the high spots, filling in the low, and scraping the brush out of the way. A few minutes spent on this at the beginning of a cutting session would make things much easier later. Jimmy could see where the crawler would be coming in and could plan his work ahead so that the logs would be oriented toward the road and would clear any obstacles as Larry pulled them in with the winch. Since he would be driving back and forth many times to clear the grove, at least part of his work was aimed at comfort. There is no suspension on a bulldozer, and the hard metal cage can give the operator a lot of punishment as the machine bangs in and out of ditches or plunges over hummocks.

Out of the corner of his eye, Larry spotted Jimmy pulling in. He was late, and this meant he was probably hung over. This was not good, since he was usually in a mean mood when his head hurt, his vision was blurry, and he occasionally had to wander out of view to be sick. Hatred of hangovers had kept Larry's beer consumption to a reasonable level through the years, and the few serious hangovers he had were usually the result of ill-advised adventures with cheap hard liquor or even cheaper red wine. He could actually remember all his bad hangovers and had not had one in some time owing largely to those unpleasant memories.

Turned out Larry was right, and this particular bout must have been pretty serious. Jimmy looked positively corpse-like, with an ashen complexion and eyes that were a deep red. Larry resolved to keep out of his way as much as possible. By lunch, he would probably be back to some semblance of humanity after sweating all morning in the heat and humidity. Larry also reasoned that he would make an extra effort to stay upwind. The cigarette smoke would be made even more rank by the smell of that rancid sweat. The combination might prove lethal.

He finished the little patch of road and headed back down to the yard. Jimmy was putting the final touches on his chain with the file. He topped the tank with mixed two-stroke gas, filled the chain oiler, and wandered groggily off toward the stand of ash. He got about halfway before being racked by dry heaves. Larry wondered how he'd even made it to work in that condition. He did not have this problem often, fortunately, but seemed convinced that he had to go to work no matter what, and here he was. It was mountain pride in action, yet again. Larry left him to work things out, thinking that a man ought to have a little privacy while vomiting bile, and anyway, he thought he'd spotted another place where a strategically cleared road would benefit.

He aimed the crawler up the slope into the thickest part of the ash grove and began clearing and grading. It was at this point that he began to feel a powerful sensation. He felt it in the same neural circuits that told him what the weather was doing and where two-by-fours or planks lay in a hemlock log. It was far stronger than anything he had felt before, however, and seemed to affect him more intimately and personally. It drowned out the background rumble that he always felt coming in along that modality in this part of the mountains—the sensation of all that water raging along, deep beneath the earth, coursing from reservoir to reservoir, and on to the City. He almost never noticed that consciously anymore, having gotten used to it. The term *extinction of response* returned to him from a psychology course he took as an undergraduate to leaven his math-and-physics load. This new sensation had the same feel as the water moving in the tunnels. Each of these curious things he perceived in this way had its own signature. The movement was close by and was distinctly passing by him vertically from great depths to great heights. The flow was titanic, and there were multiple distinct threads passing in both directions.

Whatever he was receiving was getting stronger by the second, and he knew it was coming from the center of the grove. It had no feel of quality to it; it was neither malevolent nor good. It was not directed at him, nor was there any sense that it was emanating from a sentience. His perception had never been attuned to that sort of thing in any event, so this observation was no help. There was just that overwhelming feeling he got from the deep waterways, the feeling of immense power flowing, like Alph, the sacred river—moving in its caverns, measureless to man. But one thing was becoming quite certain, and that was that at least part of the flow was beginning to interact with him; and he was frightened by this, as any rational person would be.

He did not know what to do, or if there was anything he *should* do. He backed the crawler down the slope and out of that section of the grove as quickly as possible. As soon as he was out in the clearing, the feeling abated, leaving a residual amount that he realized had been there all the time without being recognized. He had not felt it strongly enough to attribute it to a source before, but now that he had been up close to it, he was locked into it. This was a matter to think about seriously and soon. Jimmy would be cutting in there in probably two hours, if his hangover did not defeat him, and Larry needed to sort this all out before anyone started up that slope with a chainsaw. But poor Larry did not have a clue about even where to start thinking, let alone what actions he might be required to take.

He ran twitches for a while, and the remainder of that part of the stand they had started on quickly turned into logs, and the logs into a pile. Larry's road was well planned, and the logs were straight. There was now a new forest meadow where trees and deep shade had stood at the beginning of the week. Jimmy was ready to tackle the deepest part, the part where Larry had felt that immense flow of a force he could not understand. He tried to put it out of his mind. He told himself that there was nothing there but a bunch of ash trees, and he had killed a lot of ash trees. But he got no rest. He knew now that something was required of him now. "*What the hell am I supposed to fucking do?*" he almost screamed aloud.

His indecision and attempts to rationalize his newly acquired sense of duty lasted for only a short while. Larry was a man of conviction and action, and, given that he had only two choices—to stop Jimmy or not to stop Jimmy—he chose one, the former, as being the obvious answer to his question. He jumped off the crawler, which was down in the yard by the pile at this point and ran up the slope after Jimmy with one purpose in mind. There would be no cutting in this grove. How he might see to this, whether he might have a job at sunset, concerns for his personal safety, were not thoughts that troubled him at this point, given that a desired end was now in place.

Jimmy was at the end of Larry's little road by now, near the dead center of the stand. Remarkably, his hangover was almost gone. What sacrifices his battered liver might have had to make to effect this recovery did not enter his thoughts at all. His system was almost ready for that first afternoon beer. But that was not to be. Jimmy was carefully looking at the way the trees stood before cutting anything and was formulating a plan to expedite the series of cuts he would make. It was all nearly automatic for him now. But something of note grabbed his attention. At the center of the grove there stood a tree of greater age than any of the others. It was as large an ash as Jimmy had ever seen, very tall and of immense girth. Surrounding the tree was a small open area. It was curious, being almost circular in shape, about fifteen feet in diameter and ringed with round boulders and stones. The ground inside the circle thus defined was oddly flat and free of forest duff, leaves, and so forth. It almost suggested that it had been purposefully cleared, maybe by campers, but there was no sign of a firepit. He tried and failed to dismiss any thoughts about it as he kept on with his planning. He could see in his mind the felled trees and how they would lay, so he could mentally try out several schemes before even the first tree went down. But there was something new here. The lines of communication he had with the forest were open, and a message he had never felt before was tearing at his soul.

Jimmy had always lived and worked in the forest. He never felt really right when he was not surrounded by trees. His few trips to cities were short and never much fun. It was as though they were protecting him from a hostile world, and he felt safe. But this did not translate into any sense of loyalty to that forest. It gave him his livelihood and his sustenance. "Cut 'em and sell 'em" was all there was to it. It was this strong bond with the woods that made it possible for him to survive in a business where others were increasingly failing badly. The forests in this part of the Northeast had been overcut for centuries and were a scrim of their former glory. But Jimmy could find marketable timber and figure the stumpage right where others saw nothing or more than there was. It was a knack that he not only could not explain but never felt a need to. Jimmy felt for the forest just as Larry felt for things that flowed. He *felt* the timber around him. He never took a ruler or a core borer with him when he cruised a woodlot preparatory to offering a deal to the woodlot owner. He would walk the area carefully making mental notes as he went, ticking off the harvestable board feet, and once through was more than enough for his estimate.

The person Jimmy had become thought only to exploit and use, never care for. "And that is as it should be," he thought. The mountains and their forest cover seemed eternal to him, always bouncing back from whatever people did to them, an ultimate renewable resource. He would just keep taking. But now he became increasingly uneasy and angry. The woods, which were his solace, felt all wrong this day.

He was still fully caught up in this mental turmoil when Larry arrived, streaked with sweat from his run up the grade from the yard.

"Don't cut here!" was all he said.

There was no point in saying anything else. Larry knew Jimmy would not listen to any insane rant about feeling a flow, or much of anything else. Larry could tell him that the Soviets had launched a preemptive thermonuclear strike and they only had a half hour to live. Jimmy might believe him but would fire up the chainsaw anyway and get to work. There would be no point in him doing anything else at that point, as there was currently no cold beer in his cooler in the pickup bed.

There was no rational way for Larry to explain any of this, even to himself, and he did not really believe what was happening to him on that level. What he felt was in a deeper part of his brain. He knew to the very core of his being that to disturb this grove would be a great wrong. Now, there was the rub. He was not a religious person. He stopped going to church after an unfortunate incident involving his mother. But for all of that, he had a deep faith, one that was stripped down to an infinitesimal point. He knew, accepted fully now based on that, that what he did now mattered more than anything he had done before or maybe ever would again. He made no attempt to embellish this faith with gods, goddesses, creation myths, devils, or saviors. The poorly translated ancient writings of a desert-maddened tribe were of even less value to him. There was no real belief in anything necessary beyond complete acceptance of where he was at this instant. He could never justify with logic any of it. There was no evidence. He did not try to claim that he did "the right thing" for "some greater good" either. What he felt was pure Faith. He was driven by an unshakable sense of what was just.

He knew now that it was time for him to commit an act driven only by this singular faith. It was time to make his Stand. He would do something that he would never be able to explain to anyone. These were just trees, like so many that had fallen before. He didn't even really *like* trees all that much. He had burned cord after cord of ratty scrap ash wood when it was available. It was inanimate, a plant. He liked how the new sunny meadow below looked, even with all the stumps. He was not following the command of a deity with a plan for him in the universe but was acting of his own free will. What he did would matter if there was no reward in heaven, no punishment in hell—no heaven itself, no hell. It would matter even if the act was hidden forever from all of humanity, and no tangible good whatsoever resulted. Even if all this were true, it mattered.

"What the fuck are you talking about? This some kind of joke you're pulling on me?" Jimmy was too angry to find this funny if it was a joke, and he felt his hangover coming back for another round. He immediately got the overwhelming impression it was not a joke at all, but still hoped it could be true. "Get back on the crawler and stop busting my chops. You smokin' them funny cigarettes on the job?"

Larry remained firmly planted in Jimmy's path. He was just past the center of the curious circle, near the huge tree. He said nothing. He was becoming more and more convinced that nothing he said would matter, and he might need that breath for something else before this was over. Jimmy was not a person to be convinced by force of logic at the best of times, and Larry certainly had no logic to offer at this point anyway.

Jimmy could easily have headed back down the slope and started cutting near the opening of the road. If his helper had not begun acting in this bizarre manner, that is where he would have started anyway. But, for reasons he quickly pulled up from countless late-night bar brawls, he did not want to turn his back on Larry at this point. He also decided that cutting the biggest tree in the center of the grove would break this insane deadlock, and he could get on with the business of firing Larry and figuring out who he could get to help him until he could find someone else, this round maybe a grunt to exploit at minimum wage with no benefits.

But all this was going on in the part of his brain that was near the surface. The deeper parts were still riven by the by now very new and personal contact he had with the surrounding forest, and with this tree in particular. In short, he was caught up in the same strange storm that was affecting Larry, and in precisely the same way, with the same unknown ends. He was badly frightened, and fear breeds violence. If Jimmy had not become the person he was, he would have accepted the situation and let the changes that were being wrought in him go to whatever conclusion there might be. But he could not let this happen. He was a strong, stubborn man, and had fought all his life for everything he had and everything he valued. He reached deeply into himself to haul up reserves of atavistic rage to aid him in his fight against this strangeness within—and Larry without. There was no compromise, and no turning back. But whatever was going on inside continued unabated, too late to change the immediate events, but inexorable in its path.

Thunder pealed close by, and there was an intense electric field building. The hair of both the antagonists was being tugged at in a most unnerving way, and they could feel tiny currents ranging across their sweat covered skin. Rain was imminent, but that was the least of what was upon them.

"Get out of my way and off this woodlot, motherfucker! You got any shit down by the mill, you come by an get it when I'm there." Jimmy's tone was menacing, and clearly he meant business at this point. He had faced down a lot of people over the years and had no reason to doubt that Larry would fold at this point and scamper off to his truck.

"No!" That was all Larry said, and not really all that forcefully, given the situation. It was more than enough to tell Jimmy that Larry was as determined in his way as Jimmy himself. His voice was way past merely menacing. It came from a late afternoon in November, when a leaden sky spits the first snowflake of winter.

At this instant, Jimmy knew he was going to have to fight. And he would be fighting two foes at the same time. He could not back down, and he could not bluff, so he attacked. He threw the saw to one side, out of the cleared area, and sent a powerful right punch towards Larry's face. This preemptive first strike usually worked for him in bar fights. Despite the cigarettes and a roll of beer-induced fat around his gut, he was extremely strong and surprisingly quick. He could put his whole body into a blow, like a boxer. He had never had formal training, but when it came to hurting his fellow man, he was quick to learn by experience—of which he had good store, starting as a young boy. Such a punch had immense power and could end a fight by itself.

But Larry was ready. His mind was at the center of a calm place. His physical center of gravity was in the same place as that of his spirit, and he knew he could keep it there and that this would keep him safe. He was not excited, nor was he afraid. His heart rate was still at its normal fifty beats per minute, the mark of a conditioned athlete, and typical of a trained martial artist facing mortal combat. Larry was certainly the former, but not the latter. He had wrestled in high school and college, but that was about all. He had never had a fight in anger in his life. But for all of that, he was ready.

The blow was parried with ease. Larry simply swatted it out of the way. He seemed to be in a universe that was moving in slow motion. Not knowing anything else to do at this point, he rushed Jimmy and grabbed his arms—simply to prevent further blows, not really to grapple with him. In the struggle, he ended up with his left hand on Jimmy's right shoulder and his right on Jimmy's left upper arm, controlling it.

Unfamiliar with this mode of defense, preferring fists alone, Jimmy ended up with the exact same position on Larry's body to gain symmetry and keep his balance. Instantly, they were fully engaged but in a stalemate. Jimmy would have liked to free an arm to deliver a blow, but if he did so, he would be freeing Larry's arm to do the same thing to him, and he had not liked the speed and ease with which his opponent had flicked away what should have been a near-lethal blow. For the same reason, he could not kick. If he moved a leg off the ground, he would be down, and that would be fatal.

Lighting and thunder came simultaneously. Larry's predicted storm arrived pretty much on schedule. The portion of the huge frontal system that had been muttering away all morning, sending storms off to the north and south, had finally arrived in the middle and meant business. A blinding downpour started. The combatants continued on in their deadly embrace, oblivious to the elements. The standoff was perfectly even, neither man able to work to an advantage. Larry would not have struck or kicked Jimmy anyway, even given the opportunity. This was not out of any sense of not wanting to injure the man; rather, it was because his wrestling training had not pushed him in that direction, and he was uncomfortable with it. Jimmy would certainly have used anything he could to win but was stuck with the current situation. They were not motionless by any means, however. They pushed and shoved each other fiercely, but carefully. Balance was critical. If either one changed position, the leg that was not moving became the only source of stable contact with the ground, and during that instant he was vulnerable. Moving when the opponent moved was the only chance to change position safely. Both men tried to dig in more deeply, calling up images that could help turn thought into reality. While they strove against each other, a sense of the rules of engagement developed in both men. It became clear that the fight would be over when one or the other managed to throw his opponent out of the curious little circle. This was not spoken, but in the heat of the fight, it was a bargain struck and written in blood.

In the end, it was Larry's superior conditioning that won. Jimmy was at least as strong as Larry—muscles born of long, hard manual labor—but Larry was always walking the mountain trails, he did not smoke, and he ate a healthy diet, leaving him lean. He literally wore Jimmy down. Jimmy began to pant, and then his attention began to falter. He was gasping for air, and perhaps he was slightly anoxic. Whatever the reason, he tried to move without planning for his opponent's reaction. Larry sensed the instability and, in one mighty heave, threw Jimmy literally upside down and sideways onto the rocks that lined the circle.

He fell with a sickening thud in the roughest part of the pile and jerked once spasmodically. He was unconscious but not badly hurt. Larry checked him quickly for broken bones and felt none. There were no serious cuts, although he was bleeding from a few spots where the rocks had abraded him. A couple of angry bruises were in the works. Larry certainly had not wanted to harm the man. In fact, he was not at all sure just what it was he meant to do in the first place other than stop him from cutting any of these trees, and especially the big one in the circle. He could still feel its preternatural flow interacting with him in some deep, unknown places but had other matters to concern him at this point.

He did know what he had to do next. He grabbed the Homelite saw that Jimmy had discarded at the beginning of the fight and started it up. He wound it out to its maximum speed and ran the chain into the edge of a sharp piece of rock. The teeth and depth guides were stripped off in a shower of sparks and pieces of stone. Larry averted his eyes to protect them. When the saw lurched to a sickening stop as the broken chain wound up around the drive gear, he grabbed it by the bar and readied to smash it against the point of another nearby boulder. He stopped, however, and lowered the saw slowly. There was no justice in this act. Jimmy could easily afford a new chain, especially when he had the bulk of a week's wages that Larry would never now see to spend, but he could not afford a new saw. This one was only just broken in and was the top-of-the-line professional model. He had no call to impair Jimmy's livelihood and was not looking for revenge. It was he, after all, who had started this altercation with his bizarre behavior. He knew that there was nothing he could do to stop Jimmy from coming up here tomorrow and cutting everything in sight. In some odd way, he was not concerned about that in the end. What he did was done, and well done, and that was the end of it for him. He was out of it, and thankfully so. He had been weighed in the balance and not found wanting.

Which brought the matter crashing home to him. He still could not imagine what had driven him to this strange act. He had felt sure that what he was doing was Just. He knew, although the feeling was fading like a dream that you can't hold onto as you wake, that he had taken a stand as an act of Faith. But faith in what? In some sort of animist forest deity? That level of what he considered pure quill bullshit almost made him laugh despite his precarious situation. He walked past Jimmy, who was stirring by now—confirming Larry's impromptu diagnosis—and turned to the tree that had started his mind on its tortured path to an act that he could not even begin to understand. He'd want to be gone when Jimmy regained consciousness but figured he had a minute or two to spend making sense of this all before he needed to leave. He looked up at the ash tree almost in supplication, asking for answers. He received oblivion.

12

Larry did not feel the pain at first, but rather observed it from a distance with curiosity. It was certainly there, but it was obviously irrelevant to him. He puzzled over its nature and source for a period of time before it began to approach him. He was not too concerned about this at first but found he was unable to back away from its approach. As it got closer, he began to realize that it was going to catch him. Try as he might, he could not shake it. He tried to run, but his legs would not work. It quickly attached itself to him and he felt its dull presence within him now. No more running away.

It was consciousness pulling him out of his safe haven to the world of pain, and he was not even slightly happy about that fact. He wanted to go back into the cocoon that had protected him for . . . how long? He was finally in control of himself, and he started to take stock of his internal surroundings first. Was this the king of all hangovers? He did not drink like this anymore, but perhaps he was led astray in some gin mill. His mouth hurt the worst. He gingerly ran his tongue around and found the wreckage of several front teeth. His tongue touched a bit of nerve that protruded from what had been its safe haven of crystalline calcium phosphate mineral. That woke him up even more, since the pain was truly exquisite. After that calmed a bit, he explored further, noting that his tongue itself was damaged and seemed to have some stitches in it. His upper and lower lips were trussed in like manner with surgical threads.

He had a horrendous headache as well, but the back of his skull, which seemed to be heavily bandaged, was curiously numb. He tried to move his right arm to assess the damage manually, but the limb was slow to respond, and the action aggravated his headache awfully. At this point, his involuntary moan brought the attention of a nurse, who had been sitting in a chair next to his bed reading a chart. She jumped to her feet and looked at him carefully to see how he was faring.

"I'll get your wife!" she said. "I'll be back in no time. She's sleeping down in the residents' lounge. This is almost the first time she's been away from your bed. She'll be ticked off that you came out of it when she was off duty."

The woman padded off in her hospital shoes and, true to her word, returned quickly with Andrea. Andrea looked about like he felt. She was haggard, her hair was dirty, she had black circles of fatigue and worry under her eyes, and she clearly had been crying. During all of this, he was thinking about the nurse having called her his wife. He sort of liked that idea at this point. It gave him something to contemplate beyond his pain. And he would most certainly contemplate it, and maybe it could happen.

"So, you decided to live after all, you creep! What the hell have you been up to? I was sick with worry." She stifled a sob and, without thinking, started to grab him. His look of alarm stopped her, but she kept starting to reach for him unconsciously, just catching herself, which kept Larry a bit on edge. "What happened up there? There have been BCI guys here, and staties, almost nonstop. They'll be in here in no time once they hear you're awake. Do you remember anything at all?

He was about to speak when a pair of doctors, one clearly in charge and the other a resident, loomed behind Andrea. They scooted her away behind them absently and began as thorough a neurological exam on their now conscious patient as his multiple bandages and pain would allow.

"How we doing today?" the resident asked uselessly as the exam began. He could easily see how Larry was doing, and it was not well.

Larry supposed there was some kind of book that residents were given so they could develop a bedside manner. "Lesson number one: ask the patient how he or she is doing today, be pleasant and assured, never give sign of alarm at the fact that the poor son of a bitch is really all fucked up and you yourself actually just want to puke your guts out."

"Like shit." Seemed a reasonable reply.

The other physician echoed Andrea: "Do you remember anything at all about how you got here?"

"I must have tripped." He did, in fact, now begin to remember the entire affair. This, it turned out later when he did a little research on his own, was unusual for someone with a fractured skull. Almost unheard of, but not unknown. Normally, severe head trauma resulted in an amnesia about the events leading up to the injury. But, in Larry's case, he was painfully aware of what had happened, and was already thinking about a story to keep what had happened deep in the recesses of his mind. Had he been less groggy, or had he known the usual effects of a fractured skull, he would have simply lied and said he could recall nothing. But his attempt at cynical humor was not lost on the doctors, and they lost no time in reporting this fact to the detective from the Bureau of Criminal Investigation when next he inquired.

After the doctors left, he was starting to feel groggy again but wanted to ask Andrea what she knew of his condition and the condition of Jimmy Blandsford.

"How am I, really?"

"You have a fractured skull. You have been unconscious for four days. All your vital signs are good, but they are worried about clots in the damaged meninges. They did what they could to straighten out your head, but you are going to have a wicked scar, and it will be in a permanent deep depression. They could not pull the pieces of bone back into shape without causing more damage to the arachnoid. From what they were muttering about just now during your exam, there seems to be no loss of muscle function, so there was no lasting damage, but they will probably do some more extensive tests. I suspect they will want me to look for personality changes. Like they think you actually had one to start out with. You have three broken teeth, but the dentist says they are still alive and can be permanently capped. He thinks they may eventually die, and you'll need root canals, but they'll look OK and be functional, no bridge or denture work necessary. There will be a deep scar on your chin, although the plastic surgeon did a good job with what he had to work with. Rocks leave ugly wounds. I guess if you grow your hair and beard back you might not scare too many children."

"I knew having an old lady who worked in a hospital would come in handy someday."

In fact, Andrea had given the most concise, accurate, dispassionate description of his condition that he would ever hear while he was undergoing treatment. She knew her job, and she knew a few other people's jobs as well. And she was cool under fire.

"OK, your turn. Tell me what really happened.

"I told the doctors: I must have tripped."

Andrea's face clouded up "Bullshit! Blandsford's wife found you face down in those rocks after 6:00 that evening, with a considerable part of your life's blood in the soil around them. She was worried about him when he didn't come home for supper and drove out to the cutting to see what was up. She drove down to the first house on the road and called the cops from there. That motherfucker Blandsford is still nowhere to be found. He never went home that night, and that's when they called me to ask if I had seen you. I was still at work and had no idea you were out in the woods bleeding to death slowly until I got home and found the cop car in the driveway. I have not been home more than long enough to feed the pets since this happened, and I am not going to sit here and listen to a crock of shit from you. If you remember what happened, you are going to tell me now, before the cops get a chance to work you over. Me first; you fucking owe me that much!"

"It was a fight. I can't tell you really what it was over, because I don't know myself. I got this uncontrollable urge to save a tree. Big old ash tree. Like it was talking to me. It seems stupid even as I am telling you this, but I know for certain I'd do it again even knowing what was going to happen. Maybe I'll never figure it out. Who would I ask other than a shrink, and he's just going to lock me up. Jimmy obviously took exception to my attitude problem. We went at it hammer and tongs for a while. I sort of thought I'd won the fight. No, I'm sure I did. Bastard must have hit me from behind. I never saw it coming. He was probably right to take me on. I was messing things up for him, and it was his outfit. But he never should have bashed in my skull—that was uncalled for. I dunno, I might be losing it. There might have been some other weird shit going down at the same time. Can't recall much of that, probably just from getting hit. Anyway, please don't tell the cops. I don't want to get Jimmy in trouble. Even if he did whack me, I won't press charges. A fight's a fight."

The explanation was so clearly true that it stopped Andrea's quest for more information. She hoped that with time Larry would tell her more. Maybe together they could get to the bottom of what drove Larry's bizarre behavior that day. But to say she was satisfied with what she heard would be something of a mistake. She called the nurse, who came over to see if Larry was in sufficient pain to warrant some mild painkillers. Since they were reluctant to give him anything powerful owing to the nature of his injury, he figured, why take anything at all? He was feeling tired from this short stay in the land of the living and wanted to get back to the natural painkiller of sleep. Andrea tucked him in, gently kissed the less ruined side of his face, and left quietly as he drifted off.

She had indeed been briefed on looking for personality changes, mood swings, uncontrolled rages. She had seen nothing that anyone less close to him would have noticed, but what she saw in his eyes made her shiver. There was a darkness there that she had never seen before. Deep in his eyes, there had always been a bright light. She loved that light, and it had buoyed her in times of trouble or fear. His ready laugh and smile were extensions of that light, as though animated by it. But it was gone, utterly, replaced by a light of a different hue, from a more somber part of the spectrum. She hoped it was just his brush with death, or perhaps his pain, or his fear, or knowing he had been scarred for life that had temporarily stilled this essential component of the man she loved. But as year led on to year it would remain as she saw it first in these hard days. She would learn to live with it across the arc of their lives together. That strange darkness was part of why she would leave him in years hence, and it was in spite of it that she would decide to return.

The BCI detective showed up next morning. He was a cheerful-looking man and made good on the promise of his appearance. He inquired after Larry's condition in a knowing way that indicated that he had visited many bedsides and was really both interested and knowledgeable. He was rumpled, slightly overweight, and had short-cropped hair with a look that pegged him as retired military. He took his time getting around to the business at hand. In the country, and in reality the town of Liberty was certainly still country, the custom was to beat around the bush for a while. It was bad manners to walk in on someone and start right in with business. You needed to talk about the weather, the crops, the war, the crime wave in the City, the wreck in Woodbourne on Saturday night, and so forth before anything substantive could be dealt with. Detective Kowalcek was good at this, even though he was a transplant from Staten Island. He finally started to spiral in on the point of his visit.

"How's the pain? I imagine they can't give you much for it just yet. Sleeping any? That works." He clearly knew more than the docs about pain management.

"Yeah, pretty well. That's all I did for the best part of a week. I guess I'm getting good at it."

"I walked the same walk, had a similar injury. Took some shrapnel just over my right ear in Korea. Hurt like hell, but it got me home. No lasting damage. I'm no more addled now than I was before we saved the peninsula from the Red Menace. Southern half, anyway. The pain will be gone before you know it. I mostly slept it off too."

"Thanks. I'm getting more information from visitors and my old lady than I am from the staff around here. My buddy Eban was in this morning. I think my parents will be down later today from Albany."

"Well now, Mr. Vintner . . . can I call you Larry? It will make this easier for us both. You can call me Joe."

"Yeah, nobody ever calls me Mr. Vintner except cops when they pull me over and read it off my license. No offense . . ."

"None taken. I get tickets myself driving down to Florida in the winter. Pain in the ass. Who the hell can drive fifty-five miles an hour all day? Drive you nuts."

Larry had practiced his lie a bunch and was ready to rock and roll. He had tried a series of scenarios, each a bit better than the last, and made sure that he picked the simplest one. This would minimize any chances that he would be tripped up on some trivial fact that he had missed. He was really primed for it.

"OK, I suppose you want to find out about this accident, so I'll tell you what I know right off. Won't take but a second. I was setting up to cut this big old ash tree, and it was raining like hell. I figure I should have sat out the storm, it was just starting to come down hard right then, but I wanted to get going. I had graded the road, and we hadn't cut anything up in that part of the chopping yet that day. I must have slipped in the mud. It was pretty fresh from my grading."

"Right, so where was Mr. Blandsford through all this?"

"I don't recall. You know, I don't have a really clear picture of this. They say after a bad hit on the head, you tend to forget stuff."

"But you remember getting ready to cut down an ash tree."

"Yeah. Funny how that is. Anyway, maybe Jimmy was still tinkering on the old loader in the yard. It was throwing its right track about twice a day, and that can get to be a pain in the ass. You have to jack it up on that side, release the tension on the idler wheel, pry the track back on, making sure it sits right in the rollers, then set the tension back up. Takes maybe fifteen minutes once you do it twenty times or so."

"Well, that could be. We would like to talk with Jimmy to ask him that. He'd be the one to know where he was just then, don't you imagine? You don't know where he might have gone, do you? He ever talk about just heading out for parts unknown? You two must have talked a lot, working together like that all of the time. I hear lots of folks like to talk about stuff with you. You should hang out a shingle."

Larry, of course, didn't have the faintest idea what the man was talking about.

"I don't really know about that part. Anyway, he never said he was heading out. We did talk about stuff like that, I guess." Larry was beginning to see how this was going to go. This guy was good, and Larry was a poor liar at the best of times. These were not the best of times. He resolved to hang on, though, until the bitter end.

"So, let's get this all in-line: you tripped, wrecked the chainsaw as you fell, and knocked yourself out. Jimmy, in the meantime, did not notice this. He did not notice it to the extent that he just wandered off, left his pickup, all his earthly belongings, his wife, and his helper dying in the woods."

Larry was feeling sick to his stomach at this point. His lie was so outrageously weak that he was now ready to jump up and run from the room, as physically unstable and banged-up as he was.

"Beats me where Jimmy went. I was unconscious, you see."

"Right. OK, now let's talk about the rock we found with your hair and blood on it, about twenty feet from where we found you. Then there's the blood that matches Jimmy's type on some other rocks nearby. Some hair there too, but we can't match it with Jimmy's, because we can't find Jimmy. We are working on a warrant to get into his trailer to get some from one of his combs or his pillow. I suspect we'll find a match."

"I don't really have an answer, officer."

"Let's try this all over again. You are the worst liar I have ever met in my life, and I have dealt with people who lie for an infinite number of reasons every day I am on the job, and I'll even throw in the ones I meet when I am off duty. They tend to be worse. Now, I'm not asking for much here. You are not going to be charged with anything. If we ever find Jimmy, we may want to have a grand jury look at what went on. We just want to find him and get his wife off our backs. She really cares about him, and I hate to see her in such pain. I have known them both for years. If you don't press charges, we probably won't do anything but cause our Mr. Blandsford to lose a few nights' sleep. I suggest you tell me what really happened, and I'll leave you to your misery and your healing."

"Sorry. I just wanted to make it easier on him. I think the whole thing was my fault, really. I guess; I don't really know anymore. Mainly, I don't want you to throw me in the funny farm."

He told the detective as much as he was comfortable with. Leaving things out was easier than making new things up, and he could do that fairly seamlessly. He knew the man could spot the holes but doubted he would pursue them if he got what he really wanted. He ascribed his urge to protect the tree to a case of latent but temporary hippie environmental insanity boiling up, and did not shrink from describing in detail what he had done to precipitate and pursue the fight. He told the detective he could have just left, and nothing would have happened beyond his getting fired. He also told him how the fight progressed, with Jimmy thrown and stunned, and how he thought the fight was supposed to be over.

"So you had your back turned and got hit from behind?"

"Yeah. Dumb, I guess. I really thought the fight was done. I don't know why I should have thought that. It was a damn street fight, not a collegiate wrestling match. There are no rules. I should have run like hell for my car and gotten out of there as fast as I could. I wouldn't be here now, and Jimmy would be off with some new helper, explaining to him about how he can't afford health insurance."

The detective was shaking his head in disbelief.

"Now what? That's just how it went down. I'm not holding anything back." He sort of wasn't.

"I believe you about everything. But it doesn't make any sense. You know Jimmy well by now. Everyone around here knows Jimmy one way or another. You could lose your mother's tombstone dealing with that sharp bastard, but once he made a deal, he stuck with it. Of all the really strange things I have heard you say today, hearing that he busted your head with a rock, from behind after the fight was fairly won is the one that jams in my craw. Jimmy never cheated. It was like some sort of religion with him. Seems funny with all the rest of the shit he pulls around here, but on that one thing, there was no room for compromise. I just don't get it."

No one else got it, and no one would get it for a long time to come. But some seemingly intractable questions can be answered when their time comes around.

They exchanged pleasantries, and the detective left Larry alone with his thoughts and his darkness.

Two days later, they moved him out of intensive care and into a double room. As they wheeled him in, he knew there would be trouble. The room stank of the vilest cigar smoke he had ever smelled in his life. He waited awhile and thought about a strategy to cut this off at the knees. His new roommate was a small man in his sixties who had had a stroke. He could not move his arms at all and was reduced to nearly incoherent mutterings. About an hour after Larry was situated, a nurse came in and took out one of the man's cigars. It was a small black smoke that came from a box with an Italian name on it. She held it in his mouth and lit it for him as he puffed on it with great difficulty. In the mid-seventies, the sea change of public attitude in the U.S. had not yet occurred, and the default was to side with the apparent wishes of the Founding Fathers, who grew and sold tobacco, largely with slave labor. Most people thought that freedom to smoke was left out of the Bill of Rights simply because no one in their right mind would ever challenge it.

But challenge it Larry did. He was not the affable Larry of just a couple of weeks ago. He had turned hard, and the edges of where Larry stopped, and the rest of humanity began had sharpened to a crisp line. He called to the nurse to come over right away. This upset the smoker, who yelled "Haynh, whu abou my huckin sgar? Hum ha heah hod ham hyu!"

"Yes, Mr. Vintner, what's wrong? Are you OK?"

"No, I am not even close to OK. What right does that man have to smoke in this hospital?"

"The poor man, he's gravely ill, he has a right to enjoy his cigar. He has so few pleasures left." Her tone was in the manner of someone lecturing a small child about manners. This would not have been all that smart to attempt with the old Larry. It was much further from sensible with the new Larry.

"Not around me he doesn't! I can't stand that shit!" Larry was using his newfound menace to good advantage. He discovered that he could call it up from his depths at will, and its results were predictable. This poor woman began to look flustered already, and he had only just skimmed the surface of what he knew he could do.

"No need to be unpleasant—and I'm sorry, there is no reason why he can't smoke in his room." The woman was sticking with the party line; this was to her credit, but she was badly outgunned.

"Then get him another room."

"The place is full and there are no other rooms. I suggest you show some courtesy and put up with this minor annoyance." She now was back on her game and obviously was going to pull the "It's out of my hands" classic defense. Larry figured he might as well go thermonuclear.

Larry looked at her with a level gaze, and spoke with a venomously cold voice, totally devoid of emotion. That, coupled with the strangeness that sat behind his eyes, made what he said strikingly effective.

"Tonight, after lights out, I am going to get out of this bed somehow, and I am going to smother him with his own pillow." He let a tiny smile cross his ruined visage.

He said this loudly enough for the other man to hear. It had the most wondrous effect on his demeanor. He began making the most strident and exercised comments with the remnants of his verbal skills. They amounted to little more than a strangled gurgling at this point but were loud enough to make up in passion for what they lacked in intelligibility. He became nearly apoplectic when the nurse hustled out of the room.

"Hum hak heyah! Nont yeave me hwi hi hoony! Hum hak he hoo hoksukuh!"

Within an hour, Larry was in a single room and had learned a lesson in the practical value of sociopathic irascibility. Of course, it was not something you could fake, and that was the scary part.

Larry's parents arrived the next day. The meeting was grim and unpleasant, as he had expected it to be. Andrea was present, and his mother's disapproval of their relationship was a bleak basso continuo underlying the entire visit. His stepfather, a successful businessman, was his usual brusque self, constantly berating Larry for his iniquities. Larry had had the Great Confrontation with him years ago, as fathers and sons, biological or step, have done since time immemorial. He no longer bothered to answer his stepfather's barbs about how he had squandered his college education, had wasted precious years wandering around "those stupid mountains," and now was marking time in a dead-end job in the armpit of the state of New York. Thus, it was something of a shock to all, including Andrea, when Larry announced that he was planning to apply to graduate school, aiming at a PhD in physics, probably specializing in the atmosphere. The silence of the three visitors was an excellent simulacrum of a dense, solid material. Perhaps basalt would do as a metaphor.

His stepfather, true to form, finally collected himself and made a few perfunctory remarks about more wasted time, no job prospects, poor salaries for academics compared to business—but his heart was not really in it, and he wound down in just a couple of minutes. His mother was less negative. Perhaps she thought Andrea would not follow him to some unknown destination and at least five years of schooling, during which she would be working to support both of them. But by the time they left later that afternoon to return to Albany, his mother had pledged support for him until such time as he could get either a teaching assistantship or a research position. His stepfather had glumly acquiesced and agreed to provide the financing from his considerable fortune.

When they had gone, Andrea rose to a fine rage.

"So, when did you figure this shit out, asshole? When you were unconscious? The meds get to you? Maybe you forgot that I might like to have some role in what's going on. I just got blindsided in front of your mother. Who, in case you have not heard, hates my fucking guts."

"You don't like the idea?"

"Fuck you, and fuck whether I like it or not. I thought we had a partnership, and now you lay this crap on me the same time you tell your parents—whom, as far as I can tell from what you say about them, you hate as much as they hate me. How could you shut me out?"

"I just wanted it to be a nice surprise, that's all."

"More likely it was just a cynical way to put all your opponents in one spot at one time and watch the fun as they beat each other senseless. This is not going to go away anytime soon, you prick."

It was some time before they could talk about the decision and its implications for their life together in a calm way. Larry really had made a serious mistake with Andrea. He certainly had not wanted to create this mess with her and his parents; he was not a bad person, as everyone really knew. But he had to admit that he actually was trying to avoid a substantive discussion about the issue and his reasons for wanting to go back to school. He was increasingly less likely to discuss his most private thoughts with anyone, even Andrea, as his recovery plodded along. It was one more symptom of the change this evil thing had wrought in him. Getting him to sit down periodically and have a real conversation became part of a frustrating ritual for her that would end only when she ultimately threw him out of her life. And to be honest with himself, he really had no idea in the world why he suddenly wanted to do this, other than that it now "felt right."

Of Jimmy Blandsford there was never a trace.

13

It was almost a month before Larry could go home, but in the meantime he was busy on his new project. He knew he was too late for a September admission, but he thought he might be in time for a January startup. He was anxious to get going. He had wasted too much time already. He wrote for applications packages from ten schools and rated them in his mind according to how appropriate they would be for his needs. He had to take the graduate record exam as soon as possible, and there was a date that lined up with his getting out of the hospital fairly well. He had to go into the City to take the exam, but a mollified Andrea drove him down. She was never against his decision, just his tactics, and was looking forward to a change of scene. The little hospital in Liberty had very few opportunities for advancement. She was not at all displeased with the prospect of Larry earning a real salary for a change either.

In the end, he was accepted at only one school, and conditionally at that. His undergraduate record was not particularly good, and he had had little physics, just enough to fill in around the edges of his math degree. Characteristically for him, he was not ashamed of getting Ds in courses outside of his field of interest that were of no benefit to him. These dragged down the straight As he got in math and physics. He had not thought much about the future while in college and was paying his dues for that. He simply had fun with mathematics. He did manage to get two of his old professors to write him letters. They remembered him as an interesting individual with great promise and little in the way of ambition; however, when they spoke to him over the phone, they were quickly able to sense the enthusiasm and drive underlying his change in direction and were forthright in describing this. The resulting letters were uncharacteristically strong for these two people, who usually agreed to write letters only for their very best students. One was a woman, rare in mathematics in those days, who had fought hard against a serious gender bias. This fight had left her tough, mentally lean, and chary with praise. She learned in her later years that her gut feelings were dead on in Larry's case.

The other telling factor that gave Larry a second chance in academe was his performance on the entrance examination. The admissions committee at his number-seven choice was curious to see how someone who saturated all parts of the exam might do at their school, even though he was sitting on a 2.8 undergraduate GPA. They wondered aloud at the grad admissions committee meeting during which they decided to offer him acceptance, whether he might have still been able to answer literally all the questions correctly if the exam had been twice as long but with the same time limit. He was given conditional status, meaning he had to pass all his courses with a grade of B or better. This, it turned out, would not be much of a challenge for Larry.

The only drawback to the whole affair was that the only school willing to take a chance on such a dark-horse candidate was in southern California. Both he and Andrea were not ecstatic about this prospect, but by now both of them were waxing enthusiastic about the how all this could work out for them, and they came to a mutually satisfactory plan for pulling everything off. During this selfsame conversation, marriage was a topic and, in the end, agreed upon.

Andrea stayed behind in January when Larry drove out to the Coast with the lion's share of their belongings. His stepfather had spotted him a fairly good used pickup with a camper back. They sold all of their furniture that was worth selling and were travelling light. Andrea would wait until spring and sell Larry's property while saving up some money. Larry's task was to get an apartment, furnish it (with some careful instruction from Andrea), and settle into his course work. They would marry in the spring when she arrived.

It went just exactly that way, surprisingly. Both sets of parents came out to the coast for the wedding, and, for once, Larry's mother looked somewhat pleased at seeing Andrea. His stepfather was slipping into ill health by this point. He was sincerely glad to see his stepson and was almost effusive in his praise for how things were going. It was the last time Larry would see him alive; the man never saw another winter. Andrea had gotten a good job at a local hospital, in a position of greater authority than in her last job.

Larry had been more or less stable since the fight but still had periods of time when the darkness that was always lurking in the background would come out and bite them both. Andrea was becoming reconciled to these occasional mood swings, but still hoped it was a temporary effect of his injury. He went for longer and longer periods of time when the darkness did not overshadow his day-to-day life, and that was a good trend. The excitement of the move and starting school tended to drown out the ache that never left him.

Graduate school was a lot different from undergraduate. He had fewer courses, and they diminished in number as he progressed. He was required to take several undergraduate-level physics courses to make up for what he had missed as a math major, but that was beyond easy for him. He was courted by two professors to work in their labs, and had some difficulty in picking. In the end he turned down a research assistantship, settling for a teaching assistantship that would entail more inroads on his time in order to work in the lab that was doing the research most closely related to his field of interest. Within a year, he had published a paper as first author in *Physical Review Letters,* the most prestigious journal in the discipline. At this point, the graduate committee waived the requirement for a completed master's degree, and he was cleared to go directly for the PhD. His work formed the basis for a successful grant from the National Science Foundation, and he was freed from further duty teaching first-year physics labs. He had enjoyed the classroom experience, but research was a compulsion with him.

While doing ancillary reading for an advanced seminar in nonlinear dynamics, he made a chilling discovery. He thought he had largely put thoughts of his days in the Catskills behind him and was now largely able to keep from brooding over those events, but this brought it all back. He was reading a review article on nonlinear waves known as solitons, and something tweaked his memory. He was familiar with them as phenomena in optics, the curious balance of linear and nonlinear dynamics that kept white-light packets together in fiber optics. To get a feel for the physics, he decided to go back to the old sources. He was tired of looking at papers that started out with "It is obvious by inspection that:" followed by a double integral. That was not difficult for him to follow, but where was the *science*? Now he was reading the original description written in the nineteenth century.

These curious waves were initially characterized in water and had been observed for years in rivers, near their mouths, and were known as tidal bores. They were often single waves, hence the name *soliton*. Two could pass through one another and emerge intact afterwards. They had many remarkable properties, and the mathematics describing them was particularly gorgeous. The primary feature was that they were in an exact balance of forces that would dissipate them and those pulling them together-linear and non-linear.

The first recorded observation, followed later by controlled experimental work, was by a man named John Scott Russell in 1834. A team of horses was pulling a barge along a narrow canal. The teamster halted the team quickly, and the boat was stopped dead. This caused a "violent agitation" to ensue just ahead of the bow of the boat. The movement of the water was chaotic, great swirls and eddies, with no order at all. Suddenly, the commotion collected itself into a substantial mound of water that started off down the canal "at great velocity". The scientist conducting the experiment followed on his fast horse along the tow path for almost two miles. The strange wave was finally lost in the bogs where the canal widened. He called it a "wave of translation."

Larry's face was ashen. The image of a "violent agitation" pulled him out of the journal, out of his grad cubicle, and back to the seat of a bulldozer. He was pulling up on a load of logs, and as the cable drew taut, there was a chaotic, wild vibration at the far end near the logs, and a single wave took off down the line and surgically removed a man's arm. It was several days before he was able to pursue the matter on a rational level. He talked with a few professors not claiming he had actually *seen* this or offering the grisly details but offered it as a simple query about what might happen. None were very helpful on the question of whether such a thing could occur under the exact circumstances he described. Most thought not, vibrations in strings were harmonic, not chaotic. Yet it happened.

He pondered this problem over the years and looked for a chance to experience these waves. One summer, when he and Andrea were back east to announce her pregnancy to the families, they took a side trip to Nova Scotia. Andrea managed to find a place where they could almost be guaranteed a good view of a tidal bore. They drove up to the end of the Bay of Fundy and followed the detailed map they had gotten from the provincial tourist bureau to a small farm. The farmer had the best view of the river, sitting as he did on the top of a bluff that afforded a long view both up and downstream. The river made a turn right at this point and widened out over a web of sandbars. He did not charge for the privilege of sitting on a bunch of old logs to watch nature's show, but he accepted donations. The man had talked with Andrea on the phone concerning timing of the bore during their visit and had mentioned how expensive chewing tobacco was in Canada. Larry slipped him two packages of Red Man leaf, and they wandered down to the bluff, cameras at the ready.

Almost to the minute predicted by the old farmer, they heard a sound like a distant freight train. With binoculars, they could just see a dark line across the peacefully flowing river nearly three miles downstream. It was an eight-foot wall of water, travelling at a good speed, and it was boiling in their direction. The farmer by this time was regaling his audience with tales of lives lost to the bore, of daredevils who tried to navigate a surfboard or kayak up the river, of children who wandered out onto the flats. Larry supposed they were all true but was certain there was some embellishment involved at a few points.

The wall of water rushed at them, and the sound became quite loud. It was a frightening thing to watch. Larry looked at the lay of the land and tried to predict what would happen when the bore hit the rocky sand flats at the bend where they observed. The river widened out to perhaps three times its previous size, and he thought it would break up and destroy the wave. It was what would happen when the banks closed in again that interested him. He could feel the flow in his internal circuitry by now, and he was trying to combine his strange direct perception with the intellectual studies he had done on the phenomenon. He made a reasoned hypothesis based on this uneasy marriage that was counterintuitive, but which proved ultimately correct.

The wave did, indeed, break up into a chaotic mass of churning water. At this point it was no more than a foot or so high at any point. There was no order in it at all. It covered the sandbars and seethed along small, shallow channels. Lacking banks, the wave died, leaving a mass of brown eddies behind. The commotion moved inexorably upstream—the highest tides in the world were not to be denied. As the banks narrowed again and the channel deepened, a most remarkable thing occurred. The wave reformed in all its angry perfection and raced on upstream, undiminished.

Larry had not had enough. With quick driving directions from the farmer, they set off up the road to a bridge over a small stream that formed a tributary of the main channel. It was only about twenty feet across, but from the bridge, their wait was rewarded by a small wave, perhaps a foot and a half high, coursing up the stream. They found an even smaller brook a little way further upstream, and there, scaled down yet again, was another tiny offspring of the great wave.

With this single exception, thoughts of the days in the Catskills seemed to fade from the center of his mind, but they never disappeared completely. And of course, the gut-wrenching changes that had altered him when he was there remained. But he learned new ways of coping with them.

For one thing, Larry began to run. He had been an athlete in high school and college. After college, he spent several years hiking and climbing. While in the Catskills, he had added hard manual labor to the long walks. He was always in good physical shape in those days, without having to think about it. But now he was riding a desk, reading, writing, and sitting for long hours in seminars and classes. It was a surprise and a shock to him when he noticed one day that he was getting out of breath climbing stairs. This didn't make any sense to him at all. He got tired walking to the bus stop in the morning. When he and Andrea took odd hikes in the San Gabriel mountains, he got just plain exhausted. He began to notice a roll of fat forming around his middle, and that was what did the trick. He felt this loss of condition depriving him of the freedom of motion and action that he had always enjoyed and took action.

At this time, the running craze was in full swing, but he went about reinventing the wheel, so to speak. He bought a pair of tennis sneakers and went out early one morning to run three miles. This was a poor decision. Within less than two blocks he had pains in his shins and a nasty stitch in his side. He limped back to their apartment and rethought his strategy. After some deliberation, he laid out a two-mile course with the odometer of their car. He checked the distances between the power and phone poles and figured them to be about three hundred yards apart. He got up early the next morning and walked the entire course. He did that every morning for a week. At the beginning of the second week, he walked the course except for the last three hundred yards, which he ran gently. He kept that up for a week. Next week, he ran the last six hundred yards. By the end of two months, he was running the entire course. At this point, he bought a cheap stopwatch and began lowering the time it took to run the course. After a bout with shin splints, he bought some good running shoes. Distances grew and times shrank. He felt a lot better. When asked why he got up at 5:00 in the morning to run, he would answer: "No one else is up at that hour running. It gives me an edge."

The baby was born during their last year on the coast, and by now Larry was earning enough through the grants he was writing for his major professor that Andrea could afford to take some time off. They moved to a larger apartment and began to achieve a middle-class status that would have horrified both of them when they first met and were living in genuine poverty in a cabin in Claryville.

Upon graduation, Larry entered the lists with the other academic wannabes. He had been at least lucky, if not prescient, in choosing his field. By this time the whistle was being blown stridently about global warming, and Larry was at the right place at the right time. Though he had not been principal investigator on any of the grants, his mark was all over them. The grant reviewers knew this fact and were often also the same people asked to serve on faculty-hire search committees when positions in this area arose. His major professor had always given him first authorship on joint papers, and much of the substance of them was being incorporated into the most promising models of the meteorological responses to greenhouse-gas-induced climate came from him. Even if the programs *were* in FORTRAN. He was able to get a very good postdoctoral position with NOAA. He was suddenly making some real money, and things kept getting better for them.

The decision of which job offer to accept after his stint with the government was tougher. He did not like cities in general, but the prestige of the school, the startup package, and the remarkable salary were too much. They packed up for Boston.

14

There was hail rattling on the hood of Jimmy's pickup when he reached it. The storm was of an almost preternatural intensity, but Jimmy hardly noticed it around him. His one thought was of escape. He was certain he had hit the man hard enough to kill him. He was not particularly interested in staying around long enough to double check. With luck, they would not find the body until late in the day when both of them turned up missing. He guessed he had at least six hours, maybe more, to get the hell out of Dodge. But he needed a plan, and he was not thinking particularly clearly just then.

The enormity of what he had done suddenly gripped his guts in a deep spasm. The pressure rose until he bellowed out, "Fuck!" in a long, drawn-out scream of pure anguish. What was he thinking? Why did he fight the kid in the first place? He could have used the rest of the day to sleep off his throbbing hangover after firing the son of a bitch. What was one day, more or less? Then tomorrow he could have come back and cut the fucking tree down with no one to bust his chops. Now he was a murderer. He could still feel the caving sensation as the skull gave way under the rock, still felt the impact in his feet when the heavy body hit the rock pile. For a couple of seconds, he felt jubilation, raw bloodlust at the instant of the kill. But now all he had was that overwhelming pressure on his intestines and an utter numbness everywhere else. That numbness would soon pass, and the real pain would begin. It was a nightmare feeling—"How can I be here? This must be wrong. This is all wrong." But it was real, and it cut him to his very soul. The meaning of why he had fought Larry in the first place, and why he had attacked him again after he had acknowledged defeat, were questions that would take years to answer. There were answers awaiting him when he was ready, and the journey would be a long one.

But Jimmy knew nothing of this yet, and all of his attempts to recreate reality in a more familiar mold were not going to save his ass from a manslaughter charge. Jimmy was a very practical man, even under circumstances as dire as these, and a part of his brain remained strangely lucid. He was afraid to take his truck. Every cop in this part of the state would be looking for it in no time. It would not have been the first time many had looked for it for one reason or another. Leaving it here would tell them he had set off cross-country, but that did not trouble him at all. He knew these woods better than any man alive, and he could move fast along little-used trails. The rain would throw off dogs if it kept up, as an added bonus. So, with little further thought beyond getting some miles behind him, he got what he could salvage from his former life and headed northeast on a track that would take him around Slide Mountain itself and deep into the thick forest north of the highest part of the range. He was fortunate in what he had available to take with him. He always kept a .22 caliber rifle with a scope and a brick of ammunition in the truck cab. He liked to shoot and often burned up a couple of boxes of shells at a local dump, plinking rats or collecting a few squirrels for supper. He had the foul-weather coat he was wearing, a spare pair of work boots and socks, a canteen filled with water that he had thrown in to help with his hangover, and his lunch. The last one his wife would ever fix for him. He had an old woven-ash pack basket in the back of the truck with a beat-up hatchet lashed to the side, and that was about it for his kit. It would have to do. He threw all the loose stuff into the pack, adjusted the soggy leather shoulder straps, and was on his way. The rain had not yet let up and promised to keep up for some time. If he had not killed Larry, the man might have told him exactly how long.

He set a reasonable pace, having calmed down a bit by now. He did not want to end up dead himself. He would need to walk until dark. The flashlight in the truck had dead batteries, and he did not think he needed the extra weight of the heavy alloy unit. He would simply sleep when it got dark and move by daylight. But where? Just getting a few miles behind him was the easy part. Then what? He was damned if he was going to go to prison for this. It was not his fault. Was it? Was a blood rage his fault? Was he responsible for what he did in such a state? Temporary insanity? The feelings of being pulled out of his body was still fresh in his mind but would not make much of a defense, as real as it felt. Larry was well-known and well-liked in the area, even if he was a flatlander. He had never gotten into a fight that Jimmy knew about in the whole time he had been around and given his antiwar sentiments and hippy hair and beard, that was remarkable. "I am fucking toast!" he remarked to a friendly-appearing spruce tree he happened to be passing at the time. It obligingly agreed with his assessment of the situation.

The rain finally stopped, leaving an intolerable humidity behind. Small columns of mist began rising from the forest. Jimmy continued his steady pace, and the sweat poured off of his body, carrying away the poisons he had ingested the night before. His head was clearing, and he began to think about his situation in a more rational manner. "God, I need a cigarette!" he spoke aloud, but the trees here were not as forthcoming as the spruce had been. He checked his pocket and found a soggy mass of disintegrating paper tubes filled with tobacco. He started to throw it away but thought better of it and slipped the mutilated pack under a small, flat rock. People knew his brand. Shit, he smoked enough of them, he thought. Might be a long time before he tasted that sweet, resinous cloud heading for his lungs again. No matter. His addiction to this particular drug and the consequences of not having if for a while were a major thing, but not very far up on the list of problems he would be coping with in the next forty-eight hours.

As his head cleared, he began to consider his options. It was now very obvious that leaving the truck might not have been all that smart, but it was too late to go back now. So onward to the north it was. What was up there? Figuring that out was his first order of business. Then he had a flash of insight. Years back, he had gone hunting up that way with his uncle Ralph, and old Ralphie had a broken-down deer camp about twenty-five miles north of his current location. Ralph was still alive and kicking despite a serious interest in keeping the Jim Beam distillery folks happy, so maybe he had a way out of this after all. First, he would get to the camp, and then he would see if there was a way he could find out what was going on and maybe even contact Ralph. That would only work if Ralphie was sober, but it was worth a try. Better than some other things he could come up with. Jimmy always kept a few hundred dollars in his wallet so he could pick up on bargains if they turned up. He began to be a bit more optimistic, at least about the next few days into weeks. Winter would be another matter, but he had plenty of time to figure the next part of the plan before cold weather drove him down out of the high country.

He ate his bologna sandwiches with mayo, washed them down with the single soda, ate the cookies that had been packed, and hid the remains under a rock as he had done with the soggy smokes. The fact that he might never see his wife again, or his kids, began to eat at him. But how could he face anyone after his cowardly act? That was worse than the thought of prison now as more and more of his faculties that sat, often unused, above the low animal cunning that had gotten him this far in life began to fire properly again. A wave of exquisite remorse assailed him for killing this poor kid, and it hit him like a load of double-ought buckshot. This feeling settled in for a very long stay. He would deal with it during many dreary, sleepless nights in the years to come, and nothing could change that.

But Jimmy was a survivor, and he was on about the process of surviving. He knew he could not make it to the cabin before late the following day, so he planned on a bivouac when the light began to fail. He figured to maintain this pace if he could, slow it if he must, but he would move until he could not see the path or until he found a place sheltered and out of the way to stay the night. The bruises from where Larry had thrown him into the rocks had begun to hurt and swell now, and he was sore from the unaccustomed continuous walking. There was still a slight aura of nausea from his bout with the bottle the previous night, and goddamn, could he use a cigarette about now.

As darkness fell, something unusual occurred that was a harbinger of what was to come for him. He was traversing a steep, rocky slope with a great deal of exposed ledge. The path, such as it was, was no more than a vague track here, but Jimmy knew both where he was and where he was going as well as he would if he were in his own back yard. He spotted an overhang just up from the trail that promised some shelter and a dry place to sleep. He had no matches for a fire, his only pack having been as wet as the smokes, but he could not chance a fire anyway. He clambered up the slope to the overhang and found a nice shelter. It was dry and the floor was fairly level. It consisted of forest-floor duff with a coating of pine needles both thick and dry. He could not have been happier at his fortune and wondered how he deserved such luck, given the line he had crossed today. He would wonder more and more about such turns of fortune, until ultimately he would come to understand that it might not be entirely a matter of luck that such gifts from the mountains and their forests came his way. He felt almost peaceful here in this place—at least, as peaceful as his mind could be under the circumstances—and he spent a dreamless night in deep sleep.

Morning saw him up at dawn and on his way again, a hunger starting to burn in his belly. He was used to eating a gargantuan number of calories in a given day and would already have had eggs, bacon, home fried potatoes, toast, jam, and a couple of glazed doughnuts, all washed down with a quart of coffee by now. This morning, he had nothing. He would need to do something about that or he would not make it through the day, he thought. But there was nothing he could do about it, not feeling secure enough to risk a gunshot, even from a small-caliber weapon like his .22 rifle. And he was wrong. He could keep functioning for a whole day without eating anything. He would prove that many times and grow used to the sensation of gnawing hunger.

This second day progressed much as had the first, except drier. It was a nice, clear summer's day, not too humid, as the storm had wrung out the moisture and brought in a cool air mass from Canada. He covered the miles steadily, despite his lightheadedness from low blood sugar. He had never made a connection to his uncle's cabin through the woods but made no mistakes as he came to forks. He always seemed to know where the two branches would lead him. Ultimately, the path he was on joined to one he had been on before, and this revelation did not surprise him in the least. The cabin was about another five miles up into hillier country, and he covered the distance in less than two hours. That might have surprised him had his watch not been smashed in the fight, and had he thought to look in the first place. Jimmy was starting to move easily, with purpose, almost grace. Others might have seen this and been amazed.

The cabin remained in good shape. Remarkably, it had not been broken into by human weasels, nor ravaged by hungry black bears. There was a small stock of canned goods and dried soups, along with matches, kindling, and firewood for the cast-iron bulldog stove. This type of unit could be used both for heat and cooking and was popular for small camps like this one. A brook ran by about a hundred yards from the cabin, and there was even an outhouse. Jimmy contemplated whether he might avail himself of that, but he'd had so little to eat that he had really nothing in there to empty out. He set about looking for a can opener in hopes of fixing that little problem.

An hour later, Jimmy was sitting on the small-roofed porch with his hunger gone and his mind working on the next steps he would take. He had been rather surprised at how little it took to make him feel fairly full. He actually felt pretty good, which was almost astonishing. No hangover for the first time in maybe a couple of months, his wheeze seemed to be losing its edge, and the overwhelming need for a cigarette was easing faster than he thought possible.

So, what to do? He was set here for a few days. He would need to find out what happened back home and if they were looking for him. He would need to get more supplies at some small mom-and-pop market where he could pose as a fisherman or tourist, or as whatever he could put together for a disguise. That might be tough, since breaking a hundred-dollar bill could arouse suspicion. But he had some small bills for a paper and some canned stew, hash, and vegetables. Vegetables? Since when would he even *think* of buying *vegetables*? Yet he now thought that some canned peas would go nicely with his hash. Funny, that smack he got when the kid dropped him on the rocks must have done more damage than he thought. But the bruises from the fight were already healing and hardly hurt at all. That was also a bit puzzling, another tiny piece in a vast puzzle that stretched out of his sight in all directions. It was a peculiarity of his situation that he would resolve down the line, along with most of the others.

He waited a couple of days until his supplies looked ominously thin and poked around the cabin to see what might be useable to cover his identity. There was a closet that had some of Ralphie's old fishing gear and clothing in it, and Jimmy was pleased to see he was about the same size as his uncle. Ralphie had left these things here as a backup in case he got caught out in a storm and needed a change of dry clothing. There was even a fishing vest with hooks, lures, extra leader, and an old spare reel prominently displayed in a pocket. Jimmy could not believe his good fortune. Here was his disguise. He carefully composed his outfit, made a mental list of what he would need, and headed down the mountain into the tiny town below.

The old store was just as he remembered it from the last time he was there with Ralphie. He filled his list, grabbed a newspaper, and added a box of candles and more matches as an afterthought. They took him for a tourist fly fisherman, and he did not look remarkable in any way. He was even able to break one of his hundred-dollar bills without anyone batting an eye. He did not feel he could squander his money on cigarettes and beer, so he got only the bare essentials on his list, enough to keep him another week. This omission did not trouble him at all. In fact, another customer was smoking, and the smell seemed oddly unpleasant to him. One extravagance was a cheap portable radio operated by AAA batteries; of which latter commodity he bought a small extra supply. The walk back along the highway to the cabin trail was all uphill, but curiously he did not seem to be all that tired when he reached it, and the steep climb up to the cabin taxed him little more. His wheeze was almost gone, leaving the cough—which was diminishing—all by itself, and he felt better than he had in many years, at least physically. But his mind was far from easy, and his health was not uppermost in his ruminations.

The newspaper revealed much that eased his mind. On one of the back pages there was an update, almost an afterthought, about the fight. To Jimmy's cosmic relief, he found he was not a murderer. Larry was listed as being in good condition in the hospital in Liberty. He also noted that he was being sought by the police, but only for questioning. Citizens were urged to call the state police if they had any information about one James Blandsford, but there was no picture, not even a description, just his name. For some strange reason, they were not all that anxious to find him. Jimmy guessed, without proof at this point, that Larry had told them he was not interested in pressing charges. That sounded a lot like the Larry he knew. And he also knew he would not have pressed charges if the roles had been reversed. So, Jimmy could go home. “Imagine that,” he thought. “I can just go down to the store, call the cops, tell them where I am, and bingo, I can probably go home.” That relief washed over him like a warm liquid for a bit, and he began to think about doing just that. But then an odd thought began to trickle into his mind. Did he really want to go home? Why was he thinking such a thing? How could he not want to go home? He dismissed this as ridiculous. “Well, no sweat.” He said to the cabin walls. “I am outta here in the morning. First thing.”

Jimmy missed his wife and kids a lot. Unlike his odious father, he had cared for his family from day one in a genuinely thoughtful manner. They were not rich, but Jimmy worked hard and had built up a good financial base. They did not owe all that much, and even though he tended to drink heavily way too often for his own good, there was always money left for treating the wife and kids on the weekend. And he never missed a day of work. He did not mind the long, hard hours of manual labor, having grown up with this, and he figured he could keep it up until the gravediggers came for him. But the shame of what he had done started to work on his mind. He had lost a fair fight and had tried to kill someone by sneaking up from behind. This treacherous act was far from what he thought he had worked to be the core of his life. Honesty and fairness were his stock in trade. He always thought that when people figured they could count on him, they could count on him. What he'd done would be hard to live down, and he knew it would be all around town by now. Jimmy was a backstabber.

Well, he thought he might be able to live with that, given time. He would make it up to Larry somehow, hire him back, do whatever needed to be done to patch up his reputation. At least he was not a murderer.

Apparently he had not even hurt him too badly, as incredible as that sounded. Larry must be one tough son of a bitch. But there was another factor creeping into his psyche. It was obvious that he was feeling much better physically than he probably had ever in his miserable life. That was certainly part of this odd mix. But there was something even stronger at work. He assessed his mood carefully and realized that he felt entirely at home here. Not just in the cabin but in these woods and mountains. Much more so than he did back in his trailer. He really did not want to leave, and the pull to stay was growing by the hour.

"What the fuck is going on here?" He spoke softly to the cabin walls, and to the trees beyond. He got no audible answer, but he expected a reply of some sort, and a silent one was forthcoming. Talking to the trees and rocks was starting to become a habit. "Alone too long is all," he opined. But then he did not *feel* alone. He felt as he had so many times when there was a crowd of drinking buddies around him on a Saturday night, hanging out at the old bar by the dam, drinking draft beer and feeling on top of the world. But there was only the woods here, and no beer. He decided it would not hurt to hang out for a few more days, "Just until things cool down a little more, that's all." Again, there was no answer, but it was all the answer he needed. He thought that a few more days might be maybe a week. And he realized, deep in a part of his mind he was only beginning to discover, that a few more days would be years, and years would be the rest of his life. And the trees again made no answer that the ear could hear, but their agreement could not have been clearer.

Jimmy was in a curious state. He knew on one level that there had been a sea change in his life, even as he continued to plan for his return to civilization over the next few days. And he was beginning to see that it was part of the change that had started back at the chopping, on the day of the fight. It was the end of the change he had fought to forestall and had been willing to kill to prevent. But it now had become complete and permanent. An old, dying part of him said he should fight this unbelievable urge to stay, and thought he should run down the hill again and call home to assure his wife that things were OK, and that he would be home soon. But he did nothing of the sort.

He kept busy shooting small game for his meals, to supplement the oddly large cache of canned vegetables he had amassed, and started taking long hikes during the day to see more of his surroundings. He was far enough away from any other habitation or road that minor out-of-season plinking would arouse no suspicion. He liked squirrels and roasted them whole on small fires in the bulldog stove. He made a couple of stews too, which he vaguely remembered how to do from watching his wife. They were particularly delicious now that his sense of taste was recovering from its long hibernation under the pall of tobacco smoke.

"OK, this is it!" he said after a full week had passed. "Time to get your ass back and face the music. No more screwing around. Load that pack and get on the trail. You'll be home with a cold beer and a butt in your hand by sunset." Nothing from the troops. "Now, just throw your shit in that pack, put on your boots and those clean socks you washed last night, and move out, soldier." Silence. He did not move.

"We are most sorry, Mr. Blandsford," the trees responded in the silent yet eloquent way that only trees can muster, "we simply cannot allow you to go."

The funny thing was, Jimmy really could almost hear them by now.

And he knew they would not let him go. They were not in any way threatening retribution, but their powers of persuasion were most irresistible. And in that instant all pretense disappeared; Jimmy knew he would spend all his days out here. He stared out the window at the forest and knew that he was part of it now. The woods claimed him for their own, and he agreed that it was just and right that this be so. "Can I at least go down to the store for supplies?" The silent answer was plain: he could. It was not a question of trust; he himself knew beyond any doubt that he would come back. He was not a prisoner; he was a citizen. A wave of exultation washed through him like an electric shock, and he just sat for a spell, digesting all that was happening. Finally, he donned his "street clothing" to make his run down the mountain for the next few weeks' provisions.

Long-range plans were now a priority. It was all well and good to decide on the life of a hermit, but even hermits had to eat, and this cabin was not ready for winter. Where would he get money for food and supplies? Would his uncle be here for deer season this year? It must be July by now, he thought, no time at all to get ready for a long, cold winter. He counted up his remaining funds: $187.56. Not much. Not enough. He would need to get some work, but he figured he was sharp enough to do that. There was a small diesel-repair shop in the town down below, and he knew diesels upside and down. If the proprietor was like Jimmy, he would be likely to hire him without his having to surrender his social security number and all that useless folderol. A couple days a week would be all he would need, and he could survive nicely. But what about the camp? It was one thing to sit out a couple of beer-soaked weeks in November looking for deer, and quite another to live through a January of subzero weather. All things to ponder.

Jimmy was right about the mechanic. Luckily for him, the man was getting on in years, was short-handed, and quickly saw that Jimmy knew as much as he did about injectors, fuel filters, rod bearings, hydraulic cylinders, and valve tolerances. Under-the-table, green money would be fine by him. That was part one. Part two was fixing the cabin up for a winter's hunkering down. That took a bit more ingenuity. Jimmy only worked three days a week to start, but each day he would stop at the small hardware store and pick up something he would need—a roll of fiberglass insulation, or maybe some weather stripping. He picked up a high-quality bucksaw and a splitting maul to prepare his firewood. That project needed to be on the fast track to get the wood drying as soon as possible. A roll of builder's plastic and a staple gun were next. The place was soon as tight as a suburban split-level and ready for anything.

Next, he needed to know if he would be disturbed anytime in the coming months, and he hatched a simple scheme to find out. He made an anonymous call to Ralphie, who was sober for a change, and asked if he could rent that old cabin he had in the Catskills. The answer was an unequivocal no. He was planning on hanging onto it for his kids, as an investment to help his grandchildren through college in a few years, and he did not need the money or the aggravation. Sorry. A few more well-placed questions made it clear the no one was using it at all. He even made sure Ralphie would not be coming up for deer season. Too besotted to be trusted with a gun by his family, he imagined. So that solved that problem too. This was all coming out way too easy, but Jimmy, by this point, expected no less.

The year began to fade into autumn, and Jimmy figured it was time to get some new clothing. He had fallen into the routine of washing the few things he had regularly in a galvanized tub, and in fact had bought a few changes of summer garb; but nights were getting downright cold, and the first frosts had hit despite its being only late August. So, one day found him in the general store picking things out. He knew his size, of course, as he had always bought his own work clothes, being somewhat fussy about them, but for the first time he realized that was no longer useful information. Jimmy Blandsford was now a lean, tough figure of a man. He still had powerful musculature, but even the most careful observer would not see fat on his frame anywhere. He moved with an amazing litheness, almost catlike. His cough was entirely gone, and he walked with a purpose and ease that ate miles effortlessly. The other notable thing about his appearance was his hair. He had neither shaved nor cut his hair since before the "incident," as he now preferred to call it. He had a full beard and hair down past his collar. This in no way troubled him, nor did it create in him the need to deal with it other than to buy a hairbrush to keep this graying mane from snarling. So, he stacked up his new clothing in sizes he did not think possible, and he began to have thoughts of cold weather and what he would do as the iron months closed in on him. Not for the first time, he began to wonder just what it was that the forest would require in return for this incredible gift, and if he would be weighed in the balance and found wanting when the fell hour arrived.

Jimmy began to read. He had started buying a paper every time he was in town and reading it start to finish. That was fine, but he needed more than that to keep him amused on the days he did not work and during the long evenings, so he started picking up a cheap paperback at the store about once a week. There was a table filled with used books for a buck or two. You brought in the ones you were done with and threw them back on the pile. The proceeds went to the small-town library. As his speed in negotiating the printed page rapidly increased, this also became inadequate, and he started frequenting that selfsame library. He even made friends with the librarian, who worked part-time there and part-time down the mountain in a fast-food restaurant. She issued him a library card without further identification, which was irregular but very neighborly, and Jimmy moved on to more weighty tomes under her tutelage. Before the first snow had fallen, he had tackled *Moby-Dick* and emerged both victorious and totally hooked. As winter wore on, Tolstoy, Melville, Joyce, Faulkner, Dickens (around Christmas time, of course), and myriad others took the round trip up the mountain and back. The librarian was more than happy to order books from other libraries as her own stock began to appear inadequate. And the lessons in all these books were not lost on the reader. He bought used texts from the high school now, in elementary mathematics and general science as well as history, English literature, and even grammar. They were consumed in their time, to be replaced by higher-level editions. He even did the math problems, which seemed easy to him now. Jimmy's mind was becoming as lean and powerful as his body.

The snows began to disappear, and Jimmy became restless. The winter in the cabin had been pleasant, but he knew that he could not count on squatting there much longer. Further cautious research indicated that Ralphie might now be planning on selling the place to finance his grandchildren's college. In any event, he might be along anytime from early summer on to check the place out. He would be amazed at its condition. It was in perfect shape, with insulation, wallboard, new double-glazed windows (bought at a discount place, of course, but still new and sound), and a nice, new roof. Jimmy was not lazy and had little else to spend his wages on besides his meager rations, which were now almost exclusively vegetarian. Beans and greens, added to an modest ration of meat whenever he could find wild game. So, he needed a plan, and it seemed as though he ought to let his newfound colleague, the forest primeval, figure it out for him. He was not being insolent or even presumptuous, but since it had invited him to stay, it damn well ought to find another place for him to live.

He started up on his hikes again as soon as the deepest drifts had melted, just to see what might be out there. And he was not disappointed with the results. Of course, he still wondered what this was all going to cost him, and in what sort of currency the bill would be presented. But he became less and less concerned about whether he would have the means to settle up. It was obvious now to him that he was on about the business of the forest in everything that he did, and perhaps he was already making payments.

15

Jimmy's sense of where he was in the forest had always been keen. He had never been lost in the woods, despite running into bad weather, darkness, game wardens to be avoided by hightailing it—all the usual things that could get a person well and truly confounded. He just simply knew where he was. This sense of the forest had been even further heightened by his new circumstances. He could mentally lay out a day's exploration and usually get back to the cabin when he needed to. He systematically laid out a grid of day hikes, and on any day when the weather was decent and he was not needed at the repair shop, he would set out with a light pack and his new ash walking stick, which he had hewn from a young tree with his hatchet. The walks were not purposeful. He really had no idea what he was looking for, or if he really was looking at all. He just loved being out in the woods for the sake of being there, and he walked effortlessly through the thickest growth as if there were a trail.

He was patient and observant on these many walks. He began to penetrate deeper into the region, way past the point where even the local hunters might go in the fall. This part of the state park was a wasteland as far as most folks could see. It was rocky and steep, being part of the eastern foothills of the highest part of the range, and deeply fissured by ravines with running brooks coursing down through them. He bought U.S. Geological Survey maps of the area—not because he needed them to find his way around; in fact, he knew several of them to contain errors, based on his own sense of what was on the face of the earth. Rather, he wanted to judge what might become of a particular area in the future as development continued its ugly, vicious progress. His hand had been felt more than once in this arena. Crucial, well-thought-out pieces were appearing in the local papers over his nom de plume, Arnold Fisher. At public hearings and other crucial meetings, a strange, hairy man would often speak up from the back of the room with the sort of astonishing, even devastating, knowledge of facts and figures that would take the wind out of almost any developer's sails. He did not often win, but he was just getting warmed up.

Each walk was an adventure for him. His sense of wonder, lost as a child in the home of a drunken, abusive father, had returned. He had much catching up to do. He found gorges with waterfalls, he found caverns that he resolved to explore one day, he found ancient trees that the old-time loggers must have been unable to retrieve and had left to continue on into the next centuries, travelers from an antique land. And throughout, his bond with his surroundings grew deeper and more unbreakable.

It was late in May when he made his discovery. He spotted what must once have been a dirt track, passable in the old times by a horse-drawn wagon, perhaps, but nothing more substantial. It was completely overgrown, and a woodsman of lesser acuity, maybe *any* other woodsman, would have missed it completely. But it was clearly man-made, and the trees growing in the track were of a different age and type from those surrounding it. There were some declivities that had obviously been filled in, and some minor ridges that had been cut through by hand labor. It followed the contours of the shallow valley slavishly, as was always the case in the days when roadwork was not done with giant earth movers belching diesel smoke in the wake of biblical blasting with dynamite. This was from a kinder, gentler age when people let nature dictate the terms of any agreement.

The track seemed to disappear, even from Jimmy's penetrating gaze, as he looked back down the slope toward areas that people might frequent. This meant Jimmy himself would have missed it if he had been walking a mile farther down. Discovery by anyone else at any time was extremely unlikely. He turned his steps upslope to follow it without even a thought about his intentions. It was still early morning, and he had the whole day ahead of him. And the days were getting long this time of year.

He followed it for about a mile or so, whereupon it joined the course of a small creek. Jimmy thought this odd, since, on his map of the area, this creek did not exist. Yet here it was, large as life, and it was quite robust in its flow for a forest waterway now that the spring melt was long past. He intuited that this meant it had a large spring as part of its source and logged that potentially important piece of information in his memory. As he progressed, the valley became narrower and the walls steeper until it was a true ravine. There was enough of a flat area along the walls to allow for the track to continue, although he often had to wade the brook as that flat area switched sides. He looked for traces of rearrangement of stones to indicate that fords had been built, but spring floods had long ago removed any evidence. The course of the brook was eroded deeply enough that these floods had not disturbed the track in more than a few places; however, it scarcely mattered, as there was only one way to go. The ravine walls were steep enough to stop even a good climber as the soil and rock were too unstable to permit ascent.

After about another half mile, the gorge walls began to recede and the going got better. The brook's flow slowed as it widened, and the grade lessened. Immediately, Jimmy saw why. He was entering a bowl left by the vagaries of the glacier's retreat, with a very flat floor, steep sides, and a small section where the stream widened and flowed gently. The bowl contained a meadow with little in the way of new growth of trees in it, which was very puzzling. To the west, he could see the gorge reforming and could hear a waterfall, which signified the entry of the brook into the bowl. Against the north wall of the bowl, he saw something that immediately told him his search was over. He was home.

He discerned a stone house of modest proportions, with two chimneys and a separate outbuilding to the west. He went over to explore more closely. The house was roughly square in its footprint. The masonry was very old but sound. It had been carefully done by an expert craftsman. There were two fireplaces, one at either end, and their chimneys would need some work but looked sound. There was no roof, but the notches in the masonry showed that large beams had served to support a fairly simple ridged affair that could be rebuilt without a great deal of carpentry skill. The outbuilding was also sound and had obviously served as a barn for this small homestead. As the crow flew, it was not much farther from town than Ralphie's cabin, but the route was far more circuitous and would take time. He would have to plan carefully to be sure he would still be able to work. He doubted he would get to the point where he could cut civilization off entirely. If nothing else, he had gotten addicted to his books. But he knew without a doubt that this would be his home. And he also knew that no one would find him here. Even the most careful perusal of the section of the Geological Survey map offered no indication whatsoever that this place existed at all. He looked around at the forest and said a quiet "thank you" and began his plans to get this place ready before the snows of the following autumn could catch him. He would begin to move out of Uncle Ralphie's cabin immediately.

His first order of business was to make the place habitable for the summer while he worked. He did not want to meet up with his uncle and needed a reasonable shelter. He thought the old barn would suffice and started there. He convinced his boss to give him a few extra day's work, not a difficult task given the man's encroaching age and the quality of Jimmy's skills. He was well paid for his labors now, as he practically carried the business, and no taxes or other silly deductions molested the roll of green bills he got each week.

This overtime was to allow him to buy tools and materials. He first purchased some tarps to rig a shelter. This was easily effected by temporarily replacing the long-rotted ridge beams of this smaller structure with light poles and draping the tarps over them, making them fast with nylon line. He immediately moved all his worldly goods to this spot and made the place as livable as he could. It was proof against rain and wind, being well protected from storms by the steep walls of the ravine. He bought an old used bulldog stove like the one in the cabin and managed to get it up to the site on a log sledge. Even in Jimmy's condition, this was not easy, but he stuck to the job, which took three days, until it was in place and could be used for cooking and radiant heat on cold nights. He did not return again to the cabin except to keep an eye on it. Ralphie did, indeed, make a visit in July, and Jimmy watched him from a safe distance, having no interest in saying hello. Ralphie spent a few minutes scratching his head about the condition of the place, but since he was well into the first half of his day's fifth, he did not puzzle all that much. He stayed the night and left early the next day to make it back upstate before he got too drunk to drive. In his case, that was a very relative judgment that might have been questioned closely by a statie.

Jimmy added to his tools as needed, ordering some through his boss. He got a chain hoist with lots of log chain, a better handsaw—no chainsaws for him anymore—and a good adze for shaping timbers. His concession to modern building came in the roof, which he did not want to mess with ever again. He got rough-cut hemlock from a local mill, delivered in amounts that he could get in-country with his sledge in a single trip, and later bought good shingles. By cutting long poles to form tripods, he was able to raise the roofbeams up into their appointed notches with the chain fall, and by midsummer, the roof was done. He did not let up, but breathed a sigh of relief as he banged the last nail in place on the ridge cap. This was what he had been dreading, and now the hardest part was behind him. He framed out the window openings and doorways carefully, sealing the wood tight against the rough stone. A trip to the lumber yard secured what windows, doors, and casings he needed to fill those orifices, and he hauled them up the same way he had the lumber.

Despite the long hours of work at the shop and now on his dwelling, he still had time to grow a small garden. The soil was good, and he was pleased to have a ready supply of fresh vegetables. He planned the garden spot carefully and laid it out so it could be expanded in later years as time became available. Right now, his main concern was the house. He would leave the barn until the following year but thought he might need it. A small livestock holding would be good, he thought, and whenever an hour or two came by with nothing immediate on his plate, he began clearing brush from the meadow, converting it into a field for grazing and hay. He envisioned a time when his trips to town might be few and far between. They could never totally halt, however. There was no way to avoid a continuing need for money and consumer goods. That would be totally unrealistic. Likely, the diesel shop would close when the old man died or retired, but there were lots of gypsy operations that could use his talents, and he was not concerned about that. He could bullshit with the best of them. And he was not beyond the need for sex, especially given the miraculous state of this health after what he had done to his long-suffering body over the years. His friendship with the librarian was going along nicely, and he had some hope it might go very well indeed. In the meantime, he had the modest beginnings of a nest egg tucked away in his new dwelling. Even given the needs of his construction project, he had a little left over at the end of a week and thought it wise to save against a time of sickness or other problems. He was no longer trying to hide, but if he were to be found now, he might once again feel the pull of civilization and his family, and he had made his choice.

Of course, he missed his wife and family still and always would. But he knew they were really better off without him. He had been a drunken bum. She had stuck with him out of a sense of loyalty and because he was always a good provider. But love can only help you overlook so much. It would take someone with a very peculiar attitude. Now they might, but only someone with a very peculiar attitude about life and a willingness to live in the wild could have any kind of relationship with him now. But that thought always brought him up short. Who *was* he now? And, equally important, why had he become what he was? Despite a lot of time to think about such matters, no answers were forthcoming.

Certainly he could conclude that the fight with Larry had precipitated all this. That was a given. But what had actually happened that day? Why had they fought in the first place? His decision to assume this admittedly strange life was as certain on that late spring morning at the instant the rock had crushed the poor boy's skull as it could be, he now knew. It had not evolved over time with some later revelation when he found he was not being sought by the law. It was there just waiting to be discovered and acknowledged. And perhaps it had been inevitable for eons before they were born. In fact, he had, of late, been going through periods when he felt no remorse for his actions. He never thought that he was acting under some external control, or that he was not at fault; rather, he felt that what happened *needed* to happen and that he and Larry had simply obliged. They were the right people at the right place at the right time. It was an act that was generated between them and played out with unknown consequences for them both.

He came to understand that what had happened to him was only half the puzzle. What had happened to Larry afterwards? He realized that he desperately needed to know that. He also knew, conversely, that Larry needed to know what happened to him. Given that he was now in a part of the world that even the U.S. Geological Survey did not know existed, he figured it would be up to him when the time came to make the first move. In the meantime, he would keep tabs on Larry if he could. He had a hunch Larry would turn up somewhere in a very public way.

Jimmy spent the rest of that summer getting the house ready for winter. He boxed in the fireplace at the northwest end of the house with small fieldstones so that he could use the bulldog stove. Fireplaces were romantic, but terrible for heating. The other he left with a temporary plug in the chimney flue so he could use it in the normal manner when the spirit moved him. He did like a fire in the fall to heat his spirit, if not his body, as the days grew short. He furnished the place with old furniture from secondhand stores and the omnipresent yard sales. The librarian, Emma (he was now on a first-name basis with her), would drop his purchases off near the access to his trail and he would sledge them up the hill. He covered the walls with old carpets, since insulation was out of the question on the rock walls. He later learned that this was a trick done in ancient castles when his voracious reading habit took him to mediaeval history. He was able to insulate the roof, however, thanks to his wise decision to use "conventional" techniques and materials, assuming the word conventional could ever be used about anything in Jimmy's life. He amassed a large pile of good split hardwood and stored it in the barn. He put up more reinforcing poles to keep the snow from caving in the tarps and hoped for the best. It was all he could do that year. The barn would come later. Fortunately, there was ample hardwood in the valley for some time to come, and he was able to cut the wood on-site and haul it with his sledge. He would cut the following winter's wood from outside the little valley. The coming winter's snows would make hauling easier. A small pulling pony was sounding like a better and better idea. And maybe a goat for milk. That would await the finished barn and a fully functional hayfield. One purchase he made was curious. He bought a mirror. He did not shave nor cut his hair, so that was not an issue, but every morning he would get up and look at his reflection and try to assess just who it was looking back at him.

Summer ended, and he was as ready as possible. Given his capacity for work, that was more than ready enough. The winter passed as the first had, but with Jimmy reading even more. He continued his efforts to get the education he had never gotten before, and by spring, when he had to back off to get going on his various projects, he was working from college-level mathematics, biology, physics, and history texts. He was single-minded in this, so it went well. While doing this, he also began to read books on philosophy and ethics, always hoping to find an author who could tell him what was going on in his life. But that was not likely, and he knew it. If nothing else, though, it would give him the known body of information he needed so badly to carry the quest forward and make sense of it all on his own.

And his many trips to the library paid off handsomely in another way. It was now not unusual for him to spend a night under a roof in a house heated by an oil furnace, in a nice bed. And the librarian had a television, which amused him no end. And Emma, long a widow and a very bookish, introspective sort, turned out to be a match for Jimmy in many ways. Jimmy broke down and brought her up to his little valley on occasion. Though Emma had lived in this tiny town all her life, and though her dear, dead husband had been an active outdoorsman, she could not rightly say she had even heard of the place, let alone talked to anyone who had visited it. The one time she tried to surprise him with a dinner that could be warmed up, she failed utterly to find the path. Jimmy was not surprised to hear tell of this and warned her off trying it again for her own safety.

It was several years before he was able to get a lead on Larry. He ultimately called Larry's old pal Eban, disguising his voice as best he could. He said he was a friend from his days in the area and had lost track. Not really a lie. Given that he now sounded like an educated man himself, also not a lie, it was not a hard ruse to pull off. Eban told him Larry had gotten a job at a university in Cambridge, Massachusetts, and was now a physics professor. This was all Jimmy needed. He began asking Emma for help in searching journals for evidence of what he was doing. Given his new relationship with her, she put a lot more effort into it than she otherwise might have. He got her to write for a catalog from the school to see what it had to offer about the faculty. Ultimately, he began a collection of Larry's articles as they came out, and he ended up with nearly all of them, including his own copy of Larry's book on the formation of storms. Understanding them was another issue, but Jimmy was dedicated, and textbooks on the physics of the atmosphere arriving by interlibrary loan began making round trips up into the surrounding hills on a regular basis. He kept voluminous notebooks of careful documentation, all handwritten, on his studies, both scientific and otherwise. "Who woulda thunk it?" mused Jimmy.

But still there were no answers to the basic question that haunted him, nor did he expect to find them on his own. East Asian religious philosophy, the mystical Muslims called Sufis, ancient Celtic rites all were queried. There were a few leads here. The Celts had a great deal to say about the role of ash trees in their cosmology, and another glimmer penetrated the gloom when he began his trek through Jewish kabbalistic mysticism. The Zen texts held even more interest for him, and he read everything he could find. One winter's night he sat looking at a dying fire in the fireplace. He had opened it up for use just so he could see the flames, despite its obvious inefficient use of fuel. That did not matter just then. He was "dreaming the fire," as people had done since it had been tamed millennia past. He was not desperately searching for answers just now, not even really thinking about his problem, or about anything much at all. He was *mostly* at peace with himself, the person who always looked back at him from the mirror. And he was at complete peace with the forest. But he remained, as always, aware of a barrier dating back to that day in the ash grove that accounted for needing to add the "mostly." Without a sound, without warning, without fanfare or the pealing of angel's trumpets, he felt the barrier disappear into the fire.

This wrought no huge change in Jimmy. Massive real-world growth and changes had already happened over time as he had continued on his path to master the Way of the Forest. But the darkness that had begun so suddenly that day in June so long ago, and that had shadowed him over that long span of years, dropped away.

But what of Larry? He had been given the same commission and the same burden. And he had not been as fortunate as Jimmy in his choice of support group. Jimmy had the forest, Larry had Cambridge, Massachusetts, and they were not equally useful for what was afoot. Larry deserved a leg up. This new task would require more study. He had to transform from pupil to teacher. With what he now knew, he thought he could make a start. Year gave way to year, and one hot, humid day in early August, when he felt he had all the tools he could muster, he sat down and wrote out a short invitation to the dance.

16

Larry awoke to the smell of coffee brewing and spicy, sage-laden pork sausage frying. He had slept well and was relieved that there was no trace of a hangover. He and Eban had packed away quite a lot of beer last night, and he wasn't too sure how he would feel this morning. He wasn't as young as he used to be, and neither was his liver. He dressed quickly and packed his kit. He didn't want to miss a minute of time with Eban. He wished he had awakened earlier, but he must have needed the rest. He always had strange, troubling dreams when he slept past the time he should be awake, but none had come to him that he remembered. These dreams were usually of a piece. He would be doing something that was time sensitive, like trying to buy bus tickets or get a lecture prepared, and he would be constantly frustrated. It was always better just to get up and get the day going.

Eban was happily working in the kitchen. Before going to bed the night before, he had put up a batch of sourdough for pancakes. He kept a starter going, the same one that his late wife had nurtured for many years, and he could not let himself be the one to let it die after all that time. Larry had had pancakes from the selfsame starter a fair fraction of a century ago and it was old then. Eban had learned how to take care of it and how to use it properly before his wife could no longer function well enough to explain. Now, he was good at it. Larry wondered how many men would do such a thing. To keep the starter going, it needed to be used frequently, and Eban ritually made pancakes every Sunday, just for himself. For himself and his wife's ghost, Larry thought.

He took out the starter for the next batch and conveyed it to the refrigerator. Only then did he bring out the eggs, milk, and oil. If you forgot and put in those ingredients before taking out the cup or so for the future, it could spell the end of your starter; you could not have eggs and milk rotting in there. Only water, wild yeast, symbiotic bacteria, and flour were in the starter itself. With skill and patience, one might resurrect a clean culture from the starter's container, which would not be washed but simply left with its dregs on a plate covering the developing dough. He quickly beat in the other ingredients, and then put in a little sugar to make them brown, baking soda to make them rise, and salt. When he gently folded in these dry ingredients in, the batter looked even more alive than it had before, and the bowl had a curious hollow sound to it if you tapped it. He started to ladle out batter onto the griddle, which had been heating on the wood range.

"Hear the ghost last night?"

"And who might that be, Henry Hudson?"

"I thought I'd told you 'bout that. My wife and I used to call him 'the guy who's here.'"

"Oh yeah, now I remember. Been a while. No, I didn't hear him this time, but I recall I did last time I was by. Middle of the day it was too." Larry was just a little fuzzy in the head, after all. Coffee and lots of juice would help that. That and a good climb up a mountain to sweat the aldehydes out of his bloodstream.

"He comes when he wants to."

"Right. You hear a sound like a vehicle pullin' into the driveway, and then its door slams. After that, you feel absolutely sure that someone is about to knock on the door. Pretty creepy."

"We used to have a lot of fun with visitors who didn't know about it. We'd be sitting around talking, maybe having supper, maybe a few coolies, and that sound would happen. Them folks'd finally git real nervous and go to look out the window or even go to the door. Then we'd tell them all about it. Good for a laugh, but what the hell is it, really? Everyone hears it, and everyone has that same strange feeling that there is someone about to knock on the door. Hard to fool all of us ta once."

"I don't believe in ghosts, Eb. But I think we really hear something. I just don't know what it is. If we ever find out, I really do hope it is an honest-to-goodness ghost. If there are ghosts, there must be other things out there, like devils and maybe even gods."

Their conversation was punctuated by the odd car traveling down the road past Eban's farm. In the old days, these farms were built near the road to avoid snow-removal problems. Traffic had been horse-drawn back then. Perhaps it was just that it was so quiet most of the time that when a vehicle intruded, it stood out. Both Larry and Eban noticed it.

"Guess it was 'bout three years back that all traffic come to a halt here." Eban started in without preamble. "The bridge 'cross the little creek down in the ravine was getting' kinda tuckered out, so the state give the town money to replace it. They left one a them rubber hoses connected to a counter out there for a week or so and figgered they wasn't 'nuff traffic to bother 'bout tryin' to do it one lane at a time." Closed the road, they did. Took 'em all summer to finish the job too." 'Twas a God's honest blessin'."

"So how did you get to town? You must have gone all the way back around the hill and in on the county road."

"Yup, and worth ever' minute of the time. I pace my trips to town enaway."

"I'm guessing there was some entertainment value in all of this."

"Ya got that right on the money. They put up big signs sayin' the bridge was out, and that the road was open for local traffic only, in a buncha places up and down the pike. Didn't make no difference. They'd come roaring past here like they was *no way* that sign could apply to *them*! They'd screech to a halt down by the site, could tell they was all pissed off. Workers put up a coupla big piles of gravel, kinda staggered like so's ya had to go around each of 'em, ta keep folks from gittin' a run on it an' kitin' off into the drink. Creek is deep right there. For quite a while they was working on the foundation, so they wasn't nothin' goin' across the creek but air. Idiots would drive around the piles, figgerin' they would just drive over whatever was there. Wan't nothin' there. They would light up their tires and haul ass back past the house like the devil hisself was behind 'em . Kind of tapered off towards fall when word finally got around to all the cowboys. I liked the silence a lot."

"I could get used to that kind of silence myself pretty fast too."

Once again, Eban was struck by the sable light that lurked behind Larry's eyes. He had not been that way before he was hurt, and Eban always wanted to probe this, to find out what had really happened. He never did. It simply was not done in the world he inhabited. You left a man to his darkness, and if he wanted to tell you what was on his mind, he would. If you pushed, you might find out things that would be better left alone anyway. There was no ritual exorcism you could invoke. The incident with Blandsford had apparently been caged up in past, and Eban resolved to leave it so. People still talked about it once in a while. Jimmy's wife and children still lived in the area. After he had been declared legally dead, she had gotten remarried, happily, with the nice man she had been living with. She had had no more children, but she and Jimmy now had grandchildren. Wherever Jimmy had gone, he should know that. A man should know he had grandchildren. If Jimmy were anywhere and in any shape to know anything. For no special reason, Eban thought Jimmy was still out there somewhere and had one of his hunches that Jimmy knew a lot of things now that he had not known all these years gone.

The breakfast over, Larry reluctantly said his goodbyes to his old friend. As things went, the chances of seeing him again were not good. He resolved, as he always did, to make more time for the few close friends he had in this world, most dating back to the time before the fight. He did ask if he might use Eban's phone for one quick call before he left.

He checked in his pocket as he headed out for Peekamoose, almost expecting the note to be gone, a figment of his imagination, but it was still there. He carried it with him constantly, in a small plastic folder to protect it from sweat and other pocket-induced damage and puzzled over it greatly. It was his summons, his reason for being here in the Catskills again, heading out to climb a lonely mountain on the day of the autumnal equinox. It was handwritten with a fountain pen in a careful script that looked practiced, as though the writer had much occasion to write, depended on the legibility of the product, but had no access to a computer or word processing software. He knew no one with such penmanship. The note had come in August, postmarked the tenth of that month. There was no signature and no return address. The message was straightforward:

"It's been a long time, Larry, but I think the time has been well spent by us both. You and I have matters to discuss, perhaps ultimately to attend to. I shall be on top of Peekamoose on the evening of the autumnal equinox, upcoming. You should plan to stay the night. My hospitality is crude, so bring your own accommodations."

Larry was both puzzled and deeply concerned by this. There could be no doubt as to who this was from. But how could it be Jimmy? The message was clearly the work of an intelligent person, skilled in letters and no stranger to putting his thoughts down on a page in a terse, effective manner. How could a man who was a junior-high school dropout learn to avoid splitting infinitives, or care if they were or even what they were? Where did he learn that one ought to say *shall* instead of *will* with regard to all but the strongest statements of intent? Such grammatical niceties had come home to Larry only after being castigated by journal reviewers and editors in the early years of his career. It still was unnatural for him to use such precise speech in his social writing and conversation, and he did not do so. But there was no one else it could possibly be. Matters to attend to, indeed.

He headed the old Rabbit up the road toward Peekamoose Mountain—a short drive, less than half an hour. It was still relatively early, and there was frost remaining in the deeper shadows as he climbed up out of Grahamsville. The day promised to be dry and cool, good climbing weather. Only a few light clouds were in the sky at this point, but he reckoned the afternoon might bring some larger cumulus. His mind was at a slow idle as he took in the foliage. It was more advanced than in the low country he had traversed on his way over from Boston yesterday. This was a time of year that he loved a great deal. He hesitated to call it his favorite time of the year, thus denigrating other times, but other months had to work pretty hard to make equal footing with late September and early October. During these months, and even into November, he could feel the buildup toward winter and imagine the crystalline months to come. But it was all make-believe. December would bring rain and usher in four months of March. He called it "Das Gebiet ewiger März" to confer upon it a Germanic, scientific solemnity as something he loathed. There would be days in the fifties in January, and if it snowed at all, it would turn to rain and make sopping-wet slush that would freeze into dangerous ruts. Once in a while there would be a biblical blizzard, melted to brown dross in a few days. But you could still count on fall, even as the earth tumbled to its doom.

He found the pull-off for the trail, and the car crunched to a halt on the gravel which was overgrown with weeds. There were no other cars, and he had expected to see none. He rummaged around in the back of the car to get his kit together. The backpack was all ready to go, and his canteens were full. He had food and snacks enough for both days, plus a reserve for emergencies. He was an old mountain hand. This meant not that he could just jump up and head out on a moment's notice, but that he spent considerable time and care in preparation. He double-checked things he had double-checked before. He had matches, geological survey map, a compass, a whistle, bandages, painkillers, a sheath knife, and plenty of layers of clothing. Such apparent old-biddy fussiness had brought him back from mountains that had killed many who were less well prepared. They had killed some who were more prepared as well. Larry approached any mountain as he would an old friend, but one who was very strong and given to fits of bad temper.

He set up one of his many hi-tech collapsible walking sticks and he was ready.

The path was poorly marked, and only someone who knew the way would even suspect that there was a good path up the mountain at all. The path improved as it went up, but the impression one got was that the mountain was not inviting visitors. In truth, no mountain ever "invited" visitors, but you could forget that when you saw a nice well-traveled trail marked with cute little hand-carved signs and arrows made by volunteers.

His progress was slow at first. This section of the trail was both steep and soft—a bad combination. One might easily slip and terminate the hike on such terrain. He was glad to have worn his hiking boots with the deepest lug soles and the green trail conservationists be damned. The trail was visible, but no one had been through this way in a long time, certainly not in the last several weeks. The hunting was poor in this area, with little deer food and less for upland birds. If hunters did not come up this way, then the place would be very lonely indeed at this time of year. Larry's grandfather had kidded him about his choice of places to settle after college. He said the country was so poor that the bears got so hungry they had to lean them up against the trees. Larry could almost believe it as he looked around.

He hit his pace at about the time the path leveled out for a spell. His long, ground-eating strides carried him at a rate that few could match for long in this rough country, yet he did not seem to get out of breath, nor was he trying to rush. He was just geared right for what he was doing. But the sound he made in the dry newly fallen leaves was almost deafening. There would be no way to hunt this land now, even if there had been game. Only soft snow could muffle his passage, and that was more than a month away. He was not hunting anyway, and soon the sound of his rustling passage disappeared from his mind, filtered out by his aimless thoughts. He felt that he should be preparing himself for what was to come, but since he could not in any way presage what that might be, he elected to let his mind ramble to pleasant times and good friends long gone. He never felt alone in the woods, and their vastness never overwhelmed him. He was more alone on the streets of Cambridge, because the ever-present crowds served to separate him from himself, and then he was truly without a companion.

It was not long before he began to climb in earnest. The path grew steeper but was fairly dry and open. A few rocks made the going a bit slower, but with his stout staff as a prop, he could afford to take the odd chance on his next step without fear of falling. He broke into a good sweat and stopped just long enough to peel off a couple of layers. The day was warming, and now there was no trace of frost. He felt the perspiration trickle down his back where the undershirt did not contact his skin, and he relished the sensation. Unlike his (ex-)wife, who hated sweat both on herself and on him, even when exercising, he felt at his best when soaked through from the inside out. The metabolic byproducts his liver had created from the beer of the night before were soon leaching into the fabric of his clothing and troubled him no longer.

After a good solid hike upwards, he reached a steep rock wall. It was not a vertical wall or cliff, nor was it even solid rock, but for all of that, it was high angled enough. He had to climb hand over hand, taking care with his footing. There was no exposure here, as he had seen in so many climbs over his lifetime in the high places, but it was enough of a challenge to make him feel he was going to earn the summit. The pitch was soon past, and he regretted that it was so short. You could make a lot of good vertical gain in no time on such ground. And he had done so. Now he was into a markedly different part of the forest. There were fewer softwoods, although he recalled that they reached almost to the summit. But the leaves were thinner here. He had reached a later part of the season, and it looked more like mid-October than late September, even comparing things to Grahamsville. Eban's farm sat at an elevation of almost 1,800 feet, and that was far below him now. He was neither in the Rockies, nor Denali Park, nor the Andes, but high places were all part of a brotherhood and shared universal characteristics, even when their summits were not perched on the edge of outer space.

It was not long to the summit from here, but the path was still inexorably upward. He reached an area that was lightly wooded and then hit the broad, flat area that meant he was there. He had made good time: it was not yet noon. There was still a small cone to climb to the real summit, but owing to small scrub conifers there, the view from where he stood was the best the top had to offer. He dropped his pack near where he had pitched a tent in the distant past and drank deeply from his canteen to replace the water that he now carried in his clothing. He fixed part of the problem with a change of shirt and undershorts, leaving his wet things to dry in the sun. He was now comfortable and ready for the last few feet to the top.

The tiny summit cone was only perhaps twenty or thirty feet higher than where he now stood, but it held a mystery that he wanted to contemplate further. On its side, along this last remnant of the trail, there was a tiny spring. It dripped bitterly cold water into a miniature mossy grotto all summer long, even in the dry months. The water was cold and delicious, and he remembered it well from his previous climbs. The question that puzzled him, back then and now, was where the water came from. He could not feel its course, and this was unusual. He had dowsed for water several times for Eban's neighbors when he lived there. He never took a cent for the service, although he accepted the odd cold beer. Water was hard to come by in these hills. People had to drill wells to four, five, and even six hundred feet to find good veins. Sometimes they had to drop charges of dynamite down to crack open veins and use two-stage submersible pump systems just to get the water to the surface. Yet within sight of the drilling rig, there could be a spot where the water gushed right out of the ground, forming the headwaters of a small brook. Larry had been able to use his unusual skills to shave the odds when folks asked him to dowse their property. He would use the traditional forked stick, but that would just be for show. He would stick a willow branch in the ground where he thought they should drill, and that would be that. No one who called Larry to witch the ground ever drilled more than sixty feet.

But he could not feel this flow. It must be passing strange, he thought. It was a real spring. There was not enough surface for rainwater to collect above the little grotto to keep it full all year long, especially when it did not rain regularly. This was among the unsolvable mysteries that Larry treasured.

The short jaunt to the top took just a few minutes, and he stayed only a short while, solely to say he'd made it to the top. This occasioned a thought about a climb in the Himalayas he'd read about years ago. The top of that particular virgin peak was considered sacred, and the climbers gave their word that after achieving the small plateau at the summit, they would not go up the final few feet to the top of the tiny summit cone. There was no one there to attest one way or the other to their claims that they had obeyed, but Larry knew mountaineers, and he knew they had done as asked.

There was camp to make, and plenty of chances to look at the view, which was best to the south and west from here. It was difficult to see Slide and the other higher mountains to the north, but the lower hills to the south were in full color, and he was not concerned about getting a complete view at this point. The full import of what was to come had finally migrated to the center of his thoughts and now occupied most of his mind. For a practiced hand, making camp was a simple task requiring little thought. The tent went up in no time, then he unpacked his camp gear and got out his modest lunch. He cleared a wide space of forest duff and repaired the stone circle that had served generations as a fire pit. He did not have a forest warden's campfire permit, and he was in Catskill State Park, but since it was not yet deer season, and the rangers and wardens were busy with bird hunters in the cornfields and abandoned apple orchards below, in addition to the omnipresent deer jackers, he was fairly sure he could get away with a small fire. He wandered back down the trail for a quarter mile or so and got several loads of dead branches that were of no use to the trees anymore, except as fertilizer for growth several years down the line. They were nicely dry and would yield little smoke. He would need a fire for its light and warmth on his body and spirit, and his experience was such that he was not afraid of it getting away from him.

He ate his lunch and rested quietly with his thoughts. He slept a bit in the afternoon, made tea from the tiny spring's water, read a few pages in a novel he had brought along, and settled his mind into an easy space.

He was not someone with a low tolerance for boredom. He could sit and watch dawn from first light to full sunup and never feel a single moment dragging. His thoughts were rich and complex and could entertain him for hours. It was the same with driving, although he did not feel this in Boston; he was too busy fighting for his life in Boston. But on moderate-to-long trips, like the one that brought him here, he would just settle in and tell himself stories, or characterize nonlinear dynamic systems with Jacobean matrices (if he ran out of other things to do in his head). Or, perhaps, he would make up a story about wizards and dwarves that he could write up and sell one day when he finally retired. Like Mozart, he retained them once "written" in his mind, and he probably would be able to sit down at a word processor and whip out a draft as fast as he could type.

The sun was westering, and he started his small fire. He used his antique Svea stove to cook a meal of pea soup from a dry mix with some crumbled smoked meat. He promised himself that after this trip, he would eat only beans and rice, washed down with bottled spring water, until Thanksgiving. And he would throw in lots of cooked vegetables and dark-green salads too. The meal was delicious in the way such meals can only be in wild, lonely places after hard exercise. In his apartment in Cambridge, it would have been in the disposal before it was half gone, but here, it was sumptuous. He could remember many such meals scattered liberally over his long life, in those times when he was free from roofs and walls. If he really worked at it, he thought, he might be able to isolate and remember them each individually, but he knew that was an illusion. A harmless one, unlike so many others that were not.

He poured some water into the pan he had chosen from the aluminum cook set to heat the soup in, and contemplated how he might summon the energy to clean up. He had not gotten far on this mighty challenge when he heard quiet footfalls, very close. He was puzzled at how anyone could have climbed up through that deep sea of dead leaves without making a sound, and then he decided it was both unimportant and potentially unknowable. In fact, he assumed that the caller was making sound now only as a courtesy, in the manner of slamming the car door loudly in the driveway to alert the inhabitants before knocking on the door. The figure was still visible in the gathering twilight, and what Larry could see of him was of considerable interest. He walked with purpose. It was like the movement of great martial artists. Not the movie actors who trained more as gymnasts, but the truly great ones. These were the men and women who spent their lives learning to put their spirit, the very essence of their being, into their movements; "moving Zen," it had been called appropriately. It was not an arrogant swagger, as the Samurai affected, but a simple, easy walk that rooted the person to the earth for the tiniest fraction of a second each time his or her foot hit the ground. These were roots that went to the feet of the mountain and beyond; they were severed in the instant and turned to the lightness of air, only to be reformed with each step. Such a walk kept the centers of both the body and the spirit always at the point of balance. And the man seemed ageless, though he must be in his seventies.

He walked into the circle lit by the fire and sat easily and lightly across the firepit.

"Larry."

"Jimmy."

17

Jimmy was thin and wiry. He looked as though his tough hide would deflect an axe, like a knotty chunk of oak, but trying to hit him with that axe might prove both very difficult and a terribly bad idea. He had long white hair and beard, both of which appeared to have reached a point where they could grow no longer. His hair, for all its might, looked freshly washed and combed. His clothing was worn, and patched in many places, but appeared clean. He did not have the sour odor about him that spoke of a man given to sleeping in rotting underwear night after night the way urban derelicts do, and there was no crust of grime around his ears either. Larry assimilated all this in an instant, and his wonder at the sight grew into awe. So, this man, who could barely make it through the local shopping news rag in search of bargains on woods equipment, had learned that infinitives were not boldly to be split, and when he *should* use *shall.* Jimmy looked tougher and fitter than almost anyone he had ever seen, and he had seen very fit people in full measure. There were many things to be learned here, and he was anxious to start.

"I think you'll be glad to hear that I quit smoking, Larry. Happened really fast one June day, back a few years. You were there at the time, actually, but you probably don't remember it. You won't have to sidle around to get out of the effluent."

"I was that obvious?"

"Yes, and I thought it was pretty funny at the time. Don't feel embarrassed, I'd do the same now myself. You know, I used to try to get upwind to annoy you; made it kind of a game."

"Funny, I didn't catch that. Probably should have. Must have been tough back then. They have gum and patches for that now. Even my mother quit. Too late to help her any, but she did it."

"It wasn't that bad, really. My last pack was wet, and so were the matches. I wasn't anywhere where I could get another pack for a spell, and when I did get to a place I could buy them, I had kind of lost the urge. Plus, I had a whole hell of a lot of friends urging me on."

They were completely at ease with one another from the start. This surprised but did not trouble Larry. Jimmy was equally untroubled, but not at all surprised.

"So, Jimmy, where you been all these long, long years?"

"Long story. But we have time, and a short version of it is off the table. And you're not the only one with questions. I will go first."

And he did just that. And the number of questions Larry had rose exponentially.

"How in hell did you become a man of letters? Shit, I knew the note had to come from you, but how the hell did you write it? Meaning no offense, of course. I simply could not believe it on a rational level, so I kept thinking this was some practical joke. But I didn't believe that, deep down. Couldn't be. Knew it was you."

"I get down out of here regularly, even early on, and I read a lot, especially in the winter. No one remembers the "big fight" in Grahamsville up around where I hang out. I doubt more than a few people remember it in Grahamsville anymore. I even have a library card in my own name. I have the librarian too. Emma never told anyone anything after she found out about how I came to be the weird hermit everyone scares their kids with on Halloween. I had to tell her the whole nine yards. Of course, she's retired now. So, I have had some happiness and companionship, for what it's worth, which is a lot to me. We are growing old together. She moved in with me. Imagine that. Of course, she had to semi-disappear too. Took some work and a few white lies, but now we have her whole retirement and the bucks from selling her house in green money, and I don't need to go to town so much anymore. I mail off my letters to the editor, op-ed pieces, and still make the important hearings. Never met a developer I didn't hate. I have success at my task of keeping the forest safe, mostly. Not always.

"Where I live and the way I live, you can't have it both ways. I don't think even she could leave the hills now and still get back, even with me to guide her, but I am not sure. I would hate to test the rules. I even have to obey those rules. Fortunately, she is not restless. She is about my age, and for her, sitting around the fireplace and reading or dreaming the fire are good things to do, and they are a great sufficiency, to paraphrase Antonius Bloch. Me, I still need to roam the woods. I keep finding new hidden paths out here, and I don't lose the old. The new librarians know me and let me browse the Internet in their computer cluster. I even found your home page at the university. I thought I might hack it, leave a little message in there for you, but I didn't want to tip my hand until I had what I needed."

"I hope you don't mind me prying, but how the hell do you afford health care? Christ, I have a full package and I still worry."

"I don't *get* sick. And now neither does Emma. We have our own health package with my employers." Which made a lot more sense to Larry just then than it might have a few days earlier. Real sense.

"Seems like it must be pretty hard to stay hidden up here, especially in the summers or hunting season."

"There are places in these mountains that are very hard to get to for most folks, and it is not a physical barrier. You must have unlimited access to satellite images. Even the view from outer space can't see what I see." Larry used those images extensively, and would look, next chance he got.

"I know about those places Jimmy. All too well. And I also know they are even harder to get back to when you find them and then have to leave."

"I see you are more aware about this part of the world than you ever let on Larry."

"I know a lot about mountains in general, and I know a lot about these in particular. I am, as they say, a 'close study' from way back. I dreamed about them all the time as a kid, and I almost think the dreams were showing me something real."

"They were. Trust me on this, but don't ask me how I know; I have no idea. I could even take you back again to one of those places, maybe help you find the others if you could give me a description, but I don't think that would be a particularly good idea unless you have been invited. I am not authorized to send those invitations. You see, I am not in upper management. Emma was invited, and that has worked out. I think some small part of the reason she wanted to quit the town was so when her time comes she could be buried in such a spot."

"I don't think it's in the cards for me, Jimmy. And even if I did get an invitation to visit from your colleagues, the pain I felt after those dreams, every time I lost the way back, was unendurable. I might not want to leave, like your Emma. I couldn't stand that kind of pain ever again. And there are things I still have to do out in civilization. But you know that already. I bet you even know about what that might entail. It's my half of the *bargain* we made that day if that was what it was."

"And given what you know of these mountains and what they mean, you probably know more than you think about what I am all about. My part of the *bargain*, as you call it."

"So, you wander the hills and read a lot. And you visit my home page. What do you know about what I'm doing? Let's see how far we can push this into the surreal before we have to stop for a reality check."

"OK, Larry, guess it is your turn to field questions. No need to come up with a long biography; I know what you've been up to, pretty much. This place is not a prison for me, and you are not a private person when it comes to your work."

"Yeah, that part I know, but I really have tried hard to keep my personal life out of the public sector. I bet that feature in the Sunday *Globe* helped you get a handle on some of that too. It's amazing what those reporters can get out of you, even when you try to keep it pretty close to the vest."

"Yeah, got two copies of that saved. Me, privacy was not a problem.

"Some stuff got left out. You obviously know I went back to school, I managed to build a career that has meaning, Andrea and I had a kid who's actually pretty much OK. Got a few issues he could use some help with, but maybe I can get Andrea to give me a hand with that. She has gotten over the 'Larry is the root of all evil' kick. We might be able to work together again on something that important. And I love my work. I'll get out of there in a few years, though. I don't want to work much past seventy. That's a good time to open the position to the next person in line. Give another generation a chance at it. Then I can get back out here where it's real. I figure New Hampshire, maybe up near Squam Lake. No Boston traffic, lots of trees, good mountains I'll still be able to climb, get back to wood heat, and maybe, if I am lucky and don't wait too long, it will still snow up there.

"Of course, Andrea dumped me for some guy she met at work. That was a rough one for me. I am still working that one over. Still rattles me to think of them in bed, even after all this time. Fucking asshole kissing *my* old lady with that filthy ashtray he uses for a mouth. You'd think you could put that in the past, but apparently we are hardwired. Got a new woman, though, and that helps a lot. She's really nice."

"So, let's get down to business on your work. I don't have the head for math to follow you all the way, Larry. I bet I could blow you away with Kierkegaard or Lao Tzu, but functions of a complex variable are pretty rough sledding for the self-taught, even on long winter evenings with nothing else to do. But I know a lot about your field conceptually. I did read your primary textbook. Own a copy, and it is full of highlighting. You know, I have to say, you don't have what you might call a lively prose style. Meaning no offense, of course. At least you put in some words with the equations."

"I pride myself on that. We use math as a tool in our work, and as our first language to describe what we see to other physicists. It's the best way we have to discover and convey the information. But when you are talking overall driving concepts, math is not enough. You need to use a narrative to get the real meaning behind the science across. Too many papers are full of raw information and have no depth at all. I think the people who hide behind math don't really understand what they are doing at the level where real progress is made. I tried to break that mold."

"Gott sei Dank. By the way, your review in *American Scientist* in May was perfectly on target for duffers like me."

"OK, Jimmy, tell me you are a member of Sigma Xi, and I am outta here."

"No, but I talked the library into subscribing to the journal."

"I'll nominate you when I get back if you want. You can have your own subscription, comes along with the membership."

"Delivery might be a little problematic."

"Right. But you have managed to do almost everything else, why not that?"

"Why not, indeed? But let me see if I am on target about what you are doing. You have studied global warming and climate change right from early in the game. You have been in the thick of the controversy about what greenhouse gases are doing to the climate in general, but your real core work is in modeling the downstream effects of all this extra heat—the ultimate results on the face of the earth. You look at the physics underlying how storms like tornadoes, hurricanes, and microbursts form. This helps when you ask, what would the future climate cook up? Your predictive models keep being right as hard field data roll in. Your latest formulation describing the role of self-organizing atmospheric systems in the formation of killer super storms is starting to look pretty scary. And the heat differentials will grow as the climate warms.

"Tornadoes fascinate me Larry. Get a few around here, even. There was one that touched ground first in Grahamsville when I still lived there, I recall. Started right behind that biker hangout and crossed the reservoir. You can break a severe thunderstorm down into five levels, starting from the ground up. Everything has to be just right in terms of a low-level jet, a flow of cool, dry air, on up to a polar front and an upper-level jet stream at thirty thousand feet. The tornado seems to pull itself together. Seems almost alive."

By this point, Larry did not bat an eye. He felt he was at a conference talking to a colleague. And he did think briefly about the model his computer was running, even as they spoke.

"Nailed it," Larry said. "The trick is figuring out how this plays out against the global models of where the climate is headed. Severe twisters are actually rare, globally. You might not think that here in the U.S. because we have Tornado Alley, but the conditions you describe don't occur many other places. We might actually have fewer days that spawn twisters, but possibly there would be more severe twisters when they do form. That is where I come in. This is information we need.

"But let's jump up a level. What I am most concerned about is what we are going to *do* about all this. The answer, increasingly, seems like "nothing at all." I deal with people that are well-placed in the government. They know what's shaking and share with the likes of me. I am finding that science itself is becoming irrelevant out there where people vote. Climate change itself is being denied. We are told that we are just riding a wave of hysteria to get grant money, which we waste. We are accused of threatening people's livelihoods with our phony dire assessments of continued reliance on fossil fuels. So, my current doctoral student and I will publish her results, which help refine our understanding of how latent heat from seawater fuels hurricanes and what this will mean when the Gulf is the temperature of freshly served tom yum soup. It will echo down an empty hallway. No matter if multiple hurricanes that send huge storm surges along a strip from Houston to Cedar Key will be the norm. Rainfall numbers will defy imagination and might even scare Noah. I predict this atavism will only worsen and become pandemic. There are still flat-earthers, and their number grows. There are so-called scientists who must have gotten the Ph.D.s from Walmart, who are out there in the Grand Canyon trying to prove it formed in a day six thousand years ago. If you lead a protected life where real consequences of your actions never burst in, you can do that. For a while. But it is too late to discover truth when you start to feel your single-wide being lifted up into an EF5. Or when the New York subway system is permanently filled with slimy, stagnant seawater. Or when Bourbon Street in New Orleans is a very popular afternoon scuba excursion."

"Shit!"

It was the first time that Jimmy showed any sort of real emotion. For a man who seemed to be totally in charge of everything, up to and including the welfare of the entire Catskill Mountain range, he was deeply shaken for a moment, and that scared Larry too. Maybe *he* should be even more scared than he now was.

"Yeah. You got that right. Shit!"

"I guess I knew all that, down where it counts, but I desperately hoped to hear better news from you. You walk the corridors of power, after all. I imagined that maybe you saw something there that would give me hope. But as you say, it is an empty corridor with nothing but echoes.

"We are in the same line of work, Larry. You know that, nothing new here. We stand with others on the front lines in this war. You are far more influential than I, of course, but it's the same fight. I might save a few acres of old forest while you might save cities. I have had some success. But, sadly, I have started to run into the same thing. Part of it is fueled by mindless greed, but the bulk is just mindlessness, period. You tell people that clearcutting creates the danger of major flash flooding. If they said, honestly, that they didn't care and are just in it for the buck, that would not be OK, but it would make sense. You can fight that attitude with facts about the economic dangers and so forth, and people who matter will listen. But if they tell you that you are wrong about your assertions, and that you know nothing, and that they know more than you do, that means they have abandoned rational thought. You can't fight raw ignorance when facts and truth no longer mean anything to your opponents.

"I have done much preparation to be able to talk with you, to make it clear I am worth talking to. I want to find out what your work really means, directly from you. I don't think it is arrogant to assume that you have wanted the same back from me. We can link arms in an exact reciprocity. We are now there; we know where we are and what the roads we took were. But what in God's name actually happened back then, and how did it set us off on our new paths?"

Now it was time to dance.

"Let's start with some simple basics, Larry," he continued. "First off, I meant to kill you. Straight out. That's what I wanted to do when I picked up that rock. I hit you as hard as I could. I really thought you were dead. You must have one hard head, man. Shit, I was evil incarnate. That's enough to make a believer out of you."

"But was I good incarnate?"

"Yes, and I have no doubts on that matter at all."

"What are you now?"

"A man, same as you. Nothing more or less. We were only in those strange roles for a short while, by my reckoning. And I think I knew almost immediately that it wasn't you I tried to kill, or even me doing it."

"Why did you as the "Real Jimmy" hightail it, though? I could have been dying. Actually, I *was* dying. You just took off and left me there. They didn't find me until that night, like six o'clock. Maybe that's a good place to start. I'll be honest: I am still pissed off about that happening, and that was the real you by then. That was pretty fucked up, even worse than saying you were done and then popping me one. Caved in my head."

"In some part, I, as 'the real Jimmy,' panicked. No two ways about it. I just grabbed what I could and headed north. There was not much thought or contemplation involved here, Larry, just raw survival instinct. I suppose part of it was that I had no intention of going to prison for what the avatar did. But there was more than that; I knew beyond any possible doubt that my path led into the woods at that point, and I needed to go, like *right now.* Whatever strangeness drove us that morning drove both of us equally. And we were in the thick of it. As you know, you are not alone in this mystery."

"As far as the prison part is concerned, I tried to call them off. I think now, talking to you, that I must have known even then that it wasn't you who was responsible. Did my best to exonerate you, without knowing why. I should have wanted payback. Told them it was an accident, right, sure. I'm a lousy liar. Cops had me on my back wiggling in about a minute flat. I didn't press charges, and I think that helped. I ended up telling them that I would refuse to testify if they did bring you in. You could have walked back into your trailer any time after the first of July and had no more than a few papers to sign. I figured that for you to stay on the lam after you knew you were in the clear, you must have gotten on the same train I was on, and I knew as soon as I woke up, I was on that train. We have both been on it ever since. Finding out your journey was parallel to mine going forward has been truly a wild, compelling trip. But, funny thing is, none of it surprised me once I heard the details."

"I invited you up here to get us to the same place. I had to be the one to start it because I knew where you were and what you were up to all along, and you didn't know squat about where I was. Now we stand even. This is not just for comfort or healing between you and me. It's not just out of curiosity, although I am sure figuring out some answers, if there are any, will be like scratching one hell of an itch. My working vision is that we were in a ritual combat. The roles we played were not decided by us, but perhaps I was more suited to be the 'evil one.' Or maybe someone flipped a coin. But it had to be you and me. For the record, and for what it's worth—which may be nothing whatsoever—I am truly sorry for the physical harm you endured, and the other pain that continues. And I say that not as a player but as me, standing outside of who I may have been then."

"As I said, I don't blame you for what happened. Really. Neither for the fight nor for taking off. Again, that seems like it was completely out of our hands. But I am still cranky in a general way about the scars, and way more about the fucked-up teeth. I would like to know who to complain to, since it isn't you. Ever have a root canal? The eye tooth died back in '85 or '86. I can't remember now. Have a titanium screw in my jawbone holding the replacement. And the head? That dent ached like hell every time a thunderstorm was brewing until maybe '91. OK now. Mostly. But I remain concerned about the pall cast over my life since that day. And I would like to know who to blame for that as well."

"I suffered the same Darkness as you afterwards, but it has eased for me."

"Yeah, the Darkness. Uppercase *D*. I am fairly sure I have been clinically depressed at some more-or-less livable level since the fight, but I never did anything about it. Andrea was always after me to see a shrink. You know the drill: get a diagnosis and then get a 'scrip for your meds. But I don't like the idea of 'fixing' what's wrong with me with chemicals. Prozac nation and all."

"Ah, fluoxetine, a selective serotonin reuptake inhibitor."

By now, Larry did not even blink.

"Yeah, I know it works for lots of people who are now out on the street instead of in darkened bedrooms, but each of us has our own situation. In the main, I think what happens is the patients are elevated to where they should be, and who they really *are*. For them it's like filling a cavity in a tooth. For me it would be different. It's more like I have a piece of shrapnel lodged in my head that is inoperable. A chemical would not touch that, and it would just make me somebody else. I want people to see me, shrapnel, and all, not the drug."

"So that leaves the *why* of the Darkness. And I mean that for both of us, even though mine has passed."

"Bingo. It isn't just my getting my head bashed in that sits at the root—that isn't even particularly important. What has struck me as the core of it all is that finding an answer to why we had that stupid fight in the first place will help a *lot*. Can we get a handle on that?"

"Well, we have made a start by agreeing that we were not directly responsible. But if we were not, what *was*? Sadly, even if we figure it out, it may not help our personal situations in the long run. As you point out, who would we complain to for redress? Once it was all done, I chose to stay up here. I had much to figure out. The bottom line is: look at me now, and compare what you see with the hungover lout that stumbled into the chopping those long years ago. Who would you rather be of the two? And despite the weight you carry, you are far further along than that young fuckup that was happy with minimum wage, a hot chick, and a nice motorcycle. Where would you be now? Want to trade?"

"That is all on the table, no arguments there. But back to the problem—you don't have the answer to what started all this?"

"Not even close, Larry. Let's figure at least some of it out, starting with what we really know, and see where it goes. Maybe nowhere but into our own heads, but at least we will be off top dead center. Tell me what your vision of the fight is. Good place to start."

"Yeah, the fight. I don't think a single day goes by when I don't think about that, at least for a minute or two. And don't ask me why I decided you couldn't cut that accursed tree. I hate that fucking tree. I have hated it all my life. I think I hated that tree in my mother's womb or, like Ahab, a billion years before this mountain rose. And having said that out loud to you, I know it isn't true. I felt I was fighting for my life; if that tree died, I would die, and worse things were out there as well that I could not even imagine, then or now. You were a clear and present danger, an existential threat of doom. I did know at the instant it happened that I should be embracing whatever it was in that tree trunk. And I felt something outside myself there. It was new and overwhelming and a mystery."

Larry related in sharp detail his "sense of flow," relating it to the ash tree and its effect on him. This was information that Jimmy already had, in essence, but he stated it for the record, in a sense, to make it fresh and relevant and fully detailed.

"I used to try to tell Andrea about these 'feelings,' and she never really understood. It kind of freaked her out. You knew I could be counted on for a weather report—most folks did, but I never let on that I knew they were depending on me. I don't think it's anything supernatural or extrasensory. I still believe I see, hear, and feel the same things you do. Maybe by some accident of neurophysiology I process them on a different level, and that adds up to another kind of sense in sum, but it's just one manufactured by my brain from existing pieces. Another reason not to mess with the chemistry in my head. I'd hate to lose that. There was another guy in Grahamsville that seemed to be onto the same thing, so maybe it's not so rare. You at least knew about him and the biker hangout. I got a line on where the guy disappeared to, and I might try to look him up. He's up in Maine; I checked him out this morning with a call to colleagues I knew would be sitting at a computer and on the Net. He's a university professor now too: biology, mathematics, statistics, and bio-resource engineering! Some fucking biker. Ain't life grand?"

"But you felt it in spades that day coursing through the tree."

"Yeah, totally! It felt stronger by an order of magnitude than the aqueduct running under town from the Neversink to the power station. Nothing more specific than that, just that there was a flow of *something*. And as I said, I knew that it would be *bad* if it got interrupted. That's all. And I tried to stop you any way I could. No more idea than the man in the moon what it was, then or now. But the bottom line was that it was changing me, even as we fought. Hell, if that had never happened, you and I might still be cutting trees down below right now."

"Nah, I'd be dead at least twenty years by now. You know, the truth is, I felt something too, maybe something a lot like what you felt. I have a 'thing' with trees, as I told you. I have a 'sense of trees.' And I also think it could be no more than another way of looking at what sensory information I have coming in, just like your weather station. Or not . . . But I fought to destroy it, as I said, and I fell into and used my old Jimmy Blandsford role. 'Daylight in the swamp!' But you were no tree hugger, man. Shit, you made your living butchering trees just as much as I did for a spell. But that one was special, wasn't it?"

"Yeah, really special. And at that instant in time, I or whoever I was at the time was ready to give my life to keep it safe."

"I knew what was there too, in my own tree modality. And I felt I was chosen somehow to destroy it, a kind of champion of the Other Side. You fought well, we both did, with honor and by the rules, right up until the end. And you won the fight by the rules we both adopted. I had no idea where those rules came from that day, though I have since studied them in great detail in other contexts. They are very ancient rules, reserved for extraordinary combat. But after I lost, whatever gripped me and forced me into the fight also robbed me of my honor—and my soul, for a spell—and I was consumed by a blood rage that I couldn't control. I think it was an existential part of me taking on the Evil role. It was a dark atavism that I have never felt before or since and cannot fathom to this day. I could have cut down the tree right then after whacking you, but I didn't even think of doing so. I had a spare saw in the truck, sharp and ready to go. But by that point, I would not have done so, could not have done so. I was belatedly honoring your victory and your sacrifice. The blood rage had completely disappeared, and whatever bond I now have with the forest had asserted itself with the strength of high tensile steel. The act of striking you was the last, essential part of the whole thing. I will come back to the leaving-you-there part in a bit. There may well have been another force there that day, an evil one, and I was the champion of that side. The good guys won, but what a price to pay."

"Cheating on the ancient, sacred rules of the combat must have caused you some real pain over the years."

"I never went back on a deal. Just that once. It would cause me more pain to think I had any say in the matter. There had to be a blood sacrifice."

"I knew that about you and your deals. Everyone said to leave my wallet at home when I went to work or you'd have everything in it and an IOU on top, but if I ever made an agreement with you, it would make reinforced concrete look like cotton candy. Most folks aren't that obsessed with the exact limits of a bargain. There is almost always some flexibility. Why you? Why was it so central to who you were and, presumably, still are?"

"Yeah, I still am obsessed with that. And it was my fucking father that did it to me."

"Was that something that you learned from him?"

Jimmy chuckled quietly and without humor. "You might say that. Dad never honored a deal in his life. He messed around on my mother with every loose woman in a hundred-mile radius. He welched on gambling debts. He never did one thing for me that he said he would do. The man was a steaming pile of shit. I celebrated the day he died. I venerated the crash site as the place where the Grahamsville part of my life really began. The fact that he was so utterly vile was actually what gave me what chance I had in the life I led before the fight. He was so awful that I could see that there was no future in being like him. None at all. One night, he beat the hell out of my mother—after I heard him promise the night before that he would never, ever, as God was his witness, ever lay a hand on her again. That did it for me. I helped her up after he left and cleaned up her face. He really did a good job that time. Knocked out two teeth. That really . . . Oh, yeah, sorry. Sore spot, right? I have a dental plan from my employers too, by the way." He flashed a flawless smile of perfectly straight white teeth, clearly his own.

"I know your 'employers' well myself now. My sense of flow hears them talking in the forest floor. There is a whole community under our feet that I did not recognize at the time, but I know it well now. But I expect you figured that out early on. It's almost like the trees are neurons in some giant brain."

"For sure. Anyway, I swore on everything that I could think of that I would never be like my asshole dad. The one thing I could think of that would set me apart was getting a reputation for keeping my word. It worked too. I always paid my debts in full and on time. If I told you you would have so many feet of hemlock on Friday for so many dollars, *by God*, you had it. To the board inch, and all good wood. 'Jimmy Blandsford's a dumb goddamn prick, but he'll keep his word.' I figured that was good enough. Make a nice epitaph. Doubt I'll have one, though, or a grave. I kind of like that. Who needs six feet of dirt on them when they're dead, with no one around to smell the stink? Skunks and coyotes gotta eat too." The thought of a coyote grinding away disconsolately at that pile of steel-mill shavings brought a momentary flicker of a smile to Larry's face.

"Yeah, now that you mention it, when I got around to telling that detective what happened, he said—and I think these were almost his exact words: 'He went down? You turned around and Jimmy hit you on the back of the head? The *back* of your head? Jimmy? Jimmy *Blandsford* we're talking about here? Not some other Jimmy?' It seemed to really puzzle the shit out of him." He noticed the split infinitive even as he said it and looked over to catch a funny little grin on Jimmy's face.

"You had the rep you worked for."

"Well, that's a piece of evidence showing that I was not working by my usual rules that day. Not that I am going to try to duck out with a temporary-insanity defense. In 20/20 hindsight, I could have and should have wrested control back from whatever it was that was riding me. But as I have said, it was beyond my control, totally. That anomaly is a real datum, and it means we are onto something."

"And I was acting on pure faith Jimmy, something of which I am usually in very short supply. I can't usually accept faith as a driving force. So, I was not abiding by my normal guidelines either. We went for it—and here we are, decades later, trying to put the pieces back together again. You went into the woods, and I went into physics. And we both know a lot more than we did that Thursday. We are like two reagents, prepped in separate crucibles, now being introduced again to see where the reaction goes and what its products might be this time around. But the source of heat is missing, no Bunsen burner in a tree to heat things up."

"Larry don't forget that we are on borrowed time; this interval is like a special dispensation. If we hung out too long, we might find the

Bunsen burner is back. In any event, you are the physicist, my maunderings on the subject to the contrary notwithstanding. I have my own strengths, and one of the things I know a lot about on my side of the fence is Celtic mythology. It was said that there was a conduit between heaven and the underworld, but their underworld was not like our hell. This conduit passed through a sacred ash tree, Yggdrasil. There was power going both ways: up and down, Good and Evil, all mixed in."

"You think that's what we were dealing with? I thought about some forest-spirit animism and rejected it out of hand back then."

"I agree, I am not about to abandon my profound atheism in the context of the Judeo-Christian mythos to pick up some ancient religion as a substitute. Shit, if I were going to do that, I'd start drinking again and worship Bacchus. But remember where we have gotten ourselves to here. We both acknowledge that we process information differently than most folks in two specific areas, and that this does not require us to have ESP. If you perceive something, it is by definition sensory. Both of us sensed something that day through those same modalities. If the ancient Celts had people like us around, then maybe that's where the idea came from in the first place."

"Something is beginning to scratch at the back door of my so-called mind. Have you heard of nonequilibrium thermodynamics?"

"Yeah, you mean Ilya Prigogine's work, among others?"

"Right, Nobel laureate. He began to figure out why things get so interesting when systems are far from equilibrium; the reason entropy can drop to such low levels in one area spontaneously at the expense of an overall increase. Ultimately, it explains how life could form, not by chance, but because such complex systems are literally demanded by laws that govern systems in which there is a lot of energy flow."

"Sure, and I am thinking about our discussion about arguments on how a tornado forms when the right pieces collide. The storm is an area of low entropy. The systems don't just merge and go to a uniform thermal equilibrium: they get organized, and angry."

"Exactly. And I think whatever was moving through the tree that day recruited us. We were caught up as the flow organized itself into a storm. A ritual combat, as we suggested. Hot against cold and you get a whirlwind. We might have been part of a passion play."

"No way you could walk away from that kind of a shitstorm in one piece. And we didn't."

"But we still made decisions, based on who we were then, to go ahead. We were exercising free will, doing what we did for our own reasons, I think. But once we decided to accept the roles, what happened next was not under our control. We were interacting both with each other and with whatever was moving in the world right near us. And we were wielding more power than we could possibly imagine. The fight was an eddy that formed in our part of the universe."

Larry was lost in thought for several minutes, and there seemed to be a point where a bunch of pieces came together.

"Let's consider this alternate idea, Jimmy. Maybe what we felt in that tree was not even external to us at all. It *was* us. Look, we both have these curious talents. What happens when two people like us get together? Maybe the flow was around and between us. I think the fight and its consequences organized themselves in that massive flow of energy. I think the accident that took Karl's arm was part of it building. It's with us now. You can feel the buzz all around, and it's strong. But we are in control. Each of us has spent a lifetime learning how to control it. There was nothing supernatural there, it's something in our world. The tree was a lens."

"Fair enough, it can't be excluded, but consider this before ruling out some outside force. You speak of your feel for the community of trees. There is power there. Look at me now. I talk about my 'employers' jokingly but think about the last time you saw me and look at me now. You can make a case that years of spring water, organically grown pinto beans, and leaf lettuce—I *never* buy iceberg—could have done all that. But the changes proceeded at a phenomenal rate, and the odds against me being well for all this time push the statistics out to a lot of decimal places. Leaf lettuce won't do jack for non-Hodgkin's lymphoma, COPD, or congestive heart failure. And there is one more thing I need to add here. I have waited to put it all on the table until now, when I have a better feel for where you stand and if I can trust you. I told you I *meant* to kill you, and that I *thought* you were dead. That is not the full story. I have done a lot of hunting over the years, and I am good at it; I am a clean killer—no mistakes. When I was living back home, I was always getting calls from neighbors who were raising meat animals—maybe a steer, some chickens, a couple of pigs. They wanted someone to officiate who knew what they were doing; to help get them in the freezer humanely, expeditiously, and with skill. For large animals, a blow to the head was my modus operandi, and I never screwed up. I had a horrible hangover the morning of the fight, so I guess I simply forgot to throw my portable electroencephalograph equipment in the truck. I have no hard evidence, but I was and remain literally *certain* I did what needed to be done with that rock. You don't always need an EEG to see a flatline. May I call you Lazarus?

"One way or another, the incredible pain of that encounter might almost be like that of childbirth, and the offspring are our lives that started that day."

18

It was some time before either spoke as the substance of their deliberations soaked in. Larry built up the fire again, as it was now full dark, and the chill autumn air of the mountaintop was falling around them. He put on a coat, but Jimmy seemed utterly oblivious to the dropping temperature. They gazed at the flames for a while and thought about what to tackle next. They were probably at as good a point as they were going to reach in terms of an explanation of the fight itself, and the fact that they had been caught up in an unknowable storm was a workable explanation of the changes that were wrought. They might differ on the source of the force underlying it all, but this just suggested that their views were based on different hypotheses, and they could never be tested for a resolution. That would require doing it all over again and seeing if the same things happened—and taking down the data this time. This was impossible—and hardly a safe thing to try, even if there were some way to set it up. Such events would have to be very rare. But now they knew they would have to move forward with what to do about where Larry was stuck—Jimmy had clearly worked it out for himself. It now fell on him to work on the second part. They each sensed this, and Jimmy began with a simple question. He knew that back in the day, Larry had personified Good, and he had been Evil. As he saw it now, Larry was the Joker, and he was the Thief.

"Do you believe in any deity at all, Larry?"

"Nope. I can't."

"Why not?"

"I believed completely as a child. The adults I trusted told me He was there, and I believed without question. But as the years passed, I could never feel him in the way I feel some other things, and the faith faded. There were some nasty issues that helped that along too.

"Suppose there is a God who sees and knows all and is omnipotent. Let's suppose he is influencing our lives right now. Clearly, He—or She—could have set up that fight for us, right? People pray for His help all the time. They want Him to help in elections, to keep the other evil people from winning. They want His help to block gay rights amendments. They want His help to win basketball games and find parking spaces at the mall and outlaw abortion. Suppose He is the ultimate author of all. Look back on human history. Look for the hand of God. I can tell you this, if he was "helping" us along all that time, then the wildest whiskey-soaked preacher man thumping his Bible in a hot, sweaty tent in the backwoods of Alabama, screaming about the mighty hand of the Lord coming to scourge the earth, has barely scraped the surface."

"You castigate Him or Her or It for not helping us out in the face of evil. You would actually want us to be influenced and assisted for good."

"Sure. But if you have God's influence for good, you have the possibility of Satan's influence for evil. I'd rather think that we are responsible for it all, both good and evil, influenced by cold chance. Imagine an unchecked supernatural force that permits human atrocities without end. The murder of six million Jews by the Germans, the most civilized people in Europe. Unknown millions of Armenians died at the hands of the Turks, and count the millions who died in Cambodia, Russia, and China. Pick a country, pick a century. No help there. Nothing. Not even if it would have been easy. How hard would it have been to have Klara, wife of Alois Schicklgruber, have the next sperm down the line score back in Austria in 1888? She might have had a precious, warm daughter who would have brought her wonderful grandchildren. I had a Jewish colleague in my department several years back whose mother was born in Poland. She came to the U.S. when she was very young, but the Nazis exterminated every single member of her family that remained. She was not an atheist. She believed in Jehovah. And she *hated* him with great passion. Chosen people indeed. Parenthetically, if anyone were to bring up the topic of Holocaust denial, you would have been wise not to be anywhere in eastern Massachusetts, or even parts of Rhode Island or southern New Hampshire.

"What about you?" Larry asked. What was your gavotte with the heavens?

"Not much for believing in the supernatural as laid down by clergy, that's for sure. I was raised a Baptist, and at one point my mother said, 'OK, Jimmy, you are old enough now to decide for yourself if you want to continue going to church. It should be up to you.' I never went again. But I remain convinced of a few things. I don't think my life, or yours, has played out without an outside influence. Don't forget the trees. As I said, it's hard to figure how I got to be so healthy so fast and stayed that way just on my own. And how could someone who could barely read get to where he understands your papers without a tutor? And then there is Lazarus . . ."

"Point taken; you will get no argument from me there. As to formal religion in my case, I followed a more wretched pathway out. I was raised

Episcopalian. My mother and I went to church regularly, and I went to Sunday school. Even took communion; that's part of being high Episcopalian. My father died when I was seven, and I took it hard. That in itself did not shake my young faith, and I was certain Dad was looking down from heaven. My mother, possibly thinking at least to some extent that I needed a new father, took up with our neighbor. They were married in due course, after some fuss involving circumstances that I will not go into out of respect for the dead—and that I was not supposed to know about at the time. But the man in question had not been divorced from his first wife long enough when the knot was tied, and the Church found out. Why they cared enough to seek the information out I'll never know. They excommunicated her for this 'sin.' Less than a year later, the biggest Episcopal church in Albany held a wedding for a famous and very rich man. And he *himself* had been divorced for *less* time than my stepfather. Up went my middle finger. Never looked back. More globally, it convinced me that if there is a supreme being, I don't want anyone else between me and that being. I think that any advice on this matter I might get from clergy of any stripe would be, of necessity, an obstruction.

"But having said that, I have friends who are clergy, including a Catholic priest. They are extraordinarily good people. But they don't ever try to bring me into their realm. I concede that for the faithful, living with a kindly Holy Father who will be leading them to life everlasting is a wonderful thing. Helping them along is a noble way to spend one's life. But faith is not something that comes out of a faucet."

"But you clearly do have faith. You lived it when you saved the ash tree, even though you sometimes question the reality of it all. What does that look like?"

"I have pure faith without religion. I have all the faith in the world, compressed into one tiny point—a point with no dimension at all."

"A singularity."

"You have stopped surprising me, Jimmy. Somehow I expected you to know about these strange mathematical creatures."

"I like singularities. And solitons. Funny waves that don't do what ordinary waves do and don't do what you expect them to. Solitons that can't develop in twitch cables and cut off an arm, because the physics *seems* wrong. But sometimes things that 'can't' happen do."

Larry again had the odd feeling of being at a meeting of the American Physical Society.

"A singularity. They pop up all over the place. Maybe as an infinitely small domain of enormous mass, maybe part of the formation of a black hole, or a place where the rules break down unpredictably, or a place on a surface where a plotted line backs around to cross itself. Yeah, that's what my faith is. A place where the world beyond, the one that science cannot fathom, meets the one where we live and can hope for explanations. But by extension, ask, what do I *believe*? You can't 'believe' in something like a singularity *per se,* just know that it *is*. I believe that what I do matters. And that the place where you see *how* it matters is past that wall where reason can no longer go."

"You think your work on global warming matters, clearly. Objectively, you are trying to save the planet."

"True, but I don't want to be a messianic hero of any stripe. If I actually am now, in all of this, then I am a hero like Siegfried. Mighty Wotan genetically engineered him to be fearless, strong, endowed with great power, and number than a pounded thumb. He set him on the task of returning the Rheingold to the river. He did all that, but when Siegfried turned his back, Hagen was right there with his spear. 'Hagen, was tust du?' I don't want to be confused by the 'magnitude of her fury in the final hour'!

"So, not my work alone, although it may arguably be easiest to make a case for that. Everything I do matters. Not in some biblical way, with someone up there on a cloud taking down names. A cosmic Santa Claus seeing who's Naughty and Nice, uppercase *N*s. When you open this can of worms, you start off with some serious problems. I expect to die and expect to be gone forever into utter oblivion. I know that from the fifteen billion years of oblivion before I was born. Passed like a flash for us, didn't it? Remember anything from back then?

"Didn't Samuel Clemens make that comment exactly?"

"He sure did, but I figured it out for myself not long after my father passed. As I think most reasonable people would. But looking ahead, whatever I do that is good for my fellow man will be gone. And my fellow men and women and all their descendants will be gone, and all of humanity will be gone. The works of Bach will be gone. This planet is not immortal and will likely be eaten by our own dying sun as it expands into a red giant. Talk about global warming! My faith is that, even without heaven or hell or rewards, what I do in my time here matters. And I have no reason, and need none, for thinking this at all but keep trying to *see* it in its entirety."

"What we fought about matters greatly in this context, doesn't it?"

"Yes, and again, I don't know why. I have always felt cheated by not knowing what I need to know about that pivotal event that profoundly changed my life, and yours. That has been a real problem for me, as we have talked about. Faith shouldn't need hard explanations. You ought to be able just to have it, no questions asked."

"And has this brought the Darkness you feel, and that I can see in you?"

"The Darkness came on unbidden, as it did for you. Maybe I want it to continue so I can analyze it, find out its nature, and then somehow bring it to heel. But there is a barrier."

"Why have you organized all this into this singularity, this point?

"Simple: a point, without dimension, is the best way to penetrate a barrier. The wider the tip of the spear, the less chance you have to bust through. I have not given up the idea that there is something on the other side of that barrier, out where rational thought is neither useful nor even possible—where the vision of what counts lies. I think it's where the real answer sits regarding why that fight matters as much as it does. And mocks us.

"But the principle of using a sharp point to break out is solid. On the third day of the Battle of Gettysburg in 1863, Lee ordered a charge against the Union line. It failed, and Gettysburg—along with the loss at Vicksburg almost simultaneously—was the functional end of the war. Lee has been criticized down the decades for that decision. But he was not crazy, he just underestimated the resolve of the Union Army under Meade, their new commander of only a few days. The main field commander of the charge, Pickett, might have broken the Union line on the ridge that day. His line of attack concentrated to a sharp point. Scholars have some disagreement on just how this went down, or if Pickett even intended it, but the events on the battlefield are known. The units kept coalescing more and more tightly, heading to one spot. And they did start to break the line. It was only through some very tough and smart fighting by seasoned Federals that Pickett's charge did not succeed. Lee might very well have sealed the doom of the U.S.A. as we know it on that day.

"And so, I metaphorically concentrate my units, like Pickett. I throw off everything useless that can't be pulled into that point. All that ritual, all those books of scripture. They are in my way. They would make the point dull, at least for me. All that was added on by humankind. Creation myths, myths like original sin, so we can still believe in a deity when bad things happen to good people. But the way out remains tantalizingly close and always beyond my grasp. Frustratingly, I can feel a flow out across the barrier. That makes it even tougher to tolerate being stuck on this side. It's like the radiation that is known to escape a black hole. I feel it most strongly when I listen to great music. And for me, the music that seems to have the greatest flow is Bach's."

Larry related his thoughts about the Bach violin partite, and the young artist.

"That music, that particular piece of music, brings me to the edge of the known universe. I can feel the music itself crossing over the edge. But I can't ride it out. It is the work of a master, played by a master. Probably that is part of it. I understand that the great Zen masters pass that boundary: satori, enlightenment, whatever you want to call it."

"What do you think being a master of that stature might entail Larry?"

"That's a tough one Jimmy. Zen master, that's the most common example in this context. An individual meditates and studies all his or her life, achieves enlightenment and passes through the barrier. They master themselves. But there are all kinds of masters. Seems like when you use the term in a nontrivial way, you always come down to defining someone who's work transcends the simple act of doing it well and gets to the point where they can look across the line and see the part on the other side, the one I can't. Like using complex variables that have real and imaginary parts. You need that imaginary part to see how the whole system works. So, is it really imaginary if you can *use* it?

"I won't even consider the possibility that you don't know about the complex plane Jimmy. You can't take the square root of a negative number. There is a line, the *real line,* that goes from –infinity to +infinity and that's it. But, if you now define the impossible square root of –1 as *i,* you have a leg up to construct a two-dimensional plane. And you can do a lot with that."

"Sure, Fourier analysis depends on that. Vectors rotating in the complex plane."

"Right, and look at the Mandelbrot set, the most complex and beautiful mathematical object ever. The real part is just a crummy line segment! Maybe the barrier is just an inability to take the square root of –1 metaphorically. The masters see the plane. Bach must have crossed into that space to write as he did; you can feel that in the music. It's like the Mandelbrot set, reaching out to its full spectacle. I think when a person grasps that part of his or her art, they have found the Way, and then they become masters."

"So, The Way?"

"Yeah, in two senses: First, the hardcore work of learning the foundation, the unifying principles and techniques of the art. Second, the Way to unleashing the complex part that lets you see things in their entirety, maybe as they really are."

Larry didn't notice, but there was the hint of a smile playing around the stark features of Jimmy's face. He relaxed against the tree behind him and thought for few minutes. This was not the sort of conversation that needed constant attention. When he returned, he returned from long way away.

"You obviously have spent a lot of time in this area, Jimmy. Me, I am a hack, a tyro. So, how do *you* define a Way?"

"Just a path through a gateway that is actually without a closure. It is always open."

"But what makes it so special and difficult? If it's always open, I could walk through it right now. Anyone could."

"True, in principle, but you need to follow a Way to get to the gate and pass through. It could be anything Larry."

"But isn't it usually a process of meditation, or maybe even a martial art?"

"Could be anything you follow beyond the real-side perfection of the process to what lies beyond. Physics, for example. Or calligraphy. Or flower arranging."

"And music. As I said, there are times when I see a Way in music very clearly. I can't follow that Way as a performer would, but when I lose myself in it, I can follow it to the edge. You just can't ride someone else's pony out."

"True, but you can learn from what you see and hear."

"As I said, what I see is a narrowing to a point, maybe to a dimension beneath a point. Something harder than diamond and without a dimension at all. And that opens the path. But this is always just at the edge of my perception, always in my peripheral vision. Like those places here in these old mountains that you may see clearly once but can never find again. A door that opens and shows you what is on the other side, but never lets you pass."

"So, what do you think might separate someone that can use the Way from one who can't?"

"I can only speculate. I'll never know, really. But it seems the more you reach, the more you try to apply reason, the harder it gets. Seems like words are the enemy. You can find comfort in the droning of a religious ceremony, but the more words you use, the more ritual you add, the more you drag the ancient ramblings of millennia of half-mad desert tribes into the mix, the more baggage you have—and that stuff won't pass through.

"But you said physics, Jimmy. How can there be a Way of physics? It's a science. Someone even wrote a book about the Tao in the physical sciences. Physics has words, even if it is largely mathematical, and it has its own language of numbers and theories. We are talking about finding a Way that is lean and mean."

"Suppose it is not the substance of the Way, Larry, but rather just the fact that you are on it in the first place, and that you stick with it and never assume you know enough about it, no matter how proficient you become? There was a baker in Ellenville who made the best bread I have ever had. I got to know him a bit. He always told me that if he came out of his bakery after working all night and hadn't learned something, he had wasted his time. If you are a master, like your violinist or your composer or your violin maker certainly were or are, then you transcend your art by constant striving. Here's an example. You mentioned martial arts as offering a Way. In karate, there is a belt system that ranks the student. It starts with a white belt for the complete beginner, ranging through many colors—brown being the penultimate, and black the final one. But there are levels of black belts going on up as mastery continues to develop. When you achieve first-degree black belt, you are now considered a serious beginner. As one pushes on ahead, something happens to the belt. The black coloring starts to wear off and patches of white appear. If you train long enough, it becomes white again."

"But there are things we could undertake seriously that might not offer a Way. When Gödel formulated his theorem that blew the hell out of the idea of achieving perfection in number theory, he pointed out that the system had to be a substantial one, not something half-assed. In such a powerful system, Gödel showed, you can write a statement that is self-referential and creates a paradox, or that can't be proved. The result crashes the concept of perfection. So, it has to be something so challenging that its ultimate mastery is impossible for anyone. Yeah, answered my own question."

"Yup, physics seems like a good candidate."

"Why do you keep hammering away at physics? I *am* a physicist! I have been at this a good part of my life, I love it, I work at it. Don't you think I ought to have seen the door behind it by now? It's not like I haven't been looking. So maybe I am only an also-ran in that race."

"Larry, come on! I have read your work. All of it, remember? And a lot of other people's work. You are among the best. But let's leave that; it's not the core issue. I'll tell you a little story. There was a master of the tea ceremony back in the good old days in Japan. He was one of the greatest of his time, perhaps of any time. One day, while walking in town, he was lost in thought and bumped into a samurai. The warrior was deeply offended by this accident and challenged the tea master to a duel. The samurai, who had the legal right to do all this, also told him that if he did not accept, he would simply kill him. The tea master realized that he was a dead man but wished to die honorably, rather than be slaughtered. He replied that he would need to buy a sword and practice. He would then meet the samurai at the edge of town at this same time the following day.

"The tea master went to a sword shop and asked to make a purchase. The sword maker knew the tea master and knew he was no swordsman. He asked what he needed the weapon for. The tea master told him the story, and said he feared he would be dead by this time tomorrow. The sword maker told him he would give him a lesson in fighting with the sword that might help. He showed him a basic fighting stance, and the most common sword grip to use, plus a single parry and a single blow. Most important, he told him to concentrate on his opponent as hard as he could, as though he was in the tea ceremony.

"The time for the duel arrived, and true to his word, the tea master appeared, prepared for his match. The two men drew their weapons and faced off. The tea master went into a state of concentration, focused on the samurai with the same intensity he felt when preparing the tea for the ceremony. The samurai regarded this small man, sheathed his sword, and walked off without a word. Surprised at his good fortune, the tea master returned the sword and went home. When asked what he saw that day, the samurai said only, 'Death.'

"When you are a master, you are using what's on the whole plane, the nonrational part of your art. You just can't see it until it is ready to be seen. The gate is then gateless. You only feel the bond between the two sides. The minute you start thinking about it rationally, the opening drifts away. There is no magic word to open the gate, no 'open sesame.'

In fact, it is the lack of words, the calming of intellect, that lets you see the other part clearly. That's how you use the singularity you have constructed.

"Larry, you're still a cat guy, I bet."

"Yup."

"Mind telling me why?"

"My father died when I was seven, which I told you. Suddenly and without any warning. I woke up on what I later learned was St. Dunstan's Day in May. It was a school day and I looked at the clock and saw it was way late. I jumped up and looked out the front window and saw my grandparents' car parked out there. I was very confused and went downstairs to the bad news. Hit me hard. Wish I could remember more about him. I have almost nothing that was his. I have his Winchester .22, nice one, a model 62, classic. I managed to keep it out of the divorce negotiations. It means a lot to me. His Boy Scouts hatchet. A photo he took of Lake Bomoseen in the Adirondacks. A shovel. Not much else.

"What I had to help me through those times besides my living human family were my dog and cat. Loved them a lot. Up the street was this exterminator. He thought it was wise to distribute rat poison to the neighbors for free. With no instructions on safe use. Killed them both. I have a bucket list. I plan on finding where his grave is in up in Albany Rural Cemetery, going out one dark night, and taking a huge, fragrant shit on his grave."

"Good item for a bucket list."

"But cats are a good thing to bring up at this point, Jimmy. And I expect that's why you did. I have loved them as companions all my life, but beyond that, they are central to where we are in this discussion. We have been going on about our lives—how we have led them, and what we get out of them. Cats have a lot to offer as models. They seem to live in the moment. I know this has a bad rep. In the old song, the people who gave up and lived for the moment were swept away by the Deluge. But I am not talking about living *for* the moment, I am talking about living *in* it. Cats know calculus. Really, I mean that in all seriousness. We never were able fully to understand motion and the development of systems in the course of time until Newton and Leibniz. They showed that knowing what happens in literally no time at all tells us what we need to know over intervals. Why not apply that to living? When I sit in my recliner with my cat on my lap, I know he is totally unconcerned with the fact that at some point in the future, the molecules in our bodies will be reduced to atoms. The atoms themselves may be reduced to their subatomic particles, and even these may end up being pure energy. All this will be uniformly distributed across the entire universe. But in that infinitely short instant there is love, and it is immortal."

"Righteous!"

"Problem is, how do you get there? We have talked of how something like this is possible when you follow a Way. I have followed at least two: physics by doing, and music by listening. I am no closer."

"You are Larry. You have set it in a useful context with your cat calculus metaphor; why not use it? Think about exactly what Newton and Leibniz did for us. They followed the ever-decreasing intervals of time downwards and came to the inevitable barrier: you can't divide by zero; the result is meaningless. But they did a lateral arabesque around their own barrier with their use of limits."

"OK, then, Jimmy, let me take the cat calculus a few steps further, out to the point where I hit the wall. Start with a basic example: a pendulum. Look at two, side by side. One is in full swing, oscillating nicely. The other is stopped dead. Now take a snapshot of the system at the point where the weight of the moving unit is straight down and freeze it in time, the infinitely short dt. The images of the two systems are identical if you look at them at this instant, a point in time of zero dimension. They look identical. But we know the state variables. The position and angular velocity of the stationary one are both zero, but the moving one is very different. That infinitely small interval dt later, it will have moved. This is because the active pendulum has velocity and momentum, the state variables. The key is energy! The energy in the moving pendulum undergoes a regular transition from potential energy to kinetic: back and forth. We can characterize it fully and predict its movement for all time, given an ideal system with no friction.

"Now let's jump up one level and compare two *E. coli* bacteria. One is living, the other dead, but only for just an instant. We can do a similar analysis. Clearly, we will not know everything about the energy flow in the living bacterium, but we do know a lot. Things like chemical pathways, etcetera. And the key, again, is energy. The living cell has extremely low entropy, but Clausius must be obeyed: 'Die Energie der Welt ist konstant. Die Entropie der Welt strebt einem Maximum zu." The energy of the world remains constant, but the entropy strives for a maximum. The entropy in the cell is kept low by an expenditure of energy, and the ultimate result is an overall increase in entropy. The price life must pay. Prigogine characterizes this nonlinear phenomenon brilliantly. So now we have a calculus that describes life in the moment. The living bug is very different from the dead one. Energy flow. We now have hit our barriers:

how do we to define what it means to be alive. We now have a new, powerful vantage point. But what *is* this epiphenomenon of life?

"Now let's make a huge jump to a mammal."

"Hey, Larry, pick Schrödinger's cat! It's both alive and dead at the same time!"

"Cut the wisecracks . . ."

"Sorry, I couldn't resist."

"We'll jump to *Homo sapiens* and talk about the mind and consciousness. We stand on the same ground as Descartes did so long ago. He considered the mind and the body as separate, stating that there is a dualism. There has been a *lot* of thought lavished on that problem since! To get to that point, we'll look at the nervous system. A *huge mass* of living cells. In particular, the brain. How do the cranial neurons interact to form the mind, yielding what we think of as consciousness? We have switches—the synapses, and wiring—the axons. Uncountable action potentials coursing through the network. The possibility for interactions in a single brain is staggering. We know a great deal about the functions of each area of the brain in controlling physiology. What we want to understand is the mind. There is nothing supernatural about this, no dualism, and there is evidence to support this conclusion. Back in 1848, a construction foreman named Phineas Gage had a forty-three-inch steel rod blown through his head in a blasting accident. Steel and stone are a bad combination around black powder, and sparks can be struck. He survived, but his personality was totally altered. Who he *was* changed. This was a situation of some fame, interest, and study. Now, of course we have other objective examples. One 'tool' is Alzheimer's. I doubt you would have been exposed directly to this out here in the wilds, but I had a good friend and colleague at the university take this trip. It is awful. It has a lot to offer the student of mind, but the process is sort of like trying to figure out how a factory works by dropping in artillery rounds randomly and looking at how the product is affected. You start with a fully functional, conscious person and end up with a pile of protoplasm that can't even remember how to swallow. There is no mind/body dichotomy. The two are intimately related and inseparable.

"Having said that, where I want to go is to understand that relationship between all those neurons, synapses, and action potentials and from that figure out what we are. What's the connection? I sit here and think. I sit here, and I *am.* Here is where the cat calculus comes in—a solid way to formulate the problem. We look at the conscious mind in the instant, as we did with the pendulum and *E. coli.* The problem is knowing all the state variables, which is impossible. But we have reduced the system to its simplest conceptual state. We have moved up yet again to the gateless gate and still need a way *through.* The answers are all there on the other side . . ."

"That is a most excellent and concise description of the problem, Larry. And let me throw in a couple of things close to my own world. First, I am sure you have heard of Douglas Hofstadter, the *Gödel, Escher, and Bach* author. His metaphor is spot on. He speaks of an anteater whose best friend is an anthill. The individual ants fear the anteater as a mortal enemy, but the anthill itself is conscious and that consciousness arises from the interactions of the ants, much as ours comes from the interactions of neurons. Beautiful! With your talent, you surely feel the flow beneath your feet in this forest. My view is that my "employers" are the trees, and that the forest is like that anthill, conscious."

"Here is a useful way to move forward, Larry. It may sound like mere semantics, but it is light years past that. Consider the term we use to describe the science we have just been considering. Those who study living systems study *biology,* literally translated as 'the study of life.' But it is common to talk about the *biology of a system.* Like the biology of a coral reef. This refers to the system *itself,* not its study. Same with physics. Physics is the study of processes and systems, but the term is also used in the sense of 'the physics of a tornado'—literally, how the storm functions. You approach the gate when you are immersed in pure function, beyond its description and explanation, beyond words.

"Here is an example that addresses description vs. system in physics. I will ask you a simple question: What is fire?"

"Well, in the specific case of the fire separating us here, it is the oxidation, largely of cellulose and lignin, at high temperatures to CO_2 and H_2O. This involves the release of considerable energy, which allows the reaction to perpetuate to conclusion, leaving some residual unreacted carbon and mineral ash."

"Yup. That is physics in the sense of the *study* of fire. But what *is* fire? What would Leibniz, or maybe your cat, think?"

Larry said nothing for a spell. He casually picked up a dry stick sitting in the pile of wood that had been collected for fuel and held it in the flame for a bit until it caught. He stomped it out with his boot, relit it, and threw it into the fire. He sat for a long time watching it burn to ash, following it carefully as its fate played out, fully involved in the process. When he looked up, he was alone. But not really. There were a lot of trees.

19

It was an exceptionally clear night, with no clouds to keep in the earth's heat. The temperature dropped rapidly into the low twenties up where Larry camped. He burrowed deeper into his down bag as the cold strengthened and headed towards the teens. He fell asleep a bit past midnight, exhausted from the brisk hike in the cool day and the emotional turmoil of making preparations to talk with a man who had tried to kill him and had left him for dead. He was not quite ready to remove the "for" part of that sentence but was moving in that direction. The ultimate reality of that conversation was so different from what he had expected, and so much more intense, that he as yet lacked the ability to fathom the changes it had wrought in him. That was going to take some time. But, for all of that, he was not filled with anxiety. Sometimes through the years he would wake up in the middle of the night feeling an oncoming stress attack. He would be worried about losing funding, or about that funny pain in his armpit that might be cancer, or what his son might be doing right at that moment that could get him time in prison or murdered, or what Andrea was doing in bed with her lover. And he would ride out the rest of the night sweating and nursing the feeling that he was about to die. He had been told there were meds for that, but as noted, Larry was not a med kind of guy, and he would go through the next day in a zombie-like state. Larry slept deeply this night, and such dreams as he may have had dissipated.

Dawn saw him sitting up in his small tent, calm and refreshed. When planning for the trip, he'd thought he should see if he could make it through the day without coffee; hence, he had packed none. In its stead he had brought some green tea, so he would have a nice hot beverage to get the day going. He hoped the caffeine differential between the two drug-delivery systems would keep any withdrawal headache at bay. He boiled water in one of his clean pans and sat on his insulating pad, huddled over the steaming cup as though it were a precious egg to be protected rather than a source of heat and sustenance.

Breakfast was Spartan. He sipped some freeze-dried orange (-like) drink and had a bowl of cereal with instant milk and a second cup of tea. An apple topped things off, and he lay back down on his sleeping bag, resting. He made some vague plans for the rest of the day, based on not needing to go in to work on Monday at all if he did not want to. And he actually didn't need to. That thought was very pleasing. He began to think that a time when he would not need to go into the university at all was not a pipe dream. There would be no work for him to do there, and the thought did not scare him at all. He decided to spend a few hours on the summit, just relaxing, maybe thinking about the night before, maybe not thinking about anything at all.

He had always felt cheated by the really high mountains he had climbed in his distant youth. You worked desperately hard to reach the top, maybe spending days walking in before starting the actual ascent. Preparations at base camp took more time to complete. The climb itself could take several days, with as many as three or four nights spent out on the pitiless slopes. The dash to the summit always seemed to be delayed by unforeseen circumstances, and the summit was achieved hours later than the plan called for. He would turn around and head for the safety of the highest camp almost as soon as he got there, a sensible self-imposed rule that saved lives when obeyed. But the mountain never gave you anything in return for all your work, really. You had to live with the satisfaction of looking back up and knowing you had been there once and the joy of the experience. That was enough.

Mountains like this one were very different. There was no real physical or mental challenge. If you told someone you had climbed Peekamoose, even if they knew what you were talking about, they would not be impressed. If you said Aconcagua or Denali, they would look up and take your measure. But for all of that, on a mountain like this, you could take back what you paid out in full measure and with interest. You could lounge on the summit and look out on the surrounding country for hours in relative safety. You could still make mistakes and head up with a windbreaker and a pair of beach sandals to your great detriment. Mountains just love to hurt really stupid people. But if you went with respect and a humble heart, the mountain would reward you with food for your soul.

It was midmorning by the time Larry was packed and ready to head down. He took one last sip from his mysterious little spring, filled his canteens, and started down the trail. He walked slowly, not really wanting to relinquish the heights, but for him, slowly was too fast to make the hike down last long. It was scarcely noon when he closed the door of the Rabbit and let it warm up. He had a long pull from a canteen and readied the car. He still had two more stops to make, and then he would be on the way. He would get in late, but the traffic around Boston would be fairly light on a Sunday night.

As he reached back to settle some of the piles of baggage that were heaped up, he caught sight of his face in the mirror. It occurred to him that he had not shaved the previous morning. That puzzled him a bit and deserved some time for consideration. Since the day of his awakening in the hospital all those years ago, he had shaved daily. His hair was cut to a uniform two millimeters, nearly twice a month. It still covered all but the scarred part of his scalp. Andrea had assumed he would grow back the long hair and flowing beard that he had sported since she met him. His hair had been thick and heavy, and he only trimmed his beard when he could no longer eat efficiently. This had been part of who he was, even though to some, it seemed only an affectation. But it was much more than that to him. She was puzzled when he kept shaving and getting his hair cut, even after the stitches had come out and the cuts in his scalp and lips had healed.

He was puzzled at first too. He still was puzzled. People were often disturbed by the angry scars. For the first time in a while, he contemplated them honestly now. The one on his face, where he had hit the jagged rock in falling, was still a vicious-looking path travelling across his upper cheekbone, through his lips, and down to the point of his chin. The one on the back of his head was even uglier, as was the alarming depression in his skull bones. At least people could look at that those without having to pretend they were looking somewhere else; he could not see them doing it, after all. If he had grown his hair, beard, and moustache, he would have saved them some of the embarrassment of the sight, and he himself the embarrassment of trying not to notice their discomfiture. But covering them, he had concluded, would mean they had healed and no longer needed to be exposed for the physician's scrutiny. He could not really accept, over all the years, that the wounds had actually healed. But now he had no desire to shave and was equally uninterested in a haircut. He was pretty sure he would never use the disposable razors in his kit—or any others, for that matter. Another glance in the rearview mirror and he saw the shadow of the steel-gray beard to come. It would be looking rather nice, he guessed, about the time this coming winter's snows were melting. As an afterthought, he speculated on how his neighbor Carol would like him with a beard. He thought it might make him look a bit sexy for an old fart, if he could keep from looking like a dirty old man or a street person. Like his grandfather, genetics had ensured that hair covered his entire scalp with the exception of the scar tissue. He vaguely thought the crematorium would administer his next haircut.

Larry was headed up to the chopping where the fight had occurred. He had to go; he was close, and contemplating the place aroused no fear in him on this day. This was new too. There was a lot that was new. He had to backtrack through Grahamsville to get up to the site, and on his way back through town, he stopped at the small market to pick up supplies for the trek back to Cambridge. He got some pretzels, hard cheddar cheese, carrots, and an assortment of couple of apples. He had it in mind to see how it felt to be once again rolling down an interstate with a frosty-cold beer between his legs. He would stay well under the 0.08 blood-alcohol line. But ultimately decided that his luck on that issue might have finally run out. This time, to save the miles and time, he'd drop down and pick up 84, cross into Connecticut and run up to the Pike rather than going up to Albany.

While browsing the aisles he chanced upon one of the employees stocking the shelves. She was a pleasant-looking woman, maybe in her mid-forties. They struck up a brief conversation about nothing in particular. He revealed that he had shopped there many years ago, told her his name, and they talked about how much the place had changed and not changed in the decades since he left.

After he cashed out and left, the woman wandered up to the cash register. It was dead in the place right about then. Come to think of it, it was never all that lively at any time in that place, but it was a living for the family who owned it.

"Nice guy, name of Larry Vintner," she offered to the older woman at the register, who had also encountered him on his way into the store.

"I remember a guy by that name, but that was a long time back. Hard not to remember. Guy named Jimmy Blandsford almost killed the poor bastard in a fight up on Slide."

People tended to remember that incident. Jimmy was an integral member of the tight Grahamsville community in his day. He was not all that well liked, but he was well-known. His disappearance had created quite a stir, and the circumstances were not forgotten. The matter had settled down over the years, but it had staying power as a good story over a cold beer. The younger woman had moved into town only a few years back after she remarried and had not heard even a tenth of the stories this tiny town had to offer. For one reason or another, this particular narrative had not arisen, being very old news by then.

"What happened? He sure has some pretty nasty scars to show for it. Nice looking anyway. The scars don't bother me. Makes him look kind of rugged, you know, mysterious or something." She had an odd look about her that signified that Larry's presence had gotten past her outer defenses. The older woman related the tale. She added appropriate embellishments; after all, the whole matter had passed into myth.

Knowing now who the stranger was, she was somewhat surprised by his appearance. He had always had a full beard and long hair back in the day. No matter, the face was memorable and had not changed as much as you would have thought.

"Funny, it was nice just talking to him for a couple of minutes. Wish he were staying around. He told me he was up at old Eban's night before last. I know Eban pretty good."

"Probably a damn good thing he isn't, by the look you got right now, lady. You got enough problems without gettin' caught hitting on a town legend. Your husband is not known for a modern view of marriage. I've known him longer than you too."

"Just saying. No harm there at all, and really not what I was thinking. Did you catch those eyes?"

The older woman was not so much older that she had not. She was actually younger than Larry, and she had taken a really good look at his eyes as they did their bit of business at the checkout. And she had not been unaffected.

"Yeah, I did. Kind of funny how peaceful they are. Stands out. Look really cheerful."

The quiet day resumed, with canned milk being shelved, followed by some work rearranging the cold cuts in the refrigerated showcase. Small, mysterious smiles lingered on the faces of both women for most of the rest of the day.

The road up to the old cutting was impassable by vehicle after the first quarter mile, so he grabbed a day pack with some water and a light lunch of apples, crackers, and a small can of tuna fish in water with a pull-off top. Plenty. He remembered his vow concerning the beans and rice. He walked up the slope for the next mile, and slowed as the rutted old logging road became ever more treacherous. He noted that it curved sharply to the right and subconsciously planned a shortcut for the return trip that would take him through a deep ravine, but the woods were fairly open here, and he could make as good time off the overgrown trail as on it. It was almost another half mile to where the yard had been, and he was surprised that they were ever able to get their equipment up there, but then the decades of erosion and undisturbed growth had done much to return the area to its natural state.

The yard was empty. At least someone had taken the time to come up and haul off the cut wood. Probably Jimmy's wife had seen to it and gotten something out of their work. He would not have wanted the trees to go to waste after having been deprived of their lives. But the rest of the ash trees stood as he had left them. He wondered why the owner had never hired another cutter to harvest his investment. In fact, why was the forest here intact at all? It was prime land for a developer too. Then he felt the hand of Jimmy Blandsford on the land. And there was no longer any need for puzzlement. There were new trees growing in the part of the grove they had cut, and the recovery was robust. The place looked like a forest again, and that pleased him. He headed up the last road he had ever built, but it was almost invisible—just a minor unnatural smoothness in an otherwise rough forest floor. Only he and Jimmy could possibly have found it.

The grove was magnificent in its fall colors. Ash trees were not the best performers in the fall, normally yielding to the maples—especially the hard maples—but this year was special. There had been plentiful frosts, and the trees had a complex coloration that made them look like the bowls of antique meerschaum pipes with some amazing deep reds shot through them. The edges of the leaves were tipped with purple, while the inner areas, protected from the frost, were still the normal brilliant yellow. It made them look illuminated from within. The smell of the moldering leaf duff on the ground was intense and set his mind wandering to a lifetime of autumns gone. It always seemed that the best things that happened to him happened at this time of year.

The tree, the one he had come to see, was as he remembered it, but now there was no deep susurration in his mind telling him of the flow of great power up and down a conduit from heaven to earth, if that was what it had been after all. All he felt was the background rumbling of the mountain's pure water, taking its dark ride to the sewers of a blackened city that could not possibly care or even be aware of this gift. The usual feel of the forest doing its usual chatting was also apparent. He was not surprised by this relative silence. He doubted he would have felt anything unusual if he had gone back the very next day after the fight. Such things were the soul of evanescence. And now he was armed with that part of what had happened that lurked on the other side. He examined the tree and found that it was old and had not many years left. It would certainly outlive him, but not by a long stretch. His trained sawyer's eye looked for dead branches and the scars of branches that had fallen in the past, impediments to the flow of the sap, and thought it would not make many baseball bats anymore, if there was anyone left to buy wooden bats. He hoped Jimmy was on the case with the emerald ash borer and that his favorite tree would not go the way of the Dutch elm and American chestnut.

Something caught his eye almost immediately. It was an ash sapling not far from his tree, almost certainly an offspring. He had read a book about hiking many years ago, and the author had extolled the virtues of using a walking stick. It provided stability, assisted in maintaining a good rhythm in walking, helped fording streams, and could be used as an emergency shelter pole. He had always used one down the years. These were always collapsible metal offerings. But an urge came to him to make a change and here was his next stick, a throwback in the range of millennia. This would not be a walking stick, really more of a staff and would have been adequate for Moses himself. He imagined himself defending the well of Midian against brigands, striking the water to turn the Nile to blood, or perhaps waving it to part the Red Sea. More prosaically, fending off a nosy black bear. He had not the slightest twinge of regret at harvesting it, as he had recently been reminded of the friendship between an anteater and an ant colony. This was part and parcel of that metaphor. And it was one of many young around the mother tree. Few would grow to any size. And he could not shake the idea that it was a gift from the old ash.

He pulled out his heavy camp knife, razor sharp as always, and felled the sapling easily. For reasons he could not put a finger on, if he had had a saw, he would not have used it. He trimmed it down to about six feet, probably not coincidentally the length of a karate bo-- a fighting staff. Trimming off the branches took only a few moments, and he peeled the bark from a short section corresponding to where his hand would rest. When he got home, he would finish removing the bark, and after it dried over the winter, kept flat to prevent warping, a few coats of linseed oil would finish the job.

He sat with his back up against his tree and ate his small lunch, save for one nice apple. He was still hungry afterwards. Considering the great feasting on grease, salt, beer, pancakes, and other wonderful things, he thought it might take several days for his stomach to shrink back to a reasonable volume and be satisfied with such meager fare. Nonetheless, he felt sleepy after the meal. This was the time of day for him to doze, the warning shots of an old age coming up fast in his windshield. He had slept well, but not for as long as his body demanded, and that made the next turn of events inevitable. His head slipped to one side, and he fell into a restful sleep that lasted long enough to refresh him. He could sleep like this when he needed to now—a talent born of necessity. More than once in recent years, he had succumbed to the need for a little afternoon catnap while sitting propped up in front of his computer or leaning over a stack of Freshman Physics exams on his desk. Once, he had been working on a manuscript on his word processor and found he had several dozen pages of "iiiiiiiiiiiiiiiiiiiiiiiii" upon awakening. His grad students would tiptoe around the lab, hoping not to disturb him. And they would *never* ask if he'd had a nice nap. If he slept more than a few minutes, his mood could be unsavory for the rest of the day, and no one wanted to own the first face he saw when he popped awake.

This time, however, the sleep was just what he needed. He had only one dream that he could recall upon awakening, and it stuck with him for some reason. In it, there was a great blacksmith working incandescent steel on the forge. The steel was twisting and writhing under the powerful blows, sparks showering in all directions from the force. His attention was called to a curious detail that he might have missed altogether had he not been watching the torment of the metal under the maker's hand with such an interest. What occurred to him was that, between the surface of the anvil and that of the hammer, there was a space where something of lesser thickness than the billet of steel being worked would be perfectly safe from the hammer's titanic blows. Its deeper meaning, which he thought important, escaped him but seemed to hover on the edge of being revealed.

The mood of this dream stayed with him after he awoke, as such moods often do. He sat awhile in the purple shade of the ash grove and ate his apple. He rose slowly, stretched his back out carefully, and started for his car, angling off toward the shortcut through the ravine. After just a few steps with the new staff, he knew for certain he had made a friend.

The afternoon was crisp and bone-dry, as only this time of year can permit. The sun was already at a shallow angle. He recalled—felt, really, in his strange neural circuits—that the upcoming night would be just a tiny bit longer than the day had been. He really would take the whole day off tomorrow. He might even sleep until nine or ten. He could even stop and get a motel room for the night. No matter. None of that mattered now. It was his life and his time. His computer knew what to do without him for the moment. His lab crew knew what to do without him. Even he now knew what to do without him.

He reached the drop-off. The contrast of the brilliant light in the uncommonly clear air and the darkness of the ravine made it impossible for someone standing in the sun to see into what lay below. The shadowed depths appeared like the water in a deep, black mountain tarn. He stepped over the edge, and with three long strides, he was gone.

EPILOGUE

> Between the hammer and the anvil there is a space, within which something of lesser stature than the steel the master works is safe from the blows.

There are rare people who exist, but no one, especially they themselves, ever knows who they are. And because of them, and only because of them and the justice they embody, the Almighty stays His hand from destroying the world in His righteous wrath. And they see so much Darkness, it is said, that when they die, God must hold them in His arms for a thousand years to warm their souls.

ABOUT THE AUTHOR

Harold "Dusty" Dowse was born in Albany, NY and raised there and in the tiny town of Stillwater. He is a graduate of The Albany Academy, Amherst College, and New York University (Ph.D.). Upon receiving his Doctorate, he and his wife moved to Grahamsville NY, where they dwelled until moving to Maine. During this interval he worked as an electrician, short order cook, cabinet maker and then as a woodsman. He ultimately gained employment at the University of Maine and served there until retirement with professorships in Biology, Mathematics and Statistics, and Bioresource Engineering. He is now Emeritus. He has numerous refereed publications in areas of biological rhythms, signal analysis, and the molecular underpinnings of cardiology. He remains active in research. He is a published poet and writes short stories in the science fiction and fantasy genre. Dusty now operates a wood-fired artisan bakery and is a third degree blackbelt, Shotokan style, maintaining his own dojo.

Dusty Dowse